I0795583

Praise for
Channeling Marilyn

"*Channeling Marilyn* is both engaging and warmhearted, tackling fear and transformation but also delving into the unexpected ways we find courage—sometimes from the most unlikely sources."

—Booklife

"A charming novel, *Channeling Marilyn* follows a high school student's momentous senior year achievements—garnered with a bit of supernatural help."

—*Foreword Clarion Reviews*

"Mima Tipper's insightful novel will appeal to anyone who's felt torn between the opportunity to shine and the urge to disappear. Throw in the spirited ghost of Marilyn Monroe and you have an irresistible story that has all the feels – sometimes all at once. I loved it."

—Pam McGaffin, author of *Shade of Wings*

"Mima Tipper deftly navigates her characters through angst-filled situations and emotional turmoil with sensitivity and humor . . . This delightful and engaging tale of self-discovery, personal growth, and the disorienting nature of young romance is a delight to read."

—k.m. huber, author of *Call of the Owl Woman*

"Charming and so original . . . Deftly weaving a theatre story, a love triangle, and a ghostly haunting, Tipper gives us nuanced characters, spine-tingling tension, and an instantly relatable protagonist."

—Mary Pascual, author of *The Byways* and *Walk the Web Lightly*

Channeling Marilyn

Channeling Marilyn

a novel

MIMA TIPPER

SWP

SHE WRITES PRESS

Published in 2026 by
She Writes Press, an imprint of The Stable Book Group

32 Court Street, Suite 2109
Brooklyn, NY 11201
https://shewritespress.com

Library of Congress Control Number: 2026902257
ISBN: 979-8-89636-320-0
eISBN: 979-8-89636-321-7

Interior designer: Katherine Lloyd, The DESK

Printed in the United States

For Michael and Maggie,
and all those gone too soon

little soul
little stray
little drifter
now where will you stay
all pale and all alone
after the way
you used to make fun of things?

–Hadrian

Part One

Chapter One

A flash of color dazzles me, catches me, like spotting a scarlet bird across a vast wintry landscape. Oh, yes. A slash of red in my silent black-and-white world? Yes, indeed, I am caught. That red slash grows bigger and bigger, as if I am sitting on a bus or a train watching the view out the window come at me. I can't look away either, and then I see that the red is a hat sitting on the head of a person, a girl, and I want to keep watching. More than anything. Now I *am* watching. Just like that. Not the endless black-and-white reel of life carrying on. I am stopping here and watching her. The girl. The girl wearing the scarlet-red hat.

This is truly something—this difference, this change. I thought I'd already gone through the biggest change ever. I am dead, after all. Terribly, terribly dead. I don't know for sure, but I like to think I'm a spirit. A spirit who hasn't had anything to do with "change" for a good long time. Since I got here, actually. To this cloud-white place that seems to be for me. For little old, alone me. I know my living body died more than sixty years ago, and as far as I can tell, time doesn't mean anything here. Except for being able to see the world and life going by, a nonstop, silent black-and-white movie: rolling and rolling, like sleeping, like dreaming. Until this change. Being a spirit and all? I probably shouldn't use living words like "change." Except I don't know any other way to talk, and whatever this change is, it's making me talk. Somehow talking's important. Like watching the girl.

Look at her. Right now, she is a freeze-frame statue standing in a brightly lit hallway surrounded by a frozen blur of kids with books and papers clutched to their chests. High school. Honestly, some places never seem to change. Other statue kids stand near the girl, the whole group facing a bulletin board full of announcements. It's only her I need to watch, though, her I need to see, because even though everything and everyone around her remains the usual black and white, she is in color. Full, living color.

She is tall, too, and if I had to pick only one more word to describe her, I'd pick solid. Maybe because of how she fills that oversized navy peacoat, or how that nubby tan scarf loops around her neck. Or maybe it's all about that scarlet hat. How the fuzzy knit hugs her head, the pom-pom on top as big as a fist. I don't think so, though. Everything about her is solid. Her long curling brown hair fluffing over apple-cheeks. Her unsmiling, unpainted lips. Those heavy eyebrows drawn into a low V over eyes that are both green and brown. *Oh, honey,* I want to say, *you look like you want to fade into the dark, except for that mad hat and . . .*

What's this now? More colors whirling around her. Somehow, I know it's only me who sees that rainbow swirl: only me who knows they are thoughts, fears, desires. Red and gold, blue and black. My, my, the colors. Reminds me of daydreams I used to have. I can't stop looking at those colors. Not only because I haven't seen color since I got here, but somehow I know that some of those swirly colors are feelings about me.

Feelings about me. That is a puzzle. No. Correction. Not feelings about me *now*. She's thinking of who I used to be.

There, in the girl's head, I see myself from the old days, when I was famous. When I posed endlessly for the cameras. Lush body, creamy face, platinum blonde hair. My eyes, sleepy and seductive. A tiny beauty mark above my red, red lips. I was a star. Indeed, I was. A movie star—Miss Marilyn Monroe. Jeepers, Marilyn Monroe. My Marilyn. And before that my Norma Jeane. My life. My whole life. All, all a long time ago.

Oops, back to my girl. Like a director calls, "Action," movement pumps at the announcement board, the scene blazing into full technicolor and sound now. A tall boy turns and half-smiles at my girl, tucks a wisp of sunny dandelion-fluff hair behind his ear, and walks away. Others follow, congratulating my girl and moving off. Except for one dark, sultry princess who sails by my girl with an icy cold look, pulling along a dreamboat of a boy.

Then only my girl and two others are left. A string-bean boy with golden skin and black hair that looks silky as kitten fur. He pats my girl's arm. The other is a tiny Kewpie-Girl with a nose like a button and the funniest hair ever. Bobbed and bright blue. Doesn't take a college degree to know that's a wig. She throws her arm around my girl's waist.

"This kicks *ass*," Kewpie says, "you got Cherie. *Cherie!*"

"Cherie . . ." my girl echoes, her voice small and wondering, "Cherie."

Cherie. If I could smile, I would. The showgirl from *Bus Stop*. No wonder my girl's thinking of me. Thinking of me so hard I bet she isn't even listening to Kewpie going on and on. Oh, sweetie, I want to say, Cherie was one of my best parts. A sexy tainted-angel who drove an innocent young cowboy mad with desire. Honestly, this is something, all right. My girl will play Cherie, a part I played to the hilt. In the Hollywood movie version, that is. And my girl is in the play. How wonderful! I wish I could congratulate her, only . . . strangely, my girl still stands there like a block, staring at that paper tacked to that board, her eyes darting from "Cherie" across the page to . . . why, that must be her name. Alexandria Donovan.

Colors jump and explode, a tornado around my Alexandria. Scarlet shock and golden sparkles of joy. Then blue agony. Black fear. The black takes over, a cloud big enough to swallow every other color. Well, how do you like that? My Alexandria is afraid, powerfully so.

"Whoa," Kitten-Boy pipes up, "isn't Cherie like—the biggest part? You're going to have to learn mega lines, and—and sing, I think."

"She's going to kill it," says Kewpie. She hugs my Alexandria hard. "Wow! Wow! I love the whole showgirl vibe. All those feathers and glitter! I am totally going to make you the best costumes ever. I'm—"

Alexandria breaks away. "I've got to do something," she says, turning, hurrying down the hall, her quavery voice calling over her shoulder, "I'll-I'll see you guys later."

Her thoughts come at me like a storm. Everything she wants. Everything she needs. All a stew of confusion and chaos. One thing comes clear: She has to talk to a Mr. B—her teacher, her director—right this minute. *Right this minute.*

"Cool," Kewpie sings to Alexandria's retreating form, "text me later. We've got some celebrating to do!"

"Celebrate . . . yeah, sure, Em," Alexandria mutters low and troubled, not looking at . . . Em. Kewpie's name is Em. Alexandria's best friend in the world.

"Lexa, hold up!" Em's bark yanks Alexandria—no, Lexa—to a stop. "Let's do a sleepover at my house," is her command, "come over, a-sap."

With a jerking wave, Lexa rushes on, her thoughts streaming after her, confetti at a parade. *Too far.* One moment of insanity turning into a train wreck coming. But didn't she know that would happen? The second her name came out of the jar. And now? Seeing that paper on the board with her name right across from "Cherie?" She thinks of herself playing that part, and then thinks of Marilyn Monroe. How Marilyn looked and acted and sang in the movie. Marilyn. *Marilyn*. Lexa lets out an almost silent groan, her shoulders hunching, her entire body shuddering.

I watch her hurrying alone down that hall, and I don't understand a thing. How a girl gets the starring role in a play—and doesn't even want it. That *surely* never happened in my day. She gets farther away from me, smaller and smaller, and I can't help wondering, *What will she do?* Oh my, how a wanting opens up in me. Unlike anything I have ever experienced before, living or dead: wide and huge and hungry. I don't want to race by and leave this scene behind. I want to keep watching this scared, confused girl. And maybe that's a wrong thing for a spirit to want—maybe even a dangerous thing—but I *do* want it. More than anything, I want to know what Lexa Donovan is going to do.

Chapter Two

Lexa got on the bus, moving along the aisle to slump down in a rear seat. A murmur from the seat directly in front drew her attention. A youngish mom-looking woman sat with a little girl, maybe two or three years old, in her lap. The little girl's arms hugged the mom's neck, her tiny fingers patting the skin right above the collar of the mom's coat. *Patpat.* Soft and warm and comforting.

Lexa watched them, and her hands came together in her own lap, her left pointer finger going immediately to the silver ring she always wore on her right hand. She traced the familiar shape of the ring, her fingertip following the Greek key pattern, an intricate labyrinth of repeating horizontal and vertical lines. And then she twisted the ring. *Twist-twisttwist.* She nibbled her lower lip, stared out the window, the sights rushing by in a blur, her thoughts bouncing and shrieking, a party gone wild. *How did this happen?* Her mind raced, knowing *exactly* how it had happened. She saw herself on that day a couple of weeks earlier, the slip of paper clutched in her hand. It was the last Friday before the Christmas break, and her last chance. She watched herself take a deep breath, go into the school office, and drop the slip of paper into Mr. B's jar.

Lexa rested her head against the bus window now, the cold glass a welcome chill to her burning thoughts. Burning thoughts that led her to what happened a couple of weeks after the Christmas break. That freezing January morning, when she and Em had pushed inside the high school building just as the PA system crackled, the school secretary Ms. Kirk's voice blasting her high-pitched welcome back: instantly launching into announcements about picking up community service forms, yearbook deadlines for senior pictures, and then, "Seniors who submitted slips for Mr. Bertoli's spring drama are excused from homeroom and should go to the auditorium for the lottery drawing."

The lottery. Even now sitting on this jittering bus—and knowing everything that had happened since the lottery—Lexa's insides flared at how she'd felt on that cold morning when she'd heard the announcement. Scared and excited and queasy all at the same time. Like she stood on a high diving board, ready to leap. She remembered how she'd gripped Em's arm, pulling and saying, "Let's go."

Em had pulled back. "What?"

Of course, Em had been confused. She had had no idea what Lexa had done.

Lexa had persisted, though. "Mr. B's lottery!" she'd said, tugging at Em again, "let's go check it out."

And they had. Following a crowd of others into the auditorium where way down in front had stood the squat form of Mr. B, his dark curly hair flying around his head, and his bird-perch nose moving back and forth as he watched students pour in. Behind him on the stage sat two large clear plastic jars: one brimming with folded slips of paper, the other only about a quarter full. For the lottery. Where instead of letting kids fight to register for his way-too-popular spring senior drama workshop, or even holding auditions, Mr. B had invented this loony lottery system to make the whole gig completely random. No one even knew which play he'd picked. And wasn't that the craziest? How even with all that unknown, his plays crackled with an energy that was off the charts, luring seniors to put their names in those jars year after year.

Lexa'd always been glad to do backstage for Mr. B's plays, signing up freshman, sophomore, and junior years. But not this year. This year—her senior year—something she couldn't name had pushed her to step out of the shadow of backstage. Something that told her that if she didn't take some kind of action, she never would. And oh, how she'd wanted something great to happen to her for her senior year; that want had driven her to take the biggest chance of her life.

"The play I have chosen for this spring," Mr. B had begun that January day, "is William Inge's classic masterpiece *Bus Stop*, a tense story of a small group of people stranded together by a snowstorm, who must spend the night isolated at the titular bus stop. There are five male parts and three female parts. We will start with the male . . ."

And he had, each name making Lexa's belly flip and flop like she was creeping toward the razor edge of a cliff. Closer and closer.

"Now for the female roles," called Mr. B.

At the same time Lexa had seen his hand dive into the jar, she dug her fingers into Em's arm.

"Ow!" Em pushed at her hand, just as Mr. B called out a name.

"Alexandria Donovan."

Even now sitting on this bus with the heat blasting and the engine roaring, Lexa's insides thrilled remembering Mr. B calling her name. And calling it again. Because she'd just sat there, staring at him, like the two of them had slipped into some alternate dimension where unicorns lived and dreams came true.

Mr. B's voice again, that deep boom. "Miss Donovan? Ah, there you are."

Lexa's brain had turned to radio static full of *I did it. I put my name in the jar. I got picked.* Me. Me. Me.

Mr. B had gestured for her to stand and, like he was a wizard casting a spell, she got to her feet. Instantly, all attention had been on her, and her skin had torched, like she'd burn up into a tiny pile of ashes. For an instant every possible fear had surfaced, and she wished she'd do exactly what tiny ashes did when the wind blew. Disappear.

Exactly what she wanted to do right now on this juddering bus.

Lexa let her head fall back against the seat. She pulled the edge of her hat over her face, the scarlet-red wool making her eyes hot. *Man, man, man!* She was completely dumb. She could've quietly sleepwalked through the rest of senior year, saving enough money to go far, far away after graduation. That would've been the time for great things to happen. When she was on her own. Somewhere where no one knew her, and she could . . . well, where at the very least no one would be watching her up on a stage playing an impossible role. She pictured herself sitting outside a café in Paris, the Eiffel Tower rising behind her.

"Boo!"

Loud and high-pitched, that ghostly greeting startled Lexa. She lifted the red cap off one eye. The little girl from the seat in front peered at her with a wide pixie grin. A clap of tiny hands had Pixie covering her own face, only to pull her fingers away fast. "Boo," she said again.

Lexa eyed her for one frozen, leave-me-alone moment, only . . . no. Half-smile quirking, Lexa tugged her hat over her face again and yanked it up fast. "Peekaboo," she said, laughter erupting as Pixie repeated the game. *Maybe I could be a nanny*. Lexa peekabooed with the little girl again. *Maybe teach English to some cool little French kid, or—*

The bus jerked to a stop, and the young mom rose, pulling Pixie into her arms. Lexa waved, and Pixie waved back.

Left with her thoughts again, Lexa pressed her cheek to the window and realized it was her usual stop. She watched the young mom and little girl head across the parking lot toward the mini strip mall, Pixie pointing to the pink curlicue of the neon sign in the window of Film Buzz. Lexa smiled. Her Dad's beloved classic video and DVD rental shop. So retro. Her gaze traveled to the windows of the apartment above the shop, just in time to see the light in the kitchen snap off. Dad would've heard the bell on the Film Buzz door and was probably already going down the stairs. Maybe was even now in the shop, calling out his trademark, "Welcome to Film Buzz," to the mom and Pixie.

The bus moved on and, with a huffing breath, Lexa fished out her phone, needing to press extra hard over the spidery cracks in the ancient screen to tap her dad a text. "Staying at school for homework." His message came right back. "No worries."

Worries. Dad and worries. About the struggling shop maybe going under. About paying bills. About her going to college. Only those worries had faded a little. She swallowed hard. Had faded when she'd gotten home—*was it just yesterday?*—and told him about Mr. B picking her name out of the jar. How Dad had laughed with her then. About Mr. B choosing a screwy play where a young cowboy named Bo is so in love with this showgirl named Cherie that he chases her onto a bus to make her marry him, and then a storm traps the two of them and a bunch of other travelers at an isolated bus stop for the night.

Lexa slouched low on her slippery bus seat, seeing again how Dad's grizzly, graybeard face lit right up when she'd told him about the lottery, the play. How they'd both laughed because at that point she still had no idea what part she'd get. The light and the laughter were so rare for Dad, his expression always too quickly returning to sadness, the ghost that never completely went. How he'd brought the *Bus Stop* movie over then. How he'd told her that it used to be one of Mom's faves. *Oh, man!*

Lexa cringed, imagining Dad's face going tight-lipped with defeat at the news she'd tell him today. That there'd be no play for her, because she dropped out. That she had to. *Had to.* That the part Mr. B assigned her was . . . She knocked her forehead against the window, her brain swiping through clips of the Hollywood bombshell who played Cherie in the movie. Marilyn Monroe. All perfect skin and pale gold curls, every movement of her perfect body dripping sex. A low moan vibrated deep in Lexa's throat, and she tugged her hat all the way down to her nose. No choice. *Sorry, Dad.* She had to quit this play, and fast.

Chapter Three

The bus stopped, and Lexa rushed off.

A few minutes of hurried walking and she was in the driveway of a light blue one-story house with yellow shutters. Clouds of frosty breath poured through her lips and from her nose. She marched to the front door and, fingers shaking, reached for the bell. *Bing-bong*. Moments ticked and whirled and then the front door swung open revealing Mr. B, though not a version of him that Lexa recognized. A long white apron wrapped over his front, all but covering a wooly vest and tweedy pants. Lexa's nose twitched, scenting something wafting out the door. Warm and rich. Tomatoey and herby.

"Miss Donovan?" he said, his voice a low question. "This is a surprise."

Before Lexa could speak, a voice called from inside the house and Mr. B answered, "It's one of my students, Alice."

Lexa's brain registered Alice as Mr. B's wife, whom she saw once a year at the party Mr. B threw for the cast and crew. Alice's face appeared now over Mr. B's shoulder. Tall and thin, she towered over him, tiny eyes and tiny nose on a long, pale face.

"Alice," said Mr. B, "you remember Miss Donovan."

"Sure," said Alice, grinning now, with a mouth full of the biggest, whitest teeth Lexa'd ever seen.

"I'm sorry to bug you. I know I shouldn't be here," Lexa managed, "I—I need to talk to Mr. B. About this year's play."

"This is highly unusual," Mr. B said, "can't it wait until we meet on Monday?"

"No," Lexa said, "it—it can't."

"Well, then," he said, "please come in."

Lexa slinked by them into a small foyer, and Mr. B pointed to his apron and said, "You've caught me in the midst of preparing my world-famous spaghetti sauce."

"Sorry," Lexa repeated.

"Nonsense." He rubbed his palms together. "I'm thinking we should have a group dinner. Perhaps even this weekend. Oh, dear, it's already Friday. Would Sunday be too soon? We can talk about it. Now then, may I take your coat?"

"No, I mean . . ." Lexa ordered herself to get it over with. "This won't take that long. Mr. B—"

He put up a hand. "You've come all this way, Miss Donovan. We are not heathens. Is that not so?" He and Alice exchanged smiles. "We might as well be comfortable. Please, let me take your coat."

They eyed each other for one long beat. Lexa nodded and unbuttoned her coat. Hanging it, Mr. B glanced down at her ratty high tops. She plopped on a bench near the door and untied them, her fingers jerky with a bone-deep need to escape.

"Now then," said Mr. B, leading Lexa into the living room and planting himself next to her on the couch. "I'm presuming this visit has to do with the cast list."

"Yes," Lexa said, "yes, it does." The chaos and confusion in her head revved to a fever pitch, and she blurted, "There's no way I'm Cherie."

Mr. B cocked his head, a delicate, birdlike movement, and said, "That's perfectly true. Of course, you're not Cherie."

Like cameras gone wild, a dizzying explosion of red, orange, yellow, and black burst in Lexa's head. "I *knew* it was a mistake."

"Miss Donovan." Mr. B touched her wrist. "Calm yourself, please, and allow me a moment." He handed his apron to his wife. "Would you be so good as to check on the spaghetti sauce, dear?" He sounded to Lexa like a doctor, asking his nurse for a scalpel. "I'd like a private word with Miss Donovan."

"Certainly," said Nurse Alice as she rose, and Lexa winced at the concern written on Alice's wrinkled forehead.

"What I was trying to tell you," how soft Mr. B's tone was now, "is that of course you are not Cherie. *Yet.* That is the process of the workshop, and we are only at the beginning of that process. In three months, you will have found your Cherie, and for that performance, you will be her." He patted her hand.

"So . . ." Lexa swallowed. "What you're telling me is that you didn't make a mistake. About the casting."

"A mistake? Not in the least. Why would you think that?"

"Because . . ." Nervous laughter bubbled. "Look at me, Mr. B. Really look at me. I do not look like a showgirl. And don't tell me I do, because *ha*! Last night I watched *Bus Stop* and—and there's just no way."

He studied her, then stood. "Come with me. I believe the last time you were here, Alice and I were only beginning our basement renovation."

Lexa blinked. "What?"

"Yes," said Mr. B, "you of all of my students will truly appreciate what we've done, and there's a special something down there I want to show you."

To the foyer they went, where Mr. B opened a door and flicked a wall switch. The burst of light revealed carpeted steps leading down and a framed movie poster on the wall. Lexa startled, gaping at the movie poster of *The Creature from the Black Lagoon*.

"My Dad would so love that!" She whirled to Mr. B, her pleasure quickly draining to more confusion. *The play. Getting out of it.* That's what they were supposed to be talking about.

"Yes," said Mr. B, "and I adore Film Buzz. I've heard it said that small independent video and DVD stores will soon be a thing of the past, but your father has worked hard to build an admirable business and he has an enviable collection of the classics. Very niche. Please tell him I said so. Now." With a slight bow, he gestured to the stairs. "After you."

At the bottom of the stairs, the room opened to a large windowless space: more movie posters on the walls and one wall with floor-to-ceiling shelves crammed with dozens of DVDs. She couldn't focus on them, though, because what was in the room swallowed her. A bank of puffy maroon reclining chairs took up the center, and in front of them—a tremendous screen.

"Whoa." Lexa drifted closer, inhaling a whiff of popcorn. "My dad would love this, too."

Mr. B let out a rumbly laugh. "This room is my pride and joy."

"You guys must really like watching movies," Lexa said.

"Guilty as charged, though that's not why I brought you down here. Look at this."

Lexa tore her eyes from the screen. Mr. B stood in front of a poster for a film called *Some Like It Hot*, starring who else? Marilyn Monroe. Lexa groaned. Slowly she walked over, riveted to the image of Marilyn in a sheer, clinging dress all black and sparkly; eyes a half-closed invitation and full lips parted in a pout as if singing. Lexa blew out a noisy breath, saying, "See?"

"What I see," said Mr. B, "is an actress. Beautiful? Yes. Maybe made to be the most beautiful, the most desirable woman in the world. Do you think she was born looking like this? Do you think she woke up looking like this, even after she was a star? No." His curls wisped back and forth as he shook his head. "She—and the people I would call her 'handlers'—are the ones who made her look the way she did here and in *Bus Stop*, both films made at the height of her career. And we?" He spun back to Lexa, his brows beetling together. "We are the ones who made her into a goddess by worshipping her. In life. And in death."

Swallowing against a dry throat, Lexa said, "You're wrong." She reached up to touch the glass over Marilyn's sparkly skirted knee. "I mean, maybe you're right about the hair and makeup stuff, but how she played Cherie? No. She had something else in her. Some kind of magic. Magic I don't have. I can't be Cherie," she went on, dull and gray, "I can't be in the play at all."

Dusty, ringing silence filled the room.

"'Can't' is a strong and dangerous word, Miss Donovan," said Mr. B. "Now, you are understandably nervous about being *onstage* this time, instead of being part of the backstage crew. However, I would ask you to think carefully. Are you that certain of what you are and are not capable of?" His quiet tone made a shiver ripple across Lexa's skin. "Of everything that's in you?"

She opened a mouth full of *No*, only her lips trembled too hard. She shook her head instead.

"Do you think when Marilyn was your age, she knew what she would become?" he went on. "The kind of actress? The kind of symbol?"

Lexa shook her head again. "Please don't give me a life lesson," she said, hating her own broken voice. "I made a mistake. I want out."

Mr. B touched a forefinger to his lips. "I am perplexed," he said, "if this is how you feel, then why in the world did you put your name in my jar?"

"I—I don't know. I wanted . . ." she lowered her head. She couldn't say the words. *I wanted a little part. A tiny part. Just to be somebody else for a while. But not, not,* not *someone like Cherie!* She mumbled, "I don't know what I wanted."

"Why, that is truly remarkable," he whispered, and Lexa's chin shot up. "Whether you know what you wanted, or not, you put your name in the jar, and I picked you. Don't you see?" he went on, his face glowing. "This is the truest form of serendipity."

Seren-what-ity?

"Do not mistake me. I am not making light of your feelings. Only surely you don't want to turn your back on serendipity?" His eyes burned into hers. "Surely not!"

"Mr. B—"

"Please," he said, "I would ask that you reflect on what has occurred . . ."

Pop-pop went his words in Lexa's head—electric bubbles.

"Take some time. It's only Friday. Let it steep over the weekend. In your mind. Your heart. That's not so much to ask, is it?"

His reasoning exhausting her, a speechless Lexa let him lead her back upstairs.

He collected her coat as she tied on her sneakers. Alice appeared then, a wooden spoon in her hand.

Lexa stood and faced Mr. B. "I have one more question," she said. "What could I possibly have done to make you pick me for Cherie?"

"Ahhh." Mr. B shared a quick smile with Alice. "Remember that magic you referred to?" He helped Lexa with her coat. "Above all, it is Cherie's innate sweetness and yearning that make her character." He cocked his head. "During the readings in class this morning I recognized those qualities in you."

Chapter Four

S*weetiesweetiesweetness!* That's all Lexa could think during her entire walk home, her stomp up the stairs to the apartment, and her slam into her room where she repacked her backpack for her sleepover. She tried to put the whole Mr. B talk/play thing aside when she went down to say goodbye to Dad, but his hug and whisper of, "Have fun, sweetie," did not help.

Even while she trudged up the hill to Em's, her brain was full of how sweet she was—the sweetest, stupidest sucker ever. Huffing cold, smoking breath like she was some kind of dragon, a picture crystallized in Lexa's mind: her mincing in black stilettos across a stage, wearing the low-cut blouse and skin-tight skirt Marilyn wore in *Bus Stop*. She watched herself wobble and jiggle, and then the image blurred and shifted to her standing on a table singing her lungs out while spilling out of Marilyn's teensy, sprayed-on, satin-green showgirl outfit.

Oh, hell no! Lexa tried to shake away the image, shivering and cringing as she burrowed into her coat. She kicked at a hunk of dirty ice. It skittered across the sidewalk, and she marched faster, kicking and kicking, an endless loop running of her quivering flesh overflowing her costumes, jeering laughter coming at her from a dark audience. Surrounding her. Swallowing her.

She jerked to a stop. What had she done? This very morning in Mr. B's workshop? When he had spotted all that "sweetness." *What?*

As she walked on, the question nudged at her like a cold, whispery breath, making her hitch her shoulders up around her ears. *What. Had. She. Done?* She forced herself to slow her pace and take slower breaths. To think. To remember.

And there she was, this very morning, a mere one day after the lottery, sitting quiet as a mouse in that circle of desks in Mr. B's classroom. How jittery-excited she'd been. To be there. To be chosen. And, well, she had been curious—for the entire twenty-four hours since the lottery—about who would play which female role.

Across from her sat the other two female winners. Dani-Marie Alvarez and Clara Lockwood. Lexa remembered studying Dani-Marie, thinking about her cinnamon-sugary skin, how her curvy body packed into her slick varsity soccer team warmups. Athlete-bombshell. Look how Dani-Marie sat: ankle over her knee, scribbling away in a notebook. Dani-Marie was organized, focused, and drop-dead gorgeous enough to do anything.

How about Clara? Lexa saw her again. Perched sideways on her chair, bleached hair sticking up all over the place, a swatch swooping to cover half her face, gazing off over her shoulder and out the window. Dreamy. If someone had opened that window, dreamy Clara would've floated away.

Lexa remembered frown-smiling. At how random as hell this was. Then that needy truth had fizzed: Who would Mr. B ask *her* to play?

She'd taken out her copy of *Bus Stop*, flipped to the character page.

"Grace," the waitress who ran the bus stop's diner, was the smallest female part, and the most abrasive character—well, other than "Bo," the brawling young cowboy. Was that who Mr. B would ask her to play? A sharp-tongued diner lady? How about "Elma," a naïve young waitress? Lexa had nibbled her lower lip. Playing her would take serious acting, because she was the one who had to spend the most time with the strangest character in the play—and one that hadn't even made it truly into the movie—Dr. Gerald Lyman, the lonely old professor who hit on her.

God, Lexa had thought, who would play the professor? A tiny laugh had escaped as she lifted her eyes, catching Jeremy Leith's. She remembered his eyes widening, but then as if he knew she was not laughing at him, he'd studied her.

Even just the memory of that eye contact made Lexa's breaths swoop in and out now on this cold sidewalk. Shaking the memory of Jeremy's eyes away, Lexa squared her shoulders, her senses sharpening to the iciness of the air on her face, the thud of her shoes on the frozen cement.

Jeremy Leith. All Lexa really knew about him was that he'd transferred to Queen City High at the beginning of senior year, and that he wasn't what she thought of as good-looking. Still, when she caught a glimpse of him in the halls there was something about him and his lanky body that always made her look at him a beat too long. That mass of pale hair falling over his forehead. And those light blue eyes.

All but marching now, Lexa's mind ordered, *Get a grip. Think about Mr. B's class. Think about what happened this morning.*

She saw the classroom in her mind's eye again, the door scraping open, and others coming in. And then Brian McKinnon.

In full living color she again saw Brian's broad, muscular bod striding into the classroom, the buttery rasp of his voice calling over his shoulder, "Yo, Hils. Meet me after this block."

Hilary.

Lexa kicked hard at the crusty sidewalk and grimaced. Hilary Poss. Brian's super-hot forever girlfriend—well, since freshman year anyway—with a river of black hair and impossibly sharp cheekbones. Impossibly sharp everything, really, especially her tongue. Lexa was way too familiar with her sharp tongue.

"Good luck," Hilary had whispered, and man had she looked pissy. Mr. B had not picked her name from his jar. Clearly, she was not pleased.

"Thanks," Brian had said, snorting as he yanked off his ball cap, "I'll need it."

"I'm sure you *all* will," Hilary had said, glancing from Clara to Dani-Marie to—

As it had that day, Lexa's chin lifted now at the memory of staring into Hilary's razor-angry face. Not simply angry: full of disbelief, or—or something. Something Lexa couldn't totally put a finger on before Hilary huffed hard and left in a whirl of midnight hair.

Mr. B had called out, "Welcome, people. Time to get started. We've got a tick over three months together, and I'd like to begin by asking each of you to share with the group your reason for wanting to be in this workshop. Let's go around the room, starting with . . ." he looked to his immediate right, "Mr. Graham Vogel."

"Well," Graham began, his slight figure sitting straighter. He ran a hand through his tight brown curls and pushed black thick-framed glasses up his nose. "I'm going to be a film director and I thought it'd be smart to learn about what actors go through . . ."

As Graham rambled on, Lexa remembered squirming in her seat, full of *what will I say?*

He finished, and Mr. B called, "Mr. Anton Mumbare?

"Many of you know," Anton said, his voice a velvety rumble, "that my family came here from DR Congo. Being in Vermont was quite an adjustment . . ."

He'd gone on about how in the workshop all that mattered was the work. That he was only an actor. Even now Lexa couldn't help being filled up by what he'd said, and at the same time sucked dry. Then Mr. B turned to her.

"Miss Alexandria Donovan?"

"Uh . . ." After seconds that seemed like years, she'd stammered, "I—It just kind of—happened."

Silence hummed.

"Interesting," Mr. B said at last, then, "Mr. Kevin Dang?"

Lexa's gaze slid to the black-haired boy next to her as he told them about hearing someone in art club talking about the workshop before the break. When he said "someone," color flooded his cheeks, making them look like two golden ripe peaches, and he'd darted a look at Lexa. Something in Lexa unwound then, and she'd remembered him in the auditorium at the lottery. How he'd gazed at Em. The hungriest of puppies.

Mr. B called, "Mr. Brian McKinnon?"

"I guess you could say . . ." Brian hesitated, plucking at the cap sitting on his desk. His cheeks flooded red, too, but not in the sweet-Kevin way. No. This Brian was irritated as hell. "I was *convinced* this workshop was the opportunity of a lifetime."

"Is that so?" mused Mr. B. "How about Miss Clara Lockwood?"

Even as she'd shifted to Clara, Lexa had been in a fever over what Brian had said. It had to be Hilary's doing, only what could Hilary have done or said to get him to put his name in the jar?

Clara's voice had threaded into Lexa's brain then, rough and sweet. "I help out at The Wheeler School, you know, doing art projects with the kids, and I work with this one kid—Eric—who's autistic and, right before the break, he did a collage that was supposed to remind him of me. Well, it kind of freaked me out." She shook her head. "There was a girl in the middle, drawing, surrounded by these different kinds of boxes. All empty. I was like, 'Okay.' I mean, it's not like he's going to tell me what he's thinking, you know? Then a couple of days later I saw Mr. B's jars in the office and it was weird. They made me think of Eric's collage, and I had to, I don't know, *do* something different. So, I put my name in. And after I got picked?" she half-smiled, "I went to see Eric, and told him about the play, and I'm pretty sure he liked hearing about it, and—and that's all."

"That was quite a story," said Mr. B. "How about Miss Dani-Marie Alvarez?"

Lexa watched Dani-Marie's mouth moving, except she'd been full of what Clara said, and then what Anton said. Thinking of their stories now made Lexa feel as itchy and small as when she'd heard them. To at least a couple of people, Mr. B's workshop was about more than acting. Maybe not even really about acting at all.

She bit her lip as she walked, focusing back on the class, on Mr. B calling on Jeremy Leith.

Jeremy's gaze had traveled around the circle, his lips pressing tight. Not nervous. No. More like . . . curious. When he reached Lexa, the lightness and blueness of his eyes hit her clear and arrow sharp. Truth arrows. She'd looked away fast.

"I've moved around a bit. Been to a number of schools." Jeremy's voice had been soft, self-amused. "Not once have I ever been truly surprised. Your jars surprised me, Mr. B, and I thought, *I want to take a workshop with the one teacher subversive enough to do something so completely not the school norm.*" He angled a half-smile at Mr. B. "You are a brave man. To put such a motley group on a stage."

Laughter trickled around the room.

"Wonderful," Mr. B said, "I thank you all for sharing. Now then, let's turn to the play."

Then *kaboom*. The time had come to figure out who was going to play whom, and they'd started with readings. Mr. B had paired Lexa with Kevin to start with a scene between waitress Elma and Dr. Gerald Lyman, the lonely old professor.

Lexa remembered flowing into the musical chairs of shifting twosomes and Mr. B wandering around taking notes. Soon, the quiet mumble of voices reading lines, pretending to be different characters, took her far away from the classroom. She was in the diner, trapped with these few people, for this one night, while a snowstorm howled outside.

Her turn came to read the lead. Cherie, the showgirl.

The second Mr. B put her next to Brian, her whole body went noodly at one simple truth: Cherie, the class, the play, *high school* would come and go, but this moment would live in her head for eternity. This magical moment between her and Brian total-hottie McKinnon.

While Mr. B flipped through his book choosing their scene, Lexa studied Brian's profile from under her lashes. She had known him since elementary school, could even see him clearly back in the third grade: short in an oversized jean jacket. Then in eighth grade: taller for sure, his hair freshly buzzed and his big boots clomping. And then freshman year. He'd changed over the summer. She had as well. Both of them had gotten bigger and broader, except his bigger and broader made him look like one of those Roman statues. A Roman statue that, in a fingersnap, belonged to Hilary Poss. At least that's how good old Hils treated him.

Mr. B held out the play, tapping the page and saying, "This one. The scene where at last Bo apologizes to Cherie for kidnapping her on the bus."

Brian faced Lexa, his lifted brows and unsmiling lips making it dead clear that he wished he was anywhere except this room. He began riffling through his book for the assigned scene. Lexa had paged through her book too, and then . . .

She blinked now, her steps slowing again even as she shivered with the memory of the knowledge that had hit her. She and Brian were in the same boat. Neither of them 100 percent convinced they belonged in Mr. B's workshop.

Are you just angry you're here? Or . . . are you afraid, like me?

"Which is it?"

She kicked at the sidewalk, thinking of how his squint had told her she'd spoken those last words out loud.

"That's not what she says." Brian tapped his book. "And I go first anyway."

"Right. Sorry," Lexa croaked, "go ahead."

"'Cherry . . .'" Brian laid on a western twang so thick that a cartoon would laugh. "'It wasn't right a me to treat ya the way I did . . .'"

His voice relaxed. Lexa heard the change and thought of the actor playing Bo in the movie . . . thought of Brian sounding more like how she'd imagined Bo would truly sound: young and confused. Shy. She tried her hardest to follow along. Brian made that impossible. His soft, butter-toast voice had every bit of her going quivery. The words on the page danced in front of her eyes, unreadable squiggles.

Brian paused, and Lexa jolted. Her turn.

"'I—I guess . . .'" She hesitated, heat at the back of her neck telling her that Mr. B stood right behind her. Her lips shaking now, she tried again, "'I guess I been treated worse in my life.'"

"'Cherry . . .'" Brian said his line about sending Cherie home and followed the stage directions, holding out a hand as if offering her money.

Lexa reached and their fingers had bumped. She snatched back her trembling hand, read her final line, hating how her voice sounded—tiny and powdery.

Mr. B had scrawled on his clipboard and said, "Nice."

Nice? The word had twisted in Lexa's head even as she twisted away from Brian. Nice was eating ice cream and watching a movie alone in the dark. Not making a total diz-bang of herself in front of Brian McKinnon. She'd wanted the floor to crack open and swallow her whole. That was the moment she'd begun to think that being onstage instead of backstage was maybe a big, big mistake.

Ms. Kirk's voice had burst from the intercom and, after she finished a barrage of announcements, the bell rang.

"Great job, people," Mr. B had said, "I am very impressed with your readings. Please check the bulletin board next to the main office at day's end." He shot one final glance around the circle. "The cast list will be up."

Chapter Five

Lexa stood in front of Em's large pointy house, the diamond-paned windows sparkling in the frosty cold of late afternoon making the place look even grander than normal. Em's grand old house where she lived with her grand old Aunt Ann. A shadow darted across a lit-up second-floor window. Em in her room, probably already up to her ears in *Bus Stop* costume designs.

Em. Still the same since the day they'd met.

Lexa made her way up the drive and thought, as she often did, of that day in third grade when Miss Cray told them about a new kid joining the class. A kid who'd just lost both her mom and dad. In came a tiny blonde elf of a girl, and Miss Cray led her to the empty desk next to Lexa's, saying, "Lexa, I'm going to trust you to help Marvel-Ann find her way around." Only what Lexa heard was, "Lexa? I know you've still got a father, but since your mother's dead, too, I'm sure you'll be extra kind to Marvel-Ann, and make sure she has a friend."

Marvel-Ann turned her huge baby blues on Lexa, and in them Lexa saw reflected her own bigger, darker self. Along with something else. That Marvel-Ann read their shared situation perfectly. The moment Miss Cray shoved off, Marvel-Ann reached into her backpack and pulled out a pad of blank paper and a bag of colored pencils. She took a red pencil and drew a large letter M. "That's my name," she'd said, pointing the pencil at the letter. "Just Em." And even though Lexa spent that day showing her around, Em became the one who helped Lexa.

Always.

Lexa knocked on the grand old house's back door, hopeful now. If anyone could help her get out of this *Bus Stop* mess, it would be Em.

Slipping by Aunt Ann and her offer of herbal tea or a "nice fruit smoothie," Lexa rapped on Em's bedroom door, already pushing it open. The door moved only a couple of inches before stopping, blocked.

"Whoops." Em's voice came through the door, muffled and breathless. "Hold on." A flurry of shoving noises, and the door flew open. There was Em, face flushed and smiling, the sleeve of her shirt slipping off her shoulder.

"Finally," said Em, and pulled Lexa into the room fast, hugging her, right there in the middle of the piles of fabric, clothing, and huge books strewn across the floor.

"Looks like a bomb went off in here," said Lexa. "Actually, it always looks like a bomb went off."

"Ha," said Em, "you are so funny!" She pushed Lexa back, beaming at her. "I am *so* pumped. I read the play again, and I already have a million ideas for costumes." She let go of Lexa and twirled around, arms wide.

"Well, I'm glad someone's excited." Lexa dropped down on the end of Em's bed. A sharp something stabbed her butt. "Ow!" She pulled a pin cushion shaped like a tomato from under her.

Em came over, taking the pin cushion. "Sorry 'bout that." She sat next to Lexa, studying her closely. "What's up?"

Lexa threw herself back on the bed. "You have to help me."

"What's going on?" asked Em, plopping on her back beside Lexa. When Lexa didn't answer, Em rolled to her side and propped her head on her palm, facing her friend. With a confused frown she said, "That thing you had to do . . . please tell me it was *not* going to see Mr. B?"

"It was." Lexa shut her eyes hard and whispered, "I—I don't want to be in the play anymore."

"What?" said Em, her voice a shocked bark. "Why?"

"It—It's just not for me."

"Why is it not for you?" Em said.

"It just isn't," insisted Lexa. "And I told Mr. B, and he wouldn't let me drop out. He's making me think about it until Monday."

She opened her eyes, catching Em's unhappy expression.

"Is it because of that look Hilary gave you?" said Em.

"Huh?" Now Lexa was confused. She lifted up on her elbows.

"You know," Em went on, "at the cast list. Because of Brian."

Lexa's stomach squeezed and dropped. "Brian?"

"Yes, Brian," Em said, "you didn't notice? He's playing Bo."

Lexa sat up fast, her whole body blazing. She covered her face with her hands, a weak "Oh, God" expelling on a hot breath. "Please, please tell me you're joking."

"Ease up, girl." Em pulled Lexa's hands from her face. "You sound completely freaked."

"I *am* completely freaked," said Lexa. She moaned, trying to tug her hands from Em's grip.

Em didn't let go. "It's only a play, Lexa. It's going to be really fun."

"Are you kidding me? This is a nightmare." With a choked sound, Lexa managed to free her hands. She clasped them in her lap. "And if Brian is Bo, that 'nightmare' just got a thousand times worse." She twisted her ring. Twisted and twisted.

"What is the problem?" said Em, her face pinching with worry.

"The problem?" Brian flashed behind Lexa's eyes again. Reading with her in Mr. B's classroom. *Bo. Brian was cast as Bo!* "Everyone who sees me in that play will have *that* picture in their head." She tried to laugh, only the sound that came out was more like a strangled animal. "You know, me screwing up onstage while Brian McKinnon pretends to be madly in love with me. I mean, seriously, can you see me singing in front of people? Strutting it like a showgirl?"

"That's exactly it." Em nudged Lexa's arm. "It's *not* you. It's acting. Seriously, Lexa. You'll be great. I've seen you act. Uh-uh, don't shake your head at me. You know what I mean—after we watch a movie? Or when you're telling me about something you watched on one of your Film Buzz shifts? You act out the parts, making all those voices? You're really good. And totally funny."

"But all those people watching—" Lexa whispered.

Em cut her off, "All *what* people? Your dad? Aunt Ann? Come on, you know mostly only family even goes to those plays." She patted Lexa's arm, her enthusiasm sounding so much like Mr. B's that any other excuses—any other truths, to be exact—Lexa could think of died on her tongue.

Em didn't even seem to notice, her patting hand warm and full of Em-confidence. Her voice going on about Lexa being able to play any part. Kill any part. A boiling started low in Lexa's belly, and she wanted to jump up and yell, *I won't 'kill it'! I can't snap my fingers and do whatever I want. Be that girl. I'm not brilliant or gorgeous or amazing.*

As Em continued, Lexa gazed wildly around the room, at the piles of fabric and the sewing corner. At the dozens of drawings and photos of costumes and designs and clothes pinning the walls. The photos of New York City. All of them about Em and her dreams for her future life.

I'm not you. And it wasn't that Lexa wanted to be Em, but she couldn't tell Em how she truly felt. She couldn't have Em feeling all sorry for her. Or worrying about leaving her pathetic loser best friend behind.

Lexa stood abruptly, interrupting Em. "None of that matters," she said, crossing her arms over her chest, hugging herself. "I've changed my mind. I should've stuck with helping backstage. I—I don't know what I was thinking putting my name in."

"You were thinking you love Mr. B's plays, and you wanted your own shot, silly," said Em in a low tone. "How did the whole jar thing happen anyway?"

Shoulders drooping, Lexa slumped down next to Em again. After a moment, she said, "Remember that party? The one a couple of weeks before Christmas break? At the beach?"

"That super cold night? With the bonfire and everyone racing around like crazy nuts?" Em let out an amused half-sigh. "That was fun."

"You brought Cosmos in that thermos?"

"Yeah." One side of Em's mouth curved. "And I swiped a couple of Ann's clove cigarettes."

"Don't forget that cigarette holder."

Now they smiled at each other, and then Lexa said, "We talked about what we wanted to do after high school, and you started going off about New York City."

Em's smile faltered. "That was right after I sent in my application to Fashion and Design."

"Right," said Lexa.

Em went on, "I asked you what you wanted to do. Like, in life."

"And," Lexa bit her lip, "as usual—I said, 'I don't know.' Do you remember what I said next?"

"You said . . . that it wouldn't suck if at least something great happened to you before the end of senior year." Em trailed off, then blew out a breath. "And you put in your name."

"And I put in my name."

They stared at each other again, the weight of what Lexa had done like a bucket of lead between them.

"Damn," said Em at last.

"Damn." Then, with a shrug, Lexa went on, "The showgirl thing and the Brian thing are bad enough, but what's really going to stink is telling my dad. I mean, when I told him Mr. B just pulled my name out of the jar, he practically did a cartwheel. Right in the shop! He's going to be effing bummed as it is when I drop out. No way can I tell him about the part I got."

"Are you really sure about dropping, Lexa?" said Em, her voice careful. "I mean, somewhere in you, you wanted to be in a play. It's only been like not even two days since the drawing. Admit it, you were totally excited about it. Seriously, you know how the Mr. B thing goes. No one gets to choose their part. That's the whole point."

"I know. I know." Lexa groaned. "Except I thought if I even got picked, I'd get a little part."

She winced at how Em's face fell and then twisted with disbelief.

"You went into this," whispered Em, "wanting a crappy little part?"

"No," said Lexa, almost wailing. "I don't know."

She couldn't stand Em's expression, but there was no choice. "I *cannot* play Cherie. I am the *opposite* of Cherie." She shuddered. "I mean, come on. She is supposed to be so gorgeous and sexy that a guy is *obsessed* with her, and in the movie—"

"Movie?" cut in Em. "There's a movie of *Bus Stop*?"

"You haven't seen it?"

Em shook her head.

"Man," Lexa said, a gusty sigh escaping, "so, you have no idea who plays Cherie in the movie?"

Another headshake.

"Marilyn Monroe."

"Oh."

"Oh? That's all you've got? *Oh?*"

"Okay, so she's what?" Em let out a huff of air. "Supposed to be the bombshelliest bombshell of all time? What does that have to do with you?"

"That's the point." Lexa's little laugh sounded broken. "*Nothing*. She has nothing to do with me."

Em grabbed Lexa's hand. "Probably a million other girls, women, *whatever*, have played that role. Marilyn Monroe doesn't own it."

"Talk about killing it, though," said Lexa, "wait until you see—"

"No." Em shook her head hard. "I don't want to see."

"What? Why?"

"I want my *own* vision of this play, not some old Hollywood version. I wish you hadn't seen it either."

"Too late there," Lexa said, letting go of Em's fingers. "Not that I would ever in a million years think I could be any kind of a showgirl, but now that I've got Marilyn in my head? Hell, no."

"Hell, yes!" Em jumped off the bed. "You're not going to lame out and talk to Mr. B before Monday, right?"

Lexa opened her mouth, not even sure what she'd say at this point. It didn't matter. Em was on a Lexa rescue mission, and she wasn't waiting for an answer. She was lunging toward her flatscreen.

"That gives us a couple of days. What we need," said Em, clicking away with the remote as she sat back on the bed, "is more info."

"But—"

"No buts," said Em. She shifted, grabbing Lexa to pull her to her side. "Just give this a chance, okay?"

Lexa leaned into Em, the screen coming to life in front of her as Em continued with the remote. "What are you doing?

"Going to the dark side. Don't tell your dad."

Stomach twisting, Lexa watched Em load film after film to CyberFlix Instant Play, all of them starring none other than . . .

Marilyn Monroe.

Chapter Six

Lexa did not want to watch a stash of movies starring Marilyn Monroe, but she wanted even less to be doing what she was doing right now. Sitting at the dinner table with Aunt Ann. Oh, she adored Ann and normally adored having a meal with her. Not tonight. Before they went down for dinner, Lexa made Em swear not to say anything about her and the play, only that didn't stop Ann from spending the whole dinner gushing about Em being head costume designer, and wasn't it marvelous that she could add extra material to her application to "The New York Institute of Fashion and Design"—Ann *loved* saying the whole name—right up until decision day?

"*Bus Stop*," Ann went on, going dreamy. "How I loved that play." She told them about seeing it back in the day with her dear mama and papa at The Music Box in New York City.

A thought zapped Lexa then. A thought that pierced the place right behind her heart sharp as a hot, stinging arrow. After she dropped out of Mr. B's workshop—*sorry, Em, she was totally going to do that first thing Monday*—she wouldn't be able to volunteer for her usual backstage work. The burning arrow dug in. It would be too weird now. With everything she'd said to Mr. B. With the rest of the class wondering what happened. *Damn!* The burn spread to an ache. Why couldn't he have made her one of the diner waitresses? Lexa picked, picked, picked at her food. *Why?*

Later both girls curled up on Em's bed, a bowl of popcorn between them as well as a bottle of pale gold wine Em snitched from Aunt Ann's wine stash. They passed the bottle back and forth, sipping away while they watched *Some Like It Hot*. Mr. B's favorite. Lexa lost herself in the movie: thoughts of sexy-Marilyn in see-through dresses shifting to amusement over funny-Marilyn interacting with two guys in drag hiding from mobsters. She and Em laughed hard, sometimes hard enough that Lexa had to clutch her aching belly.

Halfway through the next movie, *How to Marry a Millionaire*, a light knock hit the door and quick, quick, Em tucked the almost empty wine bottle under the bed.

"You two are laughing so loud," said Ann, head poking in, "I can hear you all the way downstairs." She trailed off when she caught sight of the screen where Marilyn stood in close-up with her brand-new husband. "Why in the world are you watching this old movie?"

Em grabbed another handful of popcorn. "We're checking out Marilyn Monroe."

"Whyever for?" said Ann, coming all the way into the room now, still glued to the screen.

"Whyever . . . not?" Em gave Lexa a *your-secret's-safe-with-me* look. "I mean, these old movies are hysterical."

Ann sank down on the end of the bed. "I guess I shouldn't be surprised. *We* certainly thought they were absolutely wonderful. Oh, this part is great."

They watched an elegant actress named Lauren Bacall—playing the brains behind the marry-a-millionaire plan—fall off her diner stool when she realized that the grease-monkey beau she finally admitted to loving turned out to be a Texas oilman.

Ann hooted. "Isn't that the best ending ever? I never get tired of it."

Em clicked the remote, and the screen returned to the instant play queue. "Which one do you want to watch next," she said, facing Lexa. "*The Seven Year Itch* or *The Misfits?*"

Before Lexa answered, Ann said, "You really *are* checking Marilyn out. Oh, I get it. Because of *Bus Stop*. Why aren't you watching her in that?"

"Because." Em fiddled with the remote. "Because I don't want to wreck my own ideas for costumes and . . ."

Lexa plucked at Em's quilt. *Marilyn,* Bus Stop, *Mr. B's workshop.* She simply couldn't escape.

"That's why we're watching these other movies," Em babbled on, "since Marilyn was in *Bus Stop*, I want to get a—a sense of her showgirl-wise, costume-wise. Without, you know, stealing anything from *Bus Stop*."

"I may be able to help with that." Ann held up a finger. "I'll be right back."

After Ann left, Lexa poked Em's arm. "Thanks for not mentioning anything about me and the play. At dinner, too."

"S'okay." Em shrugged. "I guess most of what I told her is pretty true."

"Just to tell you," Lexa said, reaching for the hidden bottle and swigging. "It means a lot that you're trying to help me with my play-slash-Cherie-phobia."

"Heck yeah, of course I'm helping you. What's next?" Em wiggled the remote.

Eyeing the last couple of inches of wine in the bottle, Lexa murmured, "Why do you think she was so popular?"

"You mean Marilyn?"

Lexa rolled her eyes and drank.

"Good question," Em said, tapping her lip with the remote. She contemplated the ceiling for a second, then said, "Well . . . she *was* hot as hell."

"A lot of actresses are, *were*, hot as hell," muttered Lexa, "but none of them have anything close to the kind of following she has. I mean, what made *her* special?"

"Maybe she wasn't."

They stared at each other in silence, and then Lexa lifted her brows and Em pressed her lips together, snatching the bottle.

"What I mean," Em paused to drain the last inch, "is maybe back then, when these movies were made, she was a star and all, but she wasn't like this—this crazy *superstar*. Maybe that only happened after she died. You know, the big mystery? Did she swallow a bunch of pills by accident? Or commit suicide or . . ." Em deepened her voice, sounding to Lexa like a demented radio announcer. "Was it murder?"

Lexa made a scoffing sound. "How do you even *know* all that?"

"Her name always comes up on the internet," Em said, her voice a little sleepy-slurry. "Every time I look up old costume designers or old movies, all the big stars come up, Marilyn at the top of the list. The real question is why do *you* even care about some ancient dead movie star?"

"I don't know." Lexa lifted a shoulder. "I guess I don't, really." She rounded to the screen. "Which one do *you* want to watch next?"

"I don't care."

"Give me the remote."

Em tossed it to her, and she pointed it at the screen. "Eenie-meenie . . ."

Em mumbled, "Oh, *that's* mature," as the bedroom door swung wide.

Both girls froze, their mouths dropping open.

A woman posed in the doorway, a platinum blonde wig on her head, huge black sunglasses covering half her face, and a sheer cherry red chiffon scarf tied around her neck. "I told you I'd be right back," she said, in a breathy, cartoonish voice. She puckered bright red lipsticked lips and blew the girls a kiss.

"*Ann?*" choked Em. Ann stepped into the room and twirled, stopping to make kissy lips at herself in the bureau mirror. She plucked off the glasses and spoke to her image, "I don't know how I ever wore glasses this dark." One hand crept up to stroke a gleaming pale gold curl. "What do you think?"

Em slid off the bed, approaching. "Did you really *ever* wear this stuff?"

"Yes, indeedy," said Ann, "wigs were very popular when I was young, and we *all* wanted to look like Marilyn."

She chuckled at her reflection, then pulled off the wig, fluffing her own auburn-dyed hair. "That was a long time ago, though." She came to the bed, untying the scarf. "Here," she said, holding it out to Lexa, "smell."

Lexa breathed deep. A tangy-sweet and clean scent filled her.

"Chanel No. 5," Ann said with a small wistful smile. "That was Marilyn's signature scent. And Guerlain Rouge Diabolique," Ann went on, tapping her red-red bottom lip, "is what some magazines claimed was her signature lipstick shade."

Wearing the big black sunglasses now, Em bounced onto the bed. "How do you know all that?" she asked, taking the scarf for a sniff.

"Mostly from *Life Magazine*. Every week that magazine had the most glorious photos and stories about the lives of stars like Marilyn Monroe. And," Ann wagged her head, "we ate up every tasty bit."

"This Channel Five is nasty." Em tossed the scarf on the bed.

"I don't think so," Lexa said, picking it up. "I think it smells good, kind of like . . . roses and powder."

"And fresh, line-dried laundry," said Ann. "I don't use it much anymore, but it was my dear husband Philip's favorite." She hesitated, her attention seeming to drift off. "And he did love watching Marilyn movies."

Lexa's brain took her out on a limb, and she said, "Why do you think he . . . loved her so much?"

Still drifting, Ann let out a low laugh. "Marilyn was the epitome of everything gorgeous and funny and sexy."

"Didn't that make you jealous?"

Ann turned to Lexa, thoughtful now. "You'd think so, but no. Women loved her as much as men. There was simply something about her that made you want to, I don't know, take care of her. As if she was a little girl lost in the cold, and you wanted to pull her inside and tuck her up under a blanket near a blazing fire."

"I totally get that," said Em. "I keep wanting to put a coat on her."

"Exactly," said Ann. She smiled at the two of them. "Well then, thanks for indulging me, and enjoy your night with Marilyn." She stood and reached for the wig.

"Could you leave that?" Em said and took off the glasses. "And these? And the scarf, too? They'd help me a ton. With the costumes."

"Certainly. Good night, girls. Don't stay up too late."

"'Night," they both said.

When the door clicked shut, Em and Lexa looked at each other, then both shoved pillows over their mouths, muffling screams of amusement.

"Can you *believe* that?" said a breathless Em.

"Ann rocks. Hey," Lexa said, "let me see that."

Em tossed the wig to Lexa, and she pulled it on.

"*That's* a look. Let me fix it," Em said, adjusting the wig. "There." She studied Lexa. "That is so not you."

Lexa hadn't thought the wig would be her. Still . . . She lurched off the bed with a frown. Frowned more when she took in her reflection in the mirror. *Wrong*. No other word to describe her as a platinum blonde. None of that wrong had a thing to do with her no-makeup face, baggy T-shirt, and pajama pants either. The bright blonde hair made her skin go pasty and her eyes, nose, and mouth disappear into an undefined muddle.

"I'm totally not glam," she said, pulling off the wig. "Pretty much what I've been saying all day."

"You don't have to be blonde to be glam," said Em. "Come on, let's watch another movie, but first," she hopped off the bed, "I've got to pee."

As Em left, Lexa dropped the wig on the bureau, and the memory flashed. A memory that had visited her too many times over the past five years. She cringed. For the millionth time seeing her twelve-year-old self in this very room. When she and Em dressed for their first ever middle school dance. Even back then Em was obsessed with designing and remaking clothing, not giving a red-hot damn about what any of the other girls wore or thought. Lexa had let Em dress her in one of her cut-up shirts and a short, twirly kind of ballet dancer skirt.

Her face burned now imagining her twelve-year-old self in those clothes. It had felt like trying to squeeze into a doll's outfit, only Em had been so excited, and Lexa . . . well, Lexa did what she always did. She went along.

They'd gone to the dance and the second they'd stepped into the school gym, Lexa's stomach had sunk. The way the kids had stared! She'd gone to the girls' room and, in the mirror over the sink, tried to see how she could pull the shirt down over the skirt, hoping to cover, well, cover everything. Some girls had come in then, good old Hilary Poss in the lead. She'd stared at Lexa with those dark razor eyes and then put her hand over her mouth, pretending to hide her gasping giggles. The others had laughed, too, and then they'd all turned away to—as Hilary had said—"Give Lexa room. She needs it." Before the door closed, though, Lexa had heard Hilary say one more thing. "What does that *bovinian* think she's doing dressing like that?"

Lexa's entire body went hot at the memory of those words. She'd told Em, of course, and, furious, Em had grabbed her hand, stomping them up the hill and home, cursing those girls the whole way. How they didn't know anything about style or fashion. How *they* were a whole *herd* of cows because they all dressed alike. Lexa hadn't said much, but back in Em's room she couldn't get out of those microscopic clothes and into her own T-shirt and pajama pants fast enough.

She looked down at herself now, at the tent of T-shirt covering her from neck to thighs and the soft crumple of flannel PJ pants poking from beneath to pool over her bare feet. Guess she discovered her own style back then, too.

A loud *thud* had Lexa's head jerking up. She blinked, relaxed, the dark settling into the shadowy, familiar shapes of Em's room, and—she peeked to the other side of the wide bed—Em, stretched out, snoring softly.

Light caught the corner of Lexa's eye. The flat-screen TV pulsed on a paused black-and-white close-up of Marilyn's face. *The Misfits*. Right. Marilyn's last movie. Lexa yawned. And the one they'd fallen asleep watching.

Lexa rubbed her cheek, her other hand skating over the sheet, hunting for the remote. She frowned, not finding it, and peered over the edge of the mattress. The empty bottle gleamed. Ah, the waking thud.

Rolling off the bed, she scooped up the bottle before making her way across the minefield of the floor. She put the bottle on the desk, then slid her finger along the edge of the TV. She didn't push the "off" button right away, instead studying Marilyn. Marilyn Monroe. Sitting in front of a mirror, putting on makeup. Lexa leaned closer. Marilyn's character looked unhappy, the black-and-white film bringing out hollows, making skin too powdery, eyeliner too thick. Lexa traced a finger over that face. How was she still totally beautiful?

With a shiver, Lexa pushed the "off" button and Marilyn disappeared.

She crept back to the bed, checking the clock: 3:14 a.m. She climbed back onto the mattress and her forehead crinkled, fingers picking at something. The scarf. Gathering it up, she breathed in. The scent of Chanel No. 5 wafted, filling her brain with everything she didn't want to think about. She buried her face in the scarf. Saturday already. One more day to figure out what to do before facing Mr. B again, not to mention everyone else. With a grumble, she stared at the bed, wanting more than anything to crawl under the blankets and pass out to oblivion. She blinked one long blink. Who was she kidding? Creeping to the window, she took in the glow from the streetlight outside and, wrapping the scarf around her neck, she tiptoed out of the room and down the stairs to her coat and the back door.

Slowly, Lexa wandered to the end of the driveway, all but swallowed by the dark. She looked up and down the street, absorbed the stillness, as if the sub-zero temperatures had frozen the world to a place beyond quiet. Then she studied the sleeping giant of the Norris house, her gaze traveling across the roof to the very top of a monster-sized pine. Above, a slice of pale, icy moon dangled, cold, beautiful, and surrounded by twinkling pinprick stars.

"Mom?" The word slipped out of Lexa's mouth and she hugged herself, burrowing deeper into her coat, the wispy scarf rubbing her cheeks.

"Mom?" she said, louder this time, "I know it's crazy to try to talk to you this way, but . . . but there's no one else, and I need to say this stuff out loud, okay?" She blew out a long, foggy breath. "Here's the thing. I thought being in Mr. B's play was going to be great, like absolutely the most incredible way to end high school, you know? Finally make some tiny little mark of my own right here in good old Queen City." She sighed. "Now everything's messed up because . . . I made a mistake. The play is a mistake and I'm *afraid*, like I wish I could disappear afraid. I wish I could talk to Dad about this, *really* talk to him. I can't. I can't. All he talks about is how lucky I am to get such a good deal at State, and he's worried about Film Buzz and money. How could I tell him maybe I want to do something else? G*o* somewhere else. *Anywhere* else."

Shivering, she hugged herself harder and shook her head. "He'd be so alone, though. All alone. Man, I know he still misses you a ton. I always knew that, only this whole play thing is making it worse, because of how happy he is that I got picked. If I drop out," her lips trembled, "he'll be really sad. The last thing I want is for him to feel like he, you know, didn't do a good job." She trailed off, the backs of her eyes beginning to sting.

"I don't want to end high school as the biggest joke in the world, and I don't know what to do about it," she whispered. She shoved her hands harder under her armpits and her silver ring pinched at her cramped, frozen fingers. "I—I tried to talk to Em about it, and I know she wants to help, except she's *always* trying to help, and someone like her? She just can't understand. I wish I was brave enough to do that stupid part. I really do. I wish I had even a crumb of whatever magic Marilyn had. I don't and—I wish you were here, okay? I wish that *so much*."

She stared at the lights in the endless sky, the moon and stars suspended together like a sparkly chandelier, and she hoped for . . . she wasn't sure for what, exactly. A sign. Something, anything to tell her what to do.

All at once she jerked, searching the sky. Was that a flash? A falling star? She stared and stared. Nothing. Her gaze cut to the moon again, and her whole body shivered. She was cold. Too cold. Too small. Too alone under that sweeping sky. Then she was racing across the crunchy frozen lawn, one hand yanking the scarf from her neck, her throat swelling, choking her big and empty and hot.

Choking her with the wish she made.

Her dumb little-kid wish that could never, never come true.

There's gonna be trouble.
I kin feel it in my bones.

—Cherie, *Bus Stop*

Part Two

Chapter One

Sound woke Lexa, high and faraway, tinkly as bells.

She opened one eye, stared at the rumple of sheets, pillows, sunlight. Her hand moved, full of something hard. The remote. The one she'd been searching for in the middle of the night.

The tinkly sound came again. She listened, straining. Only the sound was now gone.

With a grunt of confusion, she rolled to face Em's side of the bed. "What was that sou…?" and trailed off. Em wasn't there.

Sitting up, Lexa stretched the stiffness from her neck and shoulders, rubbing at her chest, her belly, both feeling tight, bloated. Her brain was smooshy, too, her eyes burning. Too many movies. And that wine. She ran her tongue around the inside of her mouth. That stuff had tasted sweet as apple syrup, but it had to have been strong. Really strong. She put her hand to her woozy head, blinking at the morning light sizzling at the edges of the blinds. *Window. Outside*. She groaned. Had she honestly snuck out in the freezing dark?

A disgusted breath hissed between her lips. "Talking to the dead mom. Perfect."

That tinkling in her head again, higher, farther away. Frowning, she poked a finger inside first one ear, and then the other. Sounded like—laughter. More light caught at her. The screen. It was on again, full of Marilyn's face. Slowly and carefully, Marilyn applied eyeliner. When she finished, Marilyn's eyes widened, shifted as if searching. The screen went blank and Lexa blinked, her fingers tightening on the remote. She hadn't pushed any of the buttons. She was sure of it. Again, that tinkling laugh, like a ripple in her ears, under her skin.

Dropping the remote, she smashed both hands over her ears. "*Stop!* Stop it!" Her ears throbbed, the laughter rising. She shook her head, whispering now. "Stop, *please* stop."

The laughter went lower, muffling, like a laughing person trying to stop.

"O-kay. Ooooo-kay." Lexa could hear her own voice, crooney and soothey. "Cut it out now." She pressed her palms harder over her ears. "Man, who am I even talking to?"

"*Jesus*, Lexa. What's going on?"

Lexa swung around, her hands whipping away from her head. Em stood in the doorway, her expression covered with how nuts Lexa looked.

"I don't know," Lexa said. "I hear this . . ." She hesitated. The tinkly laughter was gone.

Em stepped into the room. "You hear . . . ?"

"It was like my brain was . . . laughing. It stopped now."

"Weird," Em said after a moment.

"Maybe I'm hungover," Lexa mumbled. "Are you?"

"No, and hey, Ann wants to know if you want one piece of French toast or two."

Bacon. The word bloomed in Lexa's head even as she smelled the scent of it cooking. For an instant, her mouth watered. Only Lexa didn't eat bacon. Ann insisted on cooking herself up a few pieces, but ages ago Em and Lexa decided together that bacon—really all red meat—was nasty.

"One's good," Lexa said. She crouched down near her pack, adding, "You go ahead. I'll be right down."

When she heard the door close, Lexa dropped to her butt, hugging her head, listening. Silence roared, only there was something. Something. The skin on the back of her neck prickled, and her hand whipped to the spot, head spinning around. She was alone, only she'd been sure . . . No. She wasn't sure. Her hand dropped from her neck, limp. Hadn't been sure of *anything* since Mr. B pulled her damn name out of that damn jar.

Maybe she was coming down with some crazy flu. At the kitchen counter island now, Lexa nibbled another bite of syrupy French toast. On nearby stools, Em and Ann talked about plans for reorganizing the mudroom closet or, rather, Ann talked about her plan to have Em "spearhead the effort." Laughing, Em kicked Lexa's shin, mouthing, "*Spearhead the effort.*" Lexa had to force out an answering laugh.

"Sorry, Ann," said Em, "Lexa and I have a ton to do today, right?"

Lexa opened her mouth to echo the expected, "Right." What came out instead was, "Oh, yeah. I totally forgot I promised to . . . go home." *Why am I saying this?* "As soon as I woke up."

Em's face wrinkled, an unhappy version of *huh?* "What? Do you have to help your dad again?"

"Yes." The word jumped out of Lexa's mouth like it had a will of its own. Then, almost like being outside her body, she watched herself slide off her stool, pile her fork and knife onto her syrupy plate, and cart the load over to the dishwasher. Near the sink, one lone piece of bacon sat on a grease-soaked paper towel. Her fingers snatched out, and she stuffed it in her mouth whole, moaning at the salty crunch.

"Sorry," she managed, wiping at her face.

Em and Ann gazed at her, open-mouthed.

"Do you . . . want more?" Ann said finally.

What Lexa wanted to say was how weird her body felt, only something pushed those words down and others out. "No, thanks. Gotta run," she said, hurrying to the stairs. "I'll get my things—"

She stopped short when Ann called, "Did you want to borrow that, dear?"

"What?"

"That scarf I showed you."

"Scarf?"

"Why, the one in your back pocket. The Marilyn scarf."

Lexa yanked the scarf out of her pocket, gaping at it, dizzy.

Her eyes snapped back to Em and Ann. Both studied her with identical worried frowns. Lexa wanted to say, "No, I don't want to borrow it and I'm *not* all right." She wanted to throw the scarf away. Except her fingers clutched at it. "Yes. I'd like to borrow it," came out of her mouth, and, "that'd be peachy." *Peachy?*

"Well, that's fine then," said Ann with a gentle nod. "That color will be good on you. Dress you up a little."

"Thanks," Lexa said with a gulp and lunged up the stairs, the scarf scrunched in her fist.

In Em's room, she grabbed her pack and shoved in the scarf, and then hurried out, only to stop at the top of the stairs. As if hypnotized, she circled to the door at the opposite end of the hall.

She crept over. Pushed open the door. A tidy four-poster bed took up the center of the room, the thin cream-colored comforter smooth, pale blue satin pillows plumped against the dark wooden headboard.

Ann's room.

Even as her brain hammered, *What are you doing?* Lexa crossed to a small pocket-door. Ann's personal bathroom. Slow and inching, she slipped in, blinked at herself in the gilt-edged mirrored cabinet. "Why are you snooping?" she mouthed to her reflection, "and why are you talking to yourself?" She didn't answer either question, instead lowering her pack to the floor. A corner of the red scarf poked out of the front pocket. She pushed at it, but the springy sheerness of the fabric made it *poof* out again. She shoved it in with clumsy fingers and zipped the pocket so fast that the fabric almost caught.

Straightening, Lexa fixed on a glass shelf above the sink. Amber-colored perfume in three pretty stoppered bottles. Her hand reached out, and she knew which one she'd pick. Chanel No. 5. She pulled the stopper and, eyelids lowering, inhaled powder and roses and sunlight.

"Mmmmm. How I *loved* that scent."

Bottle bobbling, Lexa swung around. "I'm so sorry, Ann, I—"

No one. But—but *that voice*.

She darted out to the bedroom, the only movement dust motes spiraling in a sunbeam.

At home in her own room, in her own bed, Lexa pulled the squish of her faded green down comforter up to her chin and sank into the quiet. Late morning sun washed over her walls, her door, her furniture, her rug, lighting up the colors and textures in a way that should have made them look extra solid and real. Extra normal. Except they didn't. Not today. Her gaze cut to the posters covering her walls: Greece, Spain, France, Ireland. Ages ago Dad had gotten a series of travel DVDs, and she'd snagged some of the promo posters. Looking at all these places usually warmed her up inside. Even if she and

Dad couldn't actually afford to go to any of these destinations, she liked knowing they were out there. Liked knowing that someday she'd figure out how to get out of Queen City and go somewhere new. Somewhere where *she* could be new, too.

One after another, she studied each poster. No warm feeling came.

Rubbing at her too tight chest, Lexa lay back, staring at the blank of her ceiling. Was she actually so panicked about the play thing, the Cherie thing, that she was flipping out? Or maybe . . . One hand found the other, twisting at her ring, everything she'd said to her mom in the night looping through her head.

"Queen City High senior has mental breakdown," she muttered, biting her bottom lip as a picture of Dad's worried, heartbroken face filled her brain. Em stood next to him, her expression beyond devastated. With a whimper, Lexa yanked the comforter over her head. She hadn't thought anything could be worse than the disappointment of the two people she loved most when she quit the play. Except this. This would be way worse.

"Stop it!" she said, squeezing her lids shut, "cut it out."

A new sound slipped into her consciousness.

Click, click . . . click.

Slow and steady, each *click* echoed, like . . . heels. Tapping on a tile floor. Coming toward her, as if down a long hall. Lexa didn't move. Couldn't.

There were no tile floors in the apartment. Or long halls.

No pictures played behind her eyes now, only thick darkness.

The *clicks* grew louder and her breathing, shallower and shallower. The dark behind her eyelids began to billow like a heavy curtain and, in one smooth move, pearly pink fingernails sliced through the darkness, drawing it away.

Lexa's lids flew up. *Nonono!* She wasn't thinking about *her*. Scrubbing the heels of her hands into her eyes, she tried to make the figure disappear. It didn't. *She* didn't. She just stayed smack in the middle of Lexa's head. Big as life. Marilyn Monroe.

"Hi, Kid."

Chapter Two

I am having a psychotic episode! I am having a psychotic . . . Lexa hugged her shins, pressing her face to her knees, rocking, muttering, rocking.

"Oh, honey." Marilyn stepped closer only to hesitate when Lexa shrank back. "You are not going crazy. Listen to me. Listen now."

"I am!" Lexa's whisper came out steamy hot. "I am, I am, I am!"

Marilyn put one hand to her throat, her delicate nails gleaming like flower petals.

"You can't do that!" Lexa said, chin jerking up. She didn't see her room, though, didn't see anything but Marilyn. "This doesn't happen. People can't be in my head if I don't want them there. They can't *do* stuff without me thinking it!"

"Jeepers," Marilyn blinked back, once, twice, then lifted a shoulder in an elegant shrug. "I suppose I see why you'd think all of that, but the fact is, I am here. In your head. In you."

"How can this keep getting weirder and weirder?" Lexa touched her sweaty forehead, studied her hands. "I have to be sick. Some crazy flu."

Marilyn's brow wrinkled, and then she peeked over her shoulder. The weirdness went on as all at once a tall director-type chair appeared. Marilyn *click-clicked* to the chair and perched, crossing one leg over the other. "You let me know when you're ready to talk." She clasped her knee and cuddled back against the canvas. "I'm pretty sure I've got all the time in the world."

They eyed each other, Marilyn sitting as if posing for photos, and Lexa in a full-body tremble, her thoughts warring sharp and fast.

She needed a doctor.

She needed her dad.

She needed her dad to *take* her to a doctor. Probably a therapist. A specialist who would know what it meant to have a delusion that Marilyn Monroe seemed to have taken up residence in her head.

Lexa opened her mouth, the yell for her dad that wanted to blast out of her mouth silenced by the image of his heartbroken, worried face, this time looking at her, no—no, *examining* her, and blaming himself. His poor, insane daughter strapped to a bed, writhing and screaming and—

She froze, frowning at Marilyn. "Why am I not writhing and screaming? Why are you my only . . . symptom?"

"I am no one's 'symptom' of anything. I am . . . something else." Marilyn's eyes crinkled. "What do you think I am?"

"You're." Lexa's mouth was like dust. "Dead?"

Marilyn's mouth pouted into a shocked O.

"Sorry," Lexa mumbled, "*man*, I'm not exactly used to talking to a—" What she'd been about to say knocked the wind clear out of her. "No." Her head began a slow back and forth. "Uh-uh."

"That's right," Marilyn said with a nod. "You answered the $64,000 question. I'm a . . ." Her lifted chin was a prompt.

Mouth trembling, Lexa whispered, "G-*ghost?*"

"I'm thinking 'spirit.' Isn't that a kick?" Marilyn let out a deep, delighted belly laugh and rose. "And it's swell! Why, if I'd had any idea I'd feel this way, I'd have tried being in a body again sooner." She twirled slowly. "Breathing, walking."

Lexa gawked at giggling, twirling, chattering Marilyn. This was even more insane than being insane. She had to be dreaming. Yes. *Yesyesyes. Dreaming.*

"Feeling warm, tasting French toast and bacon and coffee," Marilyn paused, took a deep breath, "smelling my favorite Chanel No. 5. Mmmmm."

The movies! That's why Lexa was having this crazy-ass dream. Look, Marilyn even had on that black lacy shirt and tight skirt from *Bus Stop*.

Facing Lexa again, Marilyn put her hand over her mouth. "Oopsie. I do apologize for sort of fooling with you earlier. Seems that sometimes I do something in here, and your body kind of follows." Her breathy amusement was too familiar after all those movies.

Wait. Could a dream Lexa was having now *remember* weirdness from that morning at Em's? More and more confused, Lexa said, "Okay, you're a spirit." She inhaled a long breath, trying to make her body relax into the dream. "What does the spirit of Marilyn Monroe want with me?"

"Why." Marilyn's amusement faded. "You don't believe me. Now you're simply playing along."

"Um, of course I believe you." Lexa made her wooden lips twist into a smile. A dream-smile.

Marilyn wandered forward, eyes slitted. "You've got a ways to go with your acting, sugar."

A snort escaping, Lexa said, "I'm not acting. Come on, work with me." She sucked in another calming dream-breath. "I'm only trying to keep the dream moving here so I can, you know, wake up."

"This is *not* a dream. I am a spirit, coming all the way to you from beyond the grave," Marilyn sputtered. "Aren't you the littlest bit curious why?"

"Fine," said Lexa, "I'm curious why you're here from"—her fingers shot out to make air quotes—"'Beyond the Grave.' Go ahead. Explain it to me."

"Don't take that snooty tone with me, young lady! I heard you calling for your mama last night." Marilyn trailed off as Lexa slumped back against the headboard. "Oh, honey," Marilyn's eyes went wide and soft, "I'm terribly sorry. I—"

"Stop." Lexa hugged her pillow. "You're right," she murmured, "I did talk to my mom last night. She's the one I wished for, so—so if you're here from the beyond, why didn't she come?"

"I've been wondering that very thing," Marilyn said, "from the second I landed in you, and all through the night while I waited for you to wake up. Wondering and wondering." She lifted her hands, palms up. "I don't know the exact answer. I've got some ideas, though." She cocked her head, "I don't think her kind can come back."

"Her—*kind*?"

"You see, your mama's probably what I'd call a regular spirit. I think spirits like me are different because . . ." Marilyn hesitated, pressing those red lips together. "I think it's because of the way you hold on to me."

"What are you even talking about?" Lexa shook her head, even more confused. "I am so not holding on to you."

"I don't mean 'you' in particular." Marilyn returned to the director's chair, hitching herself up onto the seat again. "I mean, *people*. Why, it's been years and years since I died, but you all won't let me go. I'm serious." She waved a hand. "Movies, photos, books. I'm everywhere. And I haven't even gotten started on those singers and models copy-catting my look, or all that computer stuff. Why, I have more fans now than I ever had when I was alive."

She paused, batting her lashes. Dazed, Lexa could see why her words would be true. That blonde-blonde hair, those huge eyes, that pouting mouth: all had taken a mesmerizing hold.

"Don't you see?" Marilyn pressed clasped hands to her chest, her lids lowering dreamily. "All that attention and curiosity and—and adoration. It must be like threads tying my spirit to this living world. That's probably why I could come back, but not your mama." Her hands lowered to her lap. "That's probably why I could see you in the first place. Why I could watch you. Why I *wanted* to watch you. And then when I heard you calling for your mama last night, so sweet and sad, somehow all that wanting and wishing brought me to you. I think . . . I think I'm supposed to help you."

"H-help me?"

"With the play, honey. With *Cherie*."

Belief sprang in Lexa's belly, uncoiling sharp as a wire, spearing up to wrap hot and fast around her heart. "This isn't happening," she insisted. "I don't believe in spirits, or, or ghosts." Even as Lexa spoke, her pulses thudded in her ears, the too-tight sensation in her chest and belly spreading to her arms and hands, her legs and feet. "This has to be a dream. A dream."

"A dream?" Marilyn stood, and the director's chair winked out. "I'm going to take that as my cue to give you a moment, sugar, to think deep about dreams. Dreams, and not dreams."

She disappeared.

Chapter Three

"This. Can't. Be happening!" Lexa curled up into a ball, reeling and rocking. "I cannot have a ghost in me. I mean, a spirit. I mean—"

Zap—Marilyn filled her mind again, a slam-punch that had Lexa jerking against the headboard.

"Don't *do* that!" Lexa barked.

"Sorry about that. I'm new at this," Marilyn said, settling back in her reappeared director's chair. "I'll try to make my entrances more . . . subtle."

"O—okay. Okay." Lexa uncurled from her ball. "Okay," she whispered again. The word kept coming out of her mouth like a prayer for how she wanted to feel. She lay still a moment, dazed. "I feel like I should be afraid," she tried, the slowness of her speech a kind of taking stock. "Somehow . . . I'm not."

"Thank goodness for that," said Marilyn. She regarded Lexa. "You do look whooped, though. Maybe you should take a nap. We can talk more after."

"A *nap*. The spirit of Marilyn Monroe is telling me to take a nap. Is that how this is going to work?"

Marilyn's shoulders shimmied, a delighted giggle bubbling through her lips.

"Now you're laughing at me?" Lexa said.

"I'm not laughing at you, honest," Marilyn said through more giggles. "It's being here. I told you before. I had no *idea* how good it would feel. Even you yelling at me. All that passion and youth." She hugged herself tight. "It's intoxicating."

They blinked at each other, and then Lexa said, "Can we, like . . . start over? Why me? I mean, how do you even *know* about me?"

"That is a good question." Marilyn tilted her head. "One moment I, well, let's say I was doing what I always do. The next, it was like I told you. I saw you."

"*Saw* me?"

"Standing in front of that bulletin board at school. Reading your name on that cast list."

"How? How could you see me from . . ." Lexa couldn't even come up with the words.

"Uh, uh, uh," said Marilyn, her index finger ticking side to side. "I don't know this for sure, but I think it's best if we don't talk much about," her voice went low and dramatic, "the 'other side.' I'm thinking that's got to be one of the rules."

"One of the *rules*? Now there are rules?"

"Why, of course there have to be rules, sugar. Not understanding how I got here is one thing, but now that I am, I sure don't want to mess anything up. Why the—" She slapped a hand over her mouth. "Oh, this is hard," she whispered through her fingers, "no more questions about the dead. *That's* rule number, well, rule number everything. I know, why don't you sit back and get comfy, and I'll tell you what I can."

After a moment of hesitation, Lexa said, "All right."

Marilyn sat up taller, saluting. "Thank you very much. Now go on. Get comfortable."

Punching her pillows into a puffy pile, Lexa sank against them.

"Good girl," Marilyn said. "Like I said, I was doing what I

usually do, and then there you were, standing by that bulletin board, all lit up and in color. Full of thoughts and feelings and fears. A lot of them about me. About me when I was *alive*, I mean. I couldn't seem to look away, like it was important that I see you, maybe even watch you. So, I did." Her shoulders did the quick up and down slice. "The moment I saw that you were cast as Cherie in *Bus Stop*, you catching my attention made perfect sense, except for the part where fear rolled off you in thick, dark waves. Some of that fear connected to me." Marilyn pursed her lips. "Me, when I was a movie star, that is. I did not understand all that fear, and I wanted to. So, when you ran off from your friends, I, well, I guess I stayed with you."

"Stayed with me?"

"That's what it felt like. Anyway, I wanted to know what you were going to do, and then I was able to watch you. Your life. Like a crazy movie."

"Oh," Lexa said, Marilyn's logic making her world spin even harder. "I guess that makes sense."

"I saw what happened at that Mr. B's house. How sweet you were about me. And," Marilyn's features softened, "I couldn't stop watching, because—oh, dear, I hope telling you this is a good idea."

"You couldn't stop watching," prompted Lexa.

Marilyn squared her shoulders. "When you were on the bus, and then later when you walked to your friend's house. I wanted to know why you felt the way you did and your memories simply—simply came at me. How you got in the class, what happened after."

"You." Cheeks on fire now, Lexa swallowed hard. "You *stalked* my memories?"

"I absolutely had to know," Marilyn said fast, her cheeks pinking too, "what you'd do about the play and why you were doing it."

Pressure, like a stroking hand, slid from the top of Lexa's head down her neck. She shivered, rubbing at the spot. "Look, uh, Marilyn," she said, "you being curious about me and my stupid fear of acting is sort of understandable. If you've been watching me, you already know that I'm dropping out of the play."

"Oh, honey, you can't do that now!" Marilyn's eyes got huge, like *she'd* seen a ghost. "Why I'm sure that's why I'm here. To help you with the play and—"

"No. Uh-uh!" Lexa said. "I've made up my mind about the play, and I don't want to talk about it anymore. Those are my rules."

They watched each other a moment, and then Marilyn sat back. "Well now," she said, the corners of her mouth turning down. "What am I supposed to do with that?"

"I think . . ." Lexa nodded to herself, mouth tightening. "I think you should leave. Before things get any crazier." A flashing TV-type montage careened through her mind: of her—the amazing Marilyn-spirit-in-the-head girl—on some talk show, being badgered by a fast-mouthed host; doctors all over her, more badgering, this time with needles; the tabloids, the headlines, the internet; kids from QueenHi pointing and laughing; Dad, looking rumpled and gray, his eyes buggy with shock.

"My, my, my. You have quite an imagination," Marilyn said, her voice extra breathy, "only none of that has anything to do with me."

"I don't care," Lexa said, "and stop reading my mind. I—I really appreciate you coming, but seriously, I think you should leave."

Marilyn bit her lip. "I can barely keep up with you. If that's what you want, I suppose—I suppose I don't have a choice." With an uncertain frown, she rose. "Good luck with everything."

"You too," Lexa said and, even as she wondered if luck was something spirits could use, a need spiked. "Hey, uh, Marilyn? Hold up." She blinked fast, twisting her ring. "If . . . if somehow you see my mom back there? Could you tell her I—I think about her?"

A faraway look came over Marilyn's face. "If I can, I will." She focused in on Lexa again. "You okay, honey? Your eyes look a little funny and the tip of your nose is bright red. Thinking of your mama makes you sad, doesn't it?"

"No. Yes." Lexa blew out a breath. "Yes and no. It's only that until lately I hadn't thought of her in a long time. I mean, she died when I was a baby, so it's not like I knew her, except for what my dad's told me. He doesn't like to talk about it." She circled her ring, slow and sad. "It's weird missing someone I never really got to know."

"There are lots of ways to miss someone," Marilyn said. "Believe me, I've either lived or acted all of them."

"Do you think she, my mom, is doing okay?"

"Doing okay . . . you mean, like happy?" A shadow crossed Marilyn's face, then she tilted her head. "Oh, I guess telling you this won't hurt anything. As far as I can tell, on the other side, feelings like 'happy' and 'sad' don't mean the same thing as here."

"I guess that makes sense," Lexa said slowly.

"Do you want to talk about your mama a little more? I could." Marilyn shifted to sit again.

"No." Lexa shook her head hard. "I mean, thanks. But no."

"Are you sure?"

"I'm not really sure about anything." Lexa tried to smile. "I'm sorry for being kind of a jerk before. About not believing you. Thanks for coming. Really."

"You really want me to go?" Marilyn didn't take her eyes off Lexa. "That's really and truly what you want?"

Drawing her knees to her chest, Lexa hugged them hard and nodded.

"All right then." Marilyn began walking, getting smaller and smaller, as though Lexa's brain became an ever-expanding tunnel. Holding her breath, Lexa braced. Marilyn would disappear now. Now.

Then Marilyn stopped, lifted her arms, turning in a circle. When she spoke, her voice came to Lexa as a strangled whisper. "Honey? I—I seem to be stuck."

Zap—Marilyn was right close again.

"What do you mean?" said Lexa. "Stuck?"

"I don't know. I have no idea how I got here, only I figured when it was time to leave I'd simply"—Marilyn snapped her fingers—"Poof!"

"Try again."

Marilyn balled her hands into fists at her sides and closed her eyes, her expression tight, pushing.

Nothing happened.

"Well, this is kooky," she said, her eyes opening wide. "Wait a minute. I know. If the reason I'm here is to help you with the play, then maybe I can't leave until you are done with the play."

"I *am* done," said Lexa, "I'm dropping out."

"Sure, only you haven't yet," said Marilyn with a knowing smile. "Not physically."

Lexa lunged for her pack. "I'll call Mr. B right now."

"Honey?" Marilyn's eyes went dark and liquid. "Now that we have another moment, there is one thing." She hesitated, lips parted. "One *tiny* little favor I would ask."

Lexa's pulse went into overdrive, her entire body vibrating. "You said—you said you'd leave."

Marilyn's hands went to her hips. "What happened to 'I'm not afraid of you'?"

"I—I don't know."

"That beats all!" Marilyn said. "What am I going to do with you?"

"I'm going to call Mr. B," Lexa said, scrabbling through Mr. B's handouts. "I just need to find his number. Then it'll be done and you can leave."

"Fine," Marilyn said, "I will leave—if I can." She waved a hand, encouraging Lexa to make her call. "Don't act like I was trying to scare you, though. Because I wasn't."

Number in hand, Lexa rooted for her phone. She could hear Marilyn talking to herself, a whispered rant. "You're a fool, Marilyn, a dead fool. Serves you right for wanting to help somebody, and then wanting something for yourself."

Lexa lowered the phone, watching Marilyn: Marilyn who'd come from . . . who knows where to help her. To help her, Alexandria Donovan.

Marilyn's voice was barely a mutter now. "Even if it was for only a couple of . . ."

"A couple of what?"

Marilyn's chin snapped to Lexa. "Did you say something?"

"A couple of what?" Lexa repeated, voice shaking.

Marilyn clasped her hands against her belly. "You see, I had no idea it would feel this way." Her red lips moved against her teeth as if that bit of motion would make Lexa see the truth of what she said. "This might be my only chance. To be back in the living world, feeling everything a living person feels, tastes, smells. I know I have to go back, only if you could hold that call and let me stay with you. *In you*. For a couple of days. That's all I want."

Her need burned into Lexa. Marilyn had to go back. *Of course*, she had to go back. The no-choiceness of that snaked and churned in Lexa's belly. Except . . . she was here. Her spirit was here. Now. With the living. With Lexa. The snaky writhing shifted to a curious flutter.

"A couple of days," Lexa said at last, "then I'll make the call to Mr. B, and you'll go?"

Marilyn's face bloomed. "That's right, honey, a couple of days and then I'll go. What do you say?"

Chapter Four

"I can't believe I'm doing this," Lexa whispered, "but—okay."

For one frozen second, Marilyn stared at Lexa with huge eyes. Then her arms shot over her head, and she twirled fast, squealing high and loud.

Heat and cold blasted through Lexa, and her body catapulted to the floor, careening in a circle, arms and legs flailing. Her mouth opened, a gajillion-decibel shriek blaring. Marilyn whipped to face her and, puppet-wires cut, Lexa collapsed on the rug.

"Lexa?" The bedroom door flung open, Dad rushing in. "What's going on?"

"N-nothing," Lexa managed, scrambling up.

"What was all that shouting?" Dad looked Lexa up and down. "What were you doing on the floor?"

"Floor?" It didn't take acting for Lexa to sound confused. "Shouting?"

"Yes, floor and shouting," he said, glancing around. "And I could've sworn I heard someone else in here."

"No. Only me." Lexa glanced around too, almost guiltily, like she really was hiding someone. Wait—she was hiding someone! She glared at Marilyn, both of whose hands pressed over her mouth.

Dad ran a hand over his beard. "What on earth were you doing?"

"I was . . . I was practicing. A scene. You know, for the—for the *Bus Stop* thing."

Dad's *aha* smile hit, bright as sunlight through a cloud break. "I see," he said, "that's great. Only, ah, let me know next time. When you're rehearsing. So, I don't think you're being killed in your bed."

"I sure will. Sorry 'bout that."

The second the door shut, Lexa flopped on the bed, arms wrapped around her head. "This is already a bad idea."

Marilyn's fingers fell from her mouth. "Oopsie," she whispered, "I guess I got carried away. I couldn't help it, sugar. *Thank you*. A million times thank you. Don't you worry. From now on you won't even know I'm here." She paused. "I mean, you will know I'm here, but I'll be quiet as a mouse. I'll—" she slipped into her director's chair— "I'll sit right here."

Slowly Lexa peeled her arms from her head. When Marilyn's mouth opened again, Lexa shot up her hand. "Stop! Don't say anything else. Don't *do* anything else." The leftover echoes of all that shrieking still throbbing behind her eyes, she studied Marilyn. "Before . . . you said that it was you this morning, too. Turning Em's TV on? Snarfing that bacon? Putting the scarf in my pocket?"

Marilyn nodded, her cheeks actually getting pink.

Lexa nodded too, only slower. "I didn't even know I was doing some of those things. This time? When you—when you shouted and moved around really fast? I was your totally out-of-control puppet."

"I didn't mean it," Marilyn said, her voice really small. "Like I said. I'm new at this being-in-a-body thing."

"That doesn't matter. I couldn't think because my head felt like it would pop, and my dad . . . well, you saw what happened there." Lexa sucked in a breath, the pounding in her head dulling inch by inch. "I—I want to help you, but—wait, are you controlling me now?"

Looking straight into Lexa's eyes, Marilyn said, "I would never do that. Not on purpose, that is. And I won't do it again. I'll control myself." She x-ed a pearly fingernail over her chest. "Cross my heart."

The moment expanded like a giant bubble, bursting when Lexa said, "I believe you." Steadier now, she said. "Okay, you're here for a couple of days. What do you want to do?"

"Why," Marilyn's shoulders rose, her eyes half-closing. "*Everything.*"

Letting out a quiet snort, Lexa said, "I'm not sure how much 'everything' I can offer you. I'm a high school kid, and I'm poor. You're probably used to a lot of fancy stuff."

Marilyn sat up taller. "What I'm used to, I mean, what I was used to when I was alive, well, none of that has anything to do with now. I guess this is a good time to mention my most important personal rule," she said, her smile gone. "I don't mind if you want to watch more of my old movies or look at thousands of old photos, but somehow I don't think it's a good idea to spend too much time talking about Marilyn Monroe's past."

Lexa said, "You mean you can be in my head, know all my secret thoughts, watch my every move, and I can't ask you anything?"

"Oh, you can ask me whatever you want. I'm going to be careful about what I answer is all. I don't want to mess things up. Besides." Marilyn gave her a lopsided smile. "A girl's got to have a few secrets."

"Right," Lexa said, *Whatever you say*, on the tip of her tongue. Then what Em told her about Marilyn's mysterious death splashed over her, shocking and cold as a face full of ice water.

"See what I mean? There's the biggest mess of all," Marilyn said. "And don't think I don't know I can't stop you from reading about me." Her gaze traveled, and Lexa swung around: Her laptop sat open on the desk.

"You could read about my whole life," Marilyn said, "truth and lies. Honestly? Mostly lies."

Lexa stared at the laptop a moment and then gave herself a determined shake, eyeing Marilyn again. "I won't read about you," she said, "I guess . . . somehow that seems kind of, I don't know, rude. With you right here and all."

Marilyn's smile bloomed. "Why that's nice. Nice and respectful. Thanks."

"No problem," Lexa said, and hoped that in all this crazy, that wasn't her craziest choice yet.

Chapter Five

Fresh air. Breathing it in on a long walk. That was Marilyn's idea for their first official "outing." So, when Em called, begging Lexa to talk Dad into cutting her Film Buzz shift short to meet downtown at Golden Oldies for a little costume recon expedition, Lexa jumped at the chance to get out. Out of the shop. Out of her head. Out.

The day was good for walking too, cold but not windy, and strolling along the sidewalk bundled into her peacoat was plenty warm. That's what Lexa told Em when she'd nixed her offer of a ride. Only a mile and half to downtown. A perfect amount of time to be out in the world with Marilyn before they faced Em.

On their way out the door, Lexa'd grabbed Ann's scarf. Now in the cold, the thin fabric slid silky and papery against her neck, the barest hint of Chanel perfuming the air. In Lexa's head Marilyn snuggled back on her director's chair, looking to the side as if gazing out a car window. Marilyn stroked the arms of her coat—a twin of Lexa's—and like a, well, like a ghost, Lexa felt the pressure of invisible hands rubbing against her own coat-covered arms.

"Wool is too itchy," Marilyn said, "have you ever tried fur?"

Lexa almost said, "No," out loud before catching herself. She took a quick glance around. Good. They were alone.

"When we're outside, or around other people," Lexa murmured, "try not to talk to me. It's hard not to answer, and I don't want to get caught talking to, well, to myself."

Marilyn sighed and said, "I'll try to remember, only there's so much to see and feel. Take a deep breath, sugar."

Lexa did.

"Isn't it delicious?" Marilyn's lids lowered. "All that fresh wintry air?"

Lexa rubbed her stinging nose, and Marilyn rubbed hers. They both laughed.

"Why do you look normal?" Lexa said, keeping her voice low as she trailed her fingers along the tops of a white picket fence. "I mean, I've never thought much about what a spirit *should* look like. I don't think this is what I would've expected, though."

"You mean, why am I not all spooky? Like . . . let me see. This?" Slowly Marilyn's face bled of all color, becoming transparent. "*Boo*," she said, "or . . ." In a flash, her silvery, see-through face became a twisted mass of swampy gray skin and open oozing sores.

Lexa stumbled back, her shoulder hitting the sharp tip of a picket fence. "Ew!"

"Hey!" A voice came from behind the fence. "Easy on the fence, Alexandria Donovan!"

Lexa turned to find an older gentleman frowning at her, his hands full of the holiday lights he was taking down from the front of his house. "Sorry, Mr. Licata," she called. "I slipped and—and your nice fence caught me. Thanks." She patted the fence. "Nice fence."

"Everyone's a wiseass these days," the man called after her hurrying-away form.

"Sorry." Marilyn was herself again. "Hey, you know what? We're forgetting something. I can hear your thoughts. You don't have to talk out loud."

"Oh . . . right," Lexa said, "I'll—I'll try to remember." If a mind could grumble, hers did. "It'd probably help if you didn't pull anything like that horror face again."

Marilyn pouted, saying, "I was under the impression kids today liked that zombie stuff."

What are you, nuts? That's what Lexa wanted to say; instead, barely controlling a snort, she pressed her lips together tight and said to Marilyn in her mind, "You know? You're right. Without freaking me out," she went on, her brain stumbling a bit, like she was learning a new language, "can you tell me why I see you the way I do?"

"I don't know for sure. I guess people have all kinds of ideas of how spirits are supposed to be," Marilyn said, looking out her "window" again. "I don't think there's any one way. After all, there's no 'me' to be here. Last night? While you were still asleep? While I was getting used to being 'in you,' I had time to think, and I figured you seeing me and hearing me how you expect to see and hear me would be the biggest help to you."

"What's that supposed to mean?"

"I s'pose I should tell you." Marilyn pivoted to Lexa, her expression thoughtful. "I know everything."

"Everything?"

"I already told you I know everything about *Bus Stop* and what you think of acting. What you feel about your daddy. What you think about me. And . . ." her tone slowed, going cautious. "I know what you think of yourself, too."

Lexa stared down at her walking feet. "Oh."

They came to an intersection at the edge of downtown. Lexa slapped the walk signal button. After a long moment, she said, "That explains a lot. It's—it's embarrassing. Embarrassing as hell. For you to know so much. For you of *all* people to know so much about me."

"Oh, sugar," Marilyn said, "I didn't mean to pry. All those memories kind of appeared, and I couldn't help watching. I really couldn't, like I was sitting there at the movies cemented to my seat with your life right there in front of me. And it seemed important." Her eyes widened—big, blue, and serious. "Important to understand you. I'm not explaining this very well. I'm sorry I didn't tell you before. It was a lot, and believe me, I know exactly how you feel. All those years when I was alive, people, the press, picking at my life like vultures on a fat, juicy carcass. Even after I died." Her whisper went rough and low. "Why, it's almost worse now."

"But you—you had to know that's the way it would be," Lexa mumbled, unable to help the quiet words slipping into the air, "looking the way you do? Being a star?" The light changed and she crossed. "None of that has anything to do with me."

"I didn't know anything about anything at first. Who could?" Marilyn paused, shifting as if watching out her window again. "Then it was all happening."

They walked along the sidewalk in silence and, when Lexa turned a corner, there was Em almost at the end of the next block.

"There's your friend," Marilyn said. "Are you going to tell her?"

"Tell her what?"

"About *me*, silly."

That stopped Lexa cold. At that instant Em's head swiveled. Lexa ducked back behind the corner fast, bumping into a few pedestrians before scooting out of the way. She landed in front of a shop window and leaned close, pretending her whole attention focused on the mannequins decked out in winter sports gear.

"They look warm," murmured Marilyn. "So what'll it be, sweetie? I know it's not a simple question, but I am curious."

"I—I don't know," Lexa said, "that would be . . . huge, and, I mean, you're only here for a couple of days, and then I'll tell Mr. B I'm out of the play."

"I get it. Why would you? Probably the best idea. Besides a girl's . . ."

"Got to have a few secrets," Lexa's brain whispered. They smiled at each other. "We should do this. You ready?"

Marilyn nodded.

"Remember," Lexa said, tightening her lips as she rounded the corner again, "no sudden weird spirit tricks."

Marilyn cocked her head to say, *Oh, please!*

Lexa walked the next two blocks fast and when she saw Golden Oldies, she couldn't help but shake her head at the latest bizarre window array: a blonde-wigged chick mannequin in a blowy white halter dress and mile-high stilettos whipping a red-horned devil dude's butt.

"Oh, my," Marilyn said, "see what I mean? I can't get a break."

Lexa was about to make her own comment when who should she see at the next crosswalk, hands thrust deep into the kangaroo pocket of an XXXL hoodie? Kevin Dang.

He waved at Lexa as the shop door opened and Em popped out. Like a dog on a scent, Kevin's gaze lasered to her, his smile at a million watts, his walk quickening to a jog.

Em socked Lexa's arm. "It's about time," she said.

Lifting her chin toward Kevin's approaching figure, Lexa whispered, "Coincidence?"

"What?" Em glanced over her shoulder. "Oh, good. There's Kevin. He texted me after you left this morning. Since his Sheriff Will part's pretty small, he offered to help with costumes."

A snorting giggle tickled inside Lexa's ear, and Marilyn wiggled her eyebrows. "Help with costumes."

"Hey, Em. Uh, hi Lexa." Close up now, Kevin's cheeks were so red that he looked like he'd run a marathon. "Ah, what's the plan?"

"The plan," Em said, beelining for the shop door, "is to go in here and study everything fifties, diner, showgirl and/or cowboy."

The door jingled as they went in, and two salespeople, a guy and girl with almost identical short ink-black hair, glanced their way, the guy singing out, "Let us know if you need help."

Em fished out her sketchpad and headed for a large open wardrobe. Kevin and Lexa raised their eyebrows at each other and peeled off: him through a low arch in the back to menswear and Lexa to the front for women's.

Wandering between racks of dresses and coats, a hush enveloped Lexa, muted and whispery, as if she'd closed herself into a big closet.

"Mmmmmmm," said Marilyn, her hum dreamy. "Go over to that rack of furs, will you?"

When Lexa rested her hand on the soft shoulder of a full-length fur the color of a deer, Marilyn let out another satisfied hum.

"Mink," she said, purring again. "Why don't you give this one a try?"

"I'm not really the mink type."

"Come on," Marilyn urged, "live a little. For me."

Biting her bottom lip, Lexa let her peacoat slide to the floor and draped the mink around her shoulders, drawing the collar around her face. Silky cool fur brushed her cheeks, and her eyes closed.

Marilyn's purr went low and throaty. "Isn't that the creamiest? Looks good on you, too. There's a mirror right behind you and, fond as I am of your pom-pom hat, better take it off."

Tugging the hat from her head, Lexa pivoted. The mink covered her from chin to ankle and with her hair tucked inside the collar, it looked like she'd cut it short and sleek. She held the fur lapels tight to her throat, liking how only the slenderest bit of red chiffon scarf peeked out. She looked . . . glamorous. Yes.

"Yes," Marilyn echoed, "the color is perfect on you, especially with that red scarf.

"You've got to be kidding."

Marilyn waved at her as if Lexa'd blown smoke in her face. "Look, sugar. I spent most of my adult life being poked and prodded by Hollywood's finest dressers. Believe me, I know what looks good and what doesn't."

Slipping out of the mink, Lexa whispered, "What I look good in," she shoved the coat on the hanger, "is what I have on."

"No," said Marilyn, "what you have on is what you've decided you are comfortable in. Like me wearing a big old terry-cloth robe or—or being naked."

Lexa whirled away, only to lock eyes with a curious Em. "I—I don't think any of these fur coats will work," she called, backing away quick, and hurrying toward a long rack of skirts. Snatching at the first one, she thrust it along the rack, reaching for the next.

"May I help you find something?"

"No," Lexa snapped, frowning at Marilyn.

"Honey!" Marilyn's red lips pressed tight.

Lexa peeked over her shoulder. The salesgirl stood nearby, her plucked pin-thin brows high and her black lipsticked lips pursed.

"Uh, sorry," mumbled Lexa, "I thought you were . . . never mind."

"Now that you've got her, tell her you want to try on a couple of things," Marilyn prodded, ". . . that black skirt. The camel-colored one too. And let me see—next rack over, that creamy beige twinset will do, and that jade green silk blouse."

Lexa wanted to ditch, but her feet only shuffled from the skirts to the tops as she babbled Marilyn's demands to the salesgirl.

The next thing Lexa knew she was inside a curtained dressing room, the wooden coat tree in the corner heavy with clothes. She sank down on a spindly-legged, black metal chair.

"Well?"

Lexa's chin jerked up.

"Well?" Marilyn repeated, angling her head at the hanging clothes.

"You're joking."

"Pretty please?" Marilyn's lids lowered to half-mast. "I picked those things out special, because they remind me of some of my favorite outfits. I'd give anything to feel them on me again."

"Fine." Lexa stood and began unbuttoning her flannel shirt. All at once, she stopped, hands clutching her shirt together, cheeks on fire.

"For goodness sake," Marilyn said, "you *know* I saw you this morning in your undies."

"Thanks for reminding me, only I didn't know it at the time." Lexa clutched the shirt tighter, remembering other "things" she'd done that morning. "This is *so* not okay," she sputtered.

"How about if I . . . ?" Marilyn covered her eyes with her hands.

Lexa clutched her shirt tighter. "What about when I take a shower or, you know? Everything else?"

Still blindfolding herself, Marilyn shrugged. "What would you like me to do?"

"When you disappear, I mean, when I can't see you. Can you see me then?"

Marilyn peeked through her fingers. "I could fib and say 'no,' only I promised I would tell you the truth. I can see you all the time, honey. The best I can do is swear I will do everything I can to give you your privacy."

Fingers loosening on her shirt, Lexa bit her lip. "Cover your eyes," she said at last. When Marilyn did, she peeled off her clothes and slipped on the black skirt followed by the short-sleeved part of the sweater set.

"I hope this makes you happy." Throwing her hair back, Lexa glanced toward the mirror. Froze.

"I knew it," Marilyn crooned, "they fit like a glove"—invisible hands ran over Lexa's hips and up her sides, pausing under her breasts—"and feel even better. That sweater's cashmere. Isn't it the softest thing in the world?" She made a twirling motion with her finger, and Lexa obliged, her head craning to keep all of her in sight.

"Isn't this skirt too small?" Lexa said, fascinated by how the slithery black material clung to her butt and then flared out around her knees.

Marilyn shook her head.

"This sweater is really soft," Lexa said, running her fingers up over her chest. "But it's so clingy."

"It's supposed to be. You should try a different brassiere, though, or better, nothing at all. That saggy, sporty contraption doesn't do a thing for your figure."

Lexa crossed her arms over her chest. "I doubt there's much that could do anything for my 'figure.'"

Marilyn blinked. "What on earth do you mean?"

Lexa pointed to her butt. "Chub is chub."

"Honey, the last thing you are is fat."

"We don't say 'fat' anymore," Lexa said, plucking at the skirt. "We say, 'big' or 'healthy' or 'thin-challenged.'"

Marilyn threw her head back and laughed long and loud, stopping only when Lexa moved to tug the sweater off. "Wait," Marilyn said, dabbing at her eyes. "Hold on a moment. Stand up tall. Now take a deep breath and, for goodness sake, look at yourself."

Lexa hesitated, long enough for Marilyn's brows to lift, then did as she asked.

"Now, at me." Marilyn stood too, all at once wearing exact replicas of Lexa's black skirt and cream-colored sweater, and arrowed her shoulders back, taking a deep, chest-filling breath. "Look at yourself. Good. And then at me again."

Lexa's gaze did the see-saw. Weird thing. The more she looked at herself and the more she looked at Marilyn, the less she saw an idea of Marilyn and of herself—their bodies that is—and the more Lexa simply *saw*.

"That's right, sugar," Marilyn said, "I was never really a skinny-minny. Only back then, this," she pointed first to her chest, then to her hips," was considered as good as the 'goods' get. You're a little taller and rounder than I was, but in my day? With the right clothes, you'd have had men wolf-whistling at you from here to Sunday."

"You're crazy," Lexa said on a firm headshake. "And who cares about guys whistling, or what they liked a zillion years ago. Now people have a different idea of what's . . ." An image flared. Of stick-legged Em wearing one of her signature pixie-girl outfits. "Of what's hot."

"One thing is for sure." Marilyn fluffed her platinum waves into a halo. "And you're going to be terribly mad at me for saying this. You have got to stop holding your friend there up as the be-all and end-all of 'what's beautiful.' It's not fair to you. Or to her."

Marilyn continued teasing at the tips of her hair as if oblivious to how Lexa stood there silent and stone-faced.

"Because there's not a chance of you turning into some tiny Kewpie," Marilyn went on, focusing on Lexa again. "If you want, I could give you some tips to help you be the best *you* ever. That's what you may want to try thinking about. Maybe taking a break from baggy flannel Daddy shirts and dungarees, and instead trying on some clothes that flatter you."

Lexa blinked at her reflection. At how softly the sweater fit. Sure, no way to avoid the twins on her chest, but the sweater made her shoulders look strong, kind of making everything fit together better. And her waist? Ribs curved in and hips widened out. Nothing bulgy or sausage there. Now with the black material of the skirt rounding smoothly down to balance the flared part around her knees, the whole outfit gave her the appearance of flowing curves, not chub.

"Try the blouse," Marilyn said. "That color is perfect with your eyes."

Almost in a daze, Lexa slipped off the sweater and slid on the blouse, the silk cool and magical against her skin.

"See?" said Marilyn, "sophisticated, without being fussy. And that color—"

"Lexa? You in there?" Em's head butted through the curtain. "The salesgirl said you were . . ." She trailed off, her surprise at catching Lexa playing dress-up shifting fast to a studying frown. "Hey, cool that you're really getting into this costume search. That skirt is interesting, but the blouse—a little too, kind of, dressed up." She angled her head. "Looks good on you, though. Makes your eyes really green and your skin kind of, I don't know, golden."

Kevin's face appeared over Em's shoulder. "What are you guys . . . ? Hey, nice shirt, Lexa. I—"

The salesgirl's head popped in over Em's other shoulder. "Oooooh," she said, "he is so right, girlfriend, that shirt looks amazing on you."

And, of course, salesdude. "Yes! That is totally you."

Lexa gawked at the four faces examining her every curve. A croaking, questioning "Thanks?" was all she could manage.

"Privacy, please," demanded Em, and one, two, three, the other faces disappeared.

Em looked after them, cracking up. "Talk about customer service." She turned back to Lexa. "I know I promised you a looong time ago never to give you clothing advice again, except you should totally get that blouse. Now get out here and help me!" She swished the dressing room curtain shut.

"I agree with your friend, and all your new friends," said Marilyn. "You should buy that blouse. Before you take it off, though, I want to talk hair."

"Hair?" croaked Lexa, dazed from her impromptu fashion show.

"There's simply too much of it, sugar. Pull it back."

Doing as she was told, Lexa considered what the silky green blouse plus a shorter, closer-to-her-face hairstyle equaled.

"See?" Marilyn said. "You've got cheekbones."

"But I—I really like my hair."

"It's a great feature," Marilyn said. "You know, I had long hair when I was younger, and it was darker, too. Dying it blonde, cutting it. I'm pretty sure I thought that was the classy thing to do at the time and, honestly? It was fun. Like dress-up. Besides, I could always let it grow back." That invisible hand stroked Lexa's head. "Think about it. Think about having *fun*. With your clothes, with your looks. With your—"

"I get it already," Lexa whispered, unbuttoning the shirt.

"I've got to get out there, or Em, not to mention everyone else in this store, is going to start really wondering about me."

Marilyn put her hands over her eyes, and Lexa hurried into her jeans and flannel shirt, determinedly ignoring the strange skin prickles. Her shoulders and arms already missed the cool glide of the silk blouse.

When Lexa—bag of jade silk blouse under her arm—followed Em and Kevin outside, it was snowing. Large lazy flakes drifting down. Almost in unison, they tipped their heads to the sky. The whispery cool tickle brushed Lexa's cheeks and lids. She sighed her pleasure out loud, and Marilyn's delight echoed in her mind.

A nearby giggle had Lexa turning. Tongue out, Em sprang and lunged to catch snowflakes on the tip. She stumbled against Kevin and his arms jumped out to steady her and, for a moment, it was like they were hugging. Then she *was* hugging him and laughing, and quickly pushing him away. Kevin's arms, left alone in mid-air, lowered slowly as if they hoped Em would fall into them again.

"Poor sap." Marilyn shook her head.

Lexa nodded the tiniest fraction.

"That was really helpful, guys," Em said, her expression back to business. "I'm going to do a few more sketches and then see what's in the QueenHi costume room."

A simultaneous jumble of ringing music and tones startled them.

"No way," said Kevin, "three people *together* getting texts at the same second. That's got to be a record."

"It's from Mr. B," said Em. "Looks like he's started a group chat." She read the message aloud, "*Bus Stop* dinner at casa B Sun night. 5:00 p.m. Girls bring dessert. Guys, drinks."

"Awesome," said Em and Kevin in stereo.

Part of Lexa *pinged* with how fun that dinner would be, only the time had come. "I don't think I can make it."

"What?" Kevin's face squinched as if she'd sprouted another head.

"Give us a sec," Em said to Kevin and then grabbed Lexa's arm, pulling her a little away. "Are you sure?" she whispered, "about dropping out?"

"Yes," said Lexa, hating the concerned crease etched between Em's brows. "I just can't do it, Em."

"Okay," said Em, "but let's go to the dinner. It'll be fun. After we can, you know, get you out of the play."

"Thanks." Lexa half-smiled. Em always had her back.

"It's settled then," Em said, "want a ride home?"

Something else in Lexa *pinged*, and she gripped her shopping bag tighter. "Um, no," she said, looking away from Marilyn's curiosity. "I've got a couple of other things to do downtown."

"I'll take a ride." Kevin's face was that bright glowing red again.

"Fine," said Em; then to Lexa, "Text me later?"

"You got it. Bye."

The second Em and Kevin disappeared around the corner, Marilyn poked her. "Other *things* to do?"

Instead of answering, Lexa hugged her shopping bag to her chest and looked at the sky. Soft, swirling snow slipped against her cheeks. "You said," she whispered, "you said you could give me some tips on how to be the best me ever."

Marilyn nibbled her pinkie, her lips spreading to a wide smile. "I can't think of a thing I'd enjoy more."

Chapter Six

Late Sunday afternoon found Lexa winding her way to Mr. B's. As she walked, she glanced down at the deep maroon lace-up boots with the chunky heels poking from the bottoms of her wide-legged tweedy wool pants. Next her fingers snuck up to her new black beret, only to slide down to an ear to comb through the feathery tips of freshly cut hair. "I can't believe I let you talk me into this."

"Be honest." Marilyn lounged in her director's chair. "I didn't talk you into a thing."

"Yeah, yeah," Lexa mumbled, "that wasn't you going, 'Ooh-ooh, go in there,' when we walked by J. T. Frye's Discount Emporium. Or again a few stores down when we hit Shoes4Less."

Marilyn held her hand out as if checking her manicure. "Can I help it if nothing goes better with a creamy new hairstyle, than creamy new clothes?" She winked at Lexa. "Admit it, sugar, creamy is the only way to describe how you look."

"It's just." Lexa hesitated, tucking the bag of chocolate chip cookies she'd sliced and baked for Mr. B's more firmly under her arm. "I've never done anything like this before."

Marilyn's brows lifted over genuinely bewildered eyes. "Your point is?"

"My point is?" A frustrated *chuff* slipped through Lexa's lips. "My point is that I'm pretty sure I was totally fine before any of this—this *Bus Stop* stuff happened. But now? With you in there sitting in my head? I don't know if it's me making choices, or if I'm trying to please you, or—or . . . I don't even know."

Marilyn *hmmmm*-ed.

Kicking at the half inch of new snow, Lexa bit her lip, instantly grimacing at the gluey taste of the lip gloss she'd forgotten she'd put on. That reminded her of the mascara she'd brushed on, too. What *was* all this?

Not her. That's what she kept thinking. *Not her.*

Dad's face popped into her head. He'd thought the same thing. When she walked into Film Buzz with her hair cut short, for a sec he hadn't even recognized her. Then his eyes got cartoon sparkly and his grin, big and doofy. "Nice," he'd said. "*Very* nice." She kicked more snow; he'd even rolled his Rs!

"Of course, you were totally fine before." Marilyn's voice came out low and small, "I would never want you to think you weren't, only what does changing your hair or trying some new clothes have to do with that?"

Marilyn's reasonable words made Lexa's belly churn. "Em's going to have a million questions." She groaned. "How am I going to explain?"

"You don't owe anyone any explanations," Marilyn tossed out. "Besides, no matter what you do on the outside, trust me, what's in here," an invisible finger tapped Lexa's chest, "still goes with you."

They turned onto Mr. B's street, and ahead Lexa could see that his driveway was full of cars. A second later Em's yellow Mini drove by, screeching to a halt at the curb. Lexa's legs went weak as the driver's side door cracked open.

"Lexa?" Em jumped out, hurrying closer, saying stuff like,

"No way!" and "What did you *do*?" Excited as a puppy, she circled Lexa, practically sniffing her. "Let me see your hair."

Lexa pulled off the beret.

"Whoa." Em's mouth stayed slightly open. "Your hair looks amazing. What made you decide to get it cut?"

"You'd never believe it if I told you," Lexa mumbled.

"Never mind. I don't even care. This rocks!" She grabbed Lexa's elbow, propelling her up Mr. B's front steps. "I can't wait for Mr. B to see you. He's going to be blown away. You are going to be an awesome Cherie and—"

"What does my haircut have to do with Cherie?"

"I thought . . ."

"Wait." Lexa pulled her arm away. "You thought because I cut my hair? Wrong. I only wanted a change. You know. For fun. Because I like fun." She tried to chuckle, but the rattling sound died in her throat when she caught sight of Marilyn, her lips pursing like she tasted something sour. "Maybe tomorrow I'll—I'll shave my head."

Em's face scrunched. "Bullsh—"

Heels clicked fast on the steps behind—a chirpy, satisfied voice singing out, "Hey, hey."

Em and Lexa both gawked as Hilary Poss joined them. "Shaving your head would be legit," she oozed, "you should totally do it."

"I'm sorry," said Em, bright, innocent, and dripping with sarcasm. "Lexa and I are having a private conversation."

Hilary's eyes went fake-wide as she glanced from side to side. "Exactly where I'd go for a private heart-to-heart."

"Thanks," said Em, the word coming out gooey. "Your opinion has always meant so much to me."

Hilary's brows made a V. "Marvel-Ann Norris," she said, stabbing at the doorbell. "Did you ever notice that your initials spell 'man'?"

Em smiled. "Does that get you hot?"

"You are so strange." Hilary blew out a scoffing breath. "What are you? Some kind of l—"

"Watch it." Snake-fast, Em pinched Hilary's butt. "Now you're getting *me* hot."

Before Hilary could let out more than an unhappy *yip*, the door swung open. "Welcome," said Mr. B, and the reason behind Hilary's presence was revealed instantly when she quick-shifted to gush-mode: how beyond excited she was about the article—the *feature*—she was writing about the class for the QueenHi news; how thrilled she was to be "a fly on the wall" at this kick-off dinner.

"Yes. Wonderful. Wonderful," said Mr. B, collecting coats, Hilary glued to him.

"You still hate her guts, don't you?" whispered Lexa, "because of what she said to me at that sixth-grade dance."

"That was like one of a million crappy things she's done." Em laughed low. "Whatever. I don't have the energy to hate her. She never changes, though, our *Hilarious*. As much of a dick now as ever."

"Everyone else is downstairs, ladies." Mr. B pointed to the door leading to his home theater.

Hilary shot Em a triumphant look, only then catching a full load of Lexa without hat or coat. Her eyes sharpened, and all at once Lexa knew what that expression Hilary had way back on that first day of Mr. B's was—the look of a kid whose favorite toy has been taken away. A toy she clearly wanted back. Luckily, just as Hilary opened her mouth, Mr. B came to the rescue again.

"Would you assist me a moment, Miss Donovan? Oh, you two go ahead down." He nodded at Hilary and Em. "Please tell the others dinner will be ready shortly."

Em smiled a little hopeful smile at Lexa, shoved her bag of

marshmallow dessert into Lexa's hand, and slinked off down the stairs.

"If you please, Miss Donovan?"

Trudging after Mr. B, Lexa's thoughts ricocheted like mad. *What to say?*

"Nice digs," murmured Marilyn, and Lexa let out a squeak. *How could she have forgotten about Marilyn?*

Her squeak had Mr. B swinging around. "Is everything all right?"

"What?" Lexa choked out. "Oh. Yeah. Sure, I—" She startled as invisible fingers pinched her side. *Hey!* Her brain said, and then she saw that Marilyn pointed at her own shoe, kicking it off. "Right. My boots. I—I forgot to take them off."

"Ah," said Mr. B, "thoughtful of you to remember and—" He paused, scrutinizing. "Why Miss Donovan, you've made some changes. Some very intriguing changes. That hairstyle suits you incredibly." His face lit up. "Does that mean you've chosen to accept the challenge of Cherie?"

Marilyn clasped her hands, and energy surged from Lexa's head to her belly and out to the tips of her fingers and toes. *Settle*, Lexa's brain whispered, and Marilyn nodded, her chest expanding with a deep breath. Lexa took a breath too, only she could feel her cheeks still burning. In what seemed the fingersnap of time Marilyn had been inside, Lexa had gotten used to the little pats and pokes, but when Marilyn seemed excited, those spirit-touches took on a whole different feel. More like a fiery inferno.

"I can see the excitement in your face," Mr. B continued, his voice almost bubbling. "Why I—"

"Dear?" The call came from the kitchen. "The pasta's ready."

"Our talk will have to wait," he said to Lexa. "Would you set the table, please? Forks, knives, and napkins are out.

I'll take these." He slid the cookies from under her arm and plucked the marshmallows from her fist.

As he disappeared into the kitchen, Lexa's mouth opened, closed, and opened again. "All I had to say was 'no,'" she whispered to herself, "that's all I had to say." A painful hollowness spread behind her breastbone. "I guess I would've had to leave then."

"There, there, sugar. Give yourself a break already. Plenty of time for that drama." Marilyn lifted her nose and sniffed. "*Mmmmm.* Smell that sauce. That teacher of yours is a cutie-pie. Go figure. A woman's got to love a man who loves to cook."

With no idea how to respond to that, Lexa simply stumbled to the dining room table and began doling out forks and knives.

In a surreal flash, Lexa stood in Mr. B's kitchen, waiting in the spaghetti line. Ahead of her, Em and Kevin stood rapt while Anton gesticulated wildly, talking about how colors and textures looked under stage lights. An astounding thing happened next. Anton paused and Kevin commented about how a scene's action could change—no, be *affected*—by stage lighting. Lexa waited for Em to add her own brilliant observation: She didn't. Only stood there, gazing at Kevin as if she'd never seen him before.

Behind Lexa, Clara said something and Dani-Marie cracked up.

"Innocent Elma and brassy Grace," Marilyn mused. "Those two are already getting along like a house on fire. Your Mr. B knew what he was doing casting them as the diner waitresses."

Clara cracked back up, and the dusty, coughing noise of her laugh made Lexa want to clap her between the shoulders. Jeremy Leith did actually slap Clara's back, making Dani-Marie and Clara laugh even harder. Jeremy smiled at them. Not the lip twists Lexa'd seen before either: a real smile. Real and warm.

"I know what you're thinking, and I agree," Marilyn added. "He'll be fine as fatherly cowboy Virgil Blessing to hot-headed Bo."

Weirdness, like an electric buzz, flooded Lexa, making the kitchen lights seem too bright, the edge of the counter too sharp. She looked away from Jeremy fast, catching Hilary and Brian heading to the dining table. Hilary hung onto Brian's arm while he carried their full plates.

"I wonder why he's not smiling," said Marilyn.

"Hmm," said Lexa. She watched them, frowning herself. "I wonder why they didn't show up together?"

"You could ask."

Hilary reached up on tip-toe, whispering in Brian's ear and pecking a kiss on his cheek. Brian sighed and smiled then, and floppity-drop went Lexa's stomach, a rock tossed into a pool that made something surface. Something she couldn't ignore anymore. Bo. Brian was playing Bo. The dropping sensation in her belly went quivery. Brian. Bo. And she—

"I am not changing my mind," Lexa tossed at Marilyn, plunking a heaping spoonful of spaghetti onto her plate, "but this whole thing is getting to be more and more of a bummer. Especially with Hilary worming her way in with her article."

"She's one sly little fox, I'll grant you that," said Marilyn. "Here's what I want to know, though. What will Mr. B do when you quit?"

Chapter Seven

Lexa chewed on Marilyn's worrying question as everyone took their places at the table. When all were settled, Anton raised his cup. "A toast to Mr. B," he said, "to his spring drama extravaganza. And to us, his lucky group of players." He angled his cup at each of them. "And to his illustrious minions," he finished, almost sloshing his orange soda as he pointed first to Mrs. B and then to Em.

Everyone knocked cups together, drank deep, and then dug into their spaghetti. Laughter, talk, and clinking silverware surrounded Lexa. Marilyn's eyes were closed, lips pressed together with only the hint of her tongue visible against the top one, as if savoring deliciousness.

It hit Lexa again. That she was choosing *not* to be part of this.

Marilyn's face snapped to hers and, bracing herself, Lexa said, "Don't try to get me to change my mind." Marilyn's expression went smooth as glass, and she shrugged.

"Mr. B?" Hilary's husky drawl pulled Lexa's attention. "Do you mind if I ask you a few questions for my article?" He nodded and Hilary dove in, "When did you become interested in drama?"

"Go on, dear," urged Mrs. B, and he did, telling them about

his own high school days, about how he loved his experiences in the theater. Lexa listened, but more, she watched Hilary. How she batted her lashes at Mr. B, tap-tapping what he said into her fancy phone.

When he paused, Hilary said, "That is super interesting. Here's something I'm hoping you'll address, though." Her voice went serious. "I know you know my mom is president of the school board. She told me that the budget for this workshop is under fire. Is that for real?"

Mr. B's lips curved as he finished his bite. "That could be said about every activity, class, or workshop QueenHi offers, Miss Poss."

"True. Still, not every one of those uses the whole auditorium for a whole month at the end of the school year, which is, like, the busiest time." Hilary tucked her fall of hair over her shoulder. "Isn't it also true that not very many people actually attend the performances? Why is that?"

Marilyn gave Lexa a soft nudge. "Why, she's not a sly little fox. She's a shark."

"An audience is important to any theatrical endeavor," mused Mr. B, "yes, this is true. That said, Miss Poss, for most of my performers, this is their first experience on a stage, and both the administration and the school board understand that generating audience numbers is not the point of the workshop."

The table grew silent, everyone listening to Mr. B. Lexa wanted to smack Hilary. Smack the smile on her face that boldly expressed her confidence in the limelight. Her confidence in letting Mr. B know that she—through Mommy and the schoolboard—had some kind of power over him. Lexa's gaze flicked to Brian. He frowned, toying with his soda cup.

"Of course, I can't read his mind," said Marilyn, "but 'Bo' there doesn't look like he is finding Hilary's questions amusing." She cocked her head, seeming to study Lexa. "You sure like looking at him."

Her eyes dropping fast, Lexa shifted on her seat.

"Don't bother denying it, honey," Marilyn said, her whisper tickling now. "Every time you look at that boy, your insides get all noodly."

A long cooling swig of soda did nothing to put out the fire in Lexa's cheeks, and she almost sprayed the table when Hilary asked Mr. B what would happen if someone dropped out of the play.

"Or got sick," Hilary finished.

"That's an intriguing question," Mr. B said, wiping his lips with his napkin.

Lexa looked at Marilyn, and then really looked at Em. Both stared right back.

Mr. B put his napkin down. "A question for which I have never had to find an answer." He faced Lexa now, steepling his fingers under his chin. "In all the years I've led this workshop, not *one* of my students has dropped out or missed a performance."

"That's . . . amazing," Hilary said, more unhappy than amazed.

"What *would* happen?" Lexa heard herself say, "You'd—you'd pull another name out of whichever jar, right?"

"What a clever idea," he said, as though she'd cleared up a big mystery.

Soaring on wings of relief, Lexa almost sang her thoughts to Marilyn. "Schoolboard-shmoolboard. Good old Hilarious will have to take her chances like everyone else."

"I *should* say," Mr. B continued, "what a clever idea that *would be* if I hadn't already recycled all of those little slips of paper."

Lexa slumped in her chair, relief-wings clipped.

"What would you do then?" This from Clara; some of the others chimed in with a "Yeah" or "What would happen then?"

"I believe in serendipity. In fate." Mr. B's glasses flashed as he surveyed the table. "That the luck of the draw has placed us together for *this* time. For this production. And, as fate has decided, there lies our protection. From sickness." His voice resonated with the heavy throb of a drum. "And from ill-conceived changes of heart."

Hilary cleared her throat. "If that did happen, though. If one of the players did leave the play." She regarded Lexa, her desire sharp enough to slice the air between them. "You'd still have to find a qualified person to step up."

"I suppose that would be unavoidable," Mr. B said. "I'd have to arrange an audition of some sort. After all—the show must go on. Now then, who's for dessert?"

In Mr. B's bathroom, Marilyn's face filled Lexa's mind. "You better watch your back. That Hilary's something else."

"Tell me something I don't know."

"All those deep, probing questions." Marilyn shuddered. "She should give up acting and go into politics."

"The thing is," Lexa said, now speaking aloud, to herself as much as to Marilyn, "even though I don't much like Hilary, or her . . . tactics, I know she's got what it takes to be a kickass Cherie. So. So I should be glad, right? That I'm leaving everyone in such good hands?"

"If that's what you want to think, then that's fine," Marilyn said. "No one can make you want to be in this play."

"Exactly," Lexa said, "I don't want it." She turned the faucet hard, ran her hands under the water.

Marilyn saluted her. "Aye, aye, captain."

Lexa splashed cool water on her cheeks, plucked at the thin satiny finger towel.

"Feels nice," said Marilyn. "Mr. and Mrs. B have good taste. Speaking of taste, could you pocket a couple of those lemon squares Mrs. B made? Those are too delicious, and . . ." Her words trailed off and she shrugged, one side of her mouth curving up. "After tonight the memory of that sweet's going to have to last me . . . forever, I suppose."

Her chest going tight, Lexa said, "Do you think you'll disappear the second I drop out?"

"Honestly, who knows?" Marilyn said. "I guess we'll see, and I guess this is as good a time as any to tell you how much I appreciate you letting me stay a little."

"That's okay," said Lexa, her chest tightening more, like when she was little and she didn't want Dad to turn out her light at bedtime. "Actually, it's been kind of great." She returned Marilyn's smile. "Thanks for coming. Really."

"Sure thing. This has been the swellest time ever."

"I guess we better get back out there."

When Marilyn nodded, Lexa yanked open the door and came within a hair of bumping smack into Jeremy Leith. "Sorry," she said, combing a hand over her hair.

Large almond-shaped blue eyes fastened to hers. "Who were you talking to in there?"

"W-what?"

"In there," he said, pointing his chin toward the bathroom. "I heard you talking to someone."

"Oh." Lexa folded her lower lip under her teeth, buying a second. Man, half the time when she was alone, she wasn't even aware if she talked to Marilyn out loud or in her head, and the one time she actually needed to hear herself talk? Well, at least it wasn't Hilary. She blinked at Jeremy, and the steadiness of his gaze scrambled her brain. She had a sudden intense urge to throw the truth at him.

Marilyn poked her hard, saying, "Careful, honey." Then she stood up and took a very exaggerated, swan-like bow.

"It was"—Lexa sputtered—"it was a . . . an exercise. Yeah. That's right. A theatrical exercise."

"Really?" he said. Then he reached out, tugging the ends of hair near her left ear. "Did you do this for the play? I like it. It's an unexpected change, and now I can see your face."

"Uh, thanks."

When he slipped by, Lexa caught the scent of lemons and mint. The bathroom door clicked closed after him, and her fingers crept to her neck, where he'd brushed her hair. The skin there prickled, clearly feeling the memory of his fingers.

"Well, well, well." Marilyn inhaled a long, deliberate breath. "Talk about unexpected."

Sounds of kitchen cleanup in progress greeted Lexa as she slinked through the living room, but muffled voices from the foyer behind had her scurrying to hide behind the arched opening to the dining room. Brian and Hilary, thudding up the stairs from Mr. B's movie room. When they came into sight, each held a large popcorn bowl full of predinner snack trash. Lexa watched them disappear into the kitchen, her hands balling into fists. Then she hurried over to the dining room table and began collecting crumpled napkins and scattered silverware.

"She sure is helpful," whispered Marilyn. "Already part of the group. That's what you're thinking."

"Doesn't mean I have to like it."

Em popped through the swinging kitchen door. "There you are," she said. "What's the plan?"

Lexa's plan was crystal clear, only instead of tingling with the relief of her soon-to-be freedom, she dragged. "I guess we wait until everyone else leaves and then, you know. I'll tell him I can't do the play."

"For sure Hilary's going to butt in," said Em, annoyed.

"Yup." Lexa scooped up more table trash, avoiding her eyes.

"It really would've been fun," Em's voice went soft, "to have both of us be such a big part of this final high school play."

Her raw honesty stopped Lexa in a way that no amount of begging could.

Mr. B and everyone else spilled out of the kitchen, "Goodbyes" and discussion about the next day's meeting filling the air.

Mr. B pointed at Lexa. "A moment more of your time, Miss Donovan."

She lifted her chin, smiled, and when Em grabbed her hand, giving her a "we're in this together" squeeze, Lexa whispered, "You know what? You should go."

"Huh? Hell, no."

"Hell, yes." She slipped her hand from Em's. "I have to do this myself."

Em's lips tightened, like that would hold in her disappointment. A second later, she threw her arms around Lexa, murmuring, "Whatever you say, boss. Text me after."

Hugging her back hard, Lexa let go. Then it was down to her and Mr. B. And Mrs. B, clattering dishes in the kitchen.

"And so?" he said, "I would like to hear this from your lips. The verdict, please."

It was like a metal trap caught Lexa's tongue. Flashes of Mr. B, Marilyn, Hilary, Brian, Em, Dad, even her mom jumbled together in her head, a kaleidoscope gone cuckoo. All she had to say was, "No." One word, and this moment would be over. Done.

Done. Finito. Forever.

Invisible hands massaged Lexa's shoulders. She braced herself against their warmth and looked square at Mr. B. "I guess . . . oh, God, I guess I'm in."

Marilyn jumped up from her chair so fast that it fell over

behind her. She didn't move again. Only stood there, eyes huge, hands clasped. Lexa's whole body squeezed tight, as if between those pressing hands.

"Excellent. I knew you wouldn't disappoint me." Mr. B beamed, herding Lexa to the front door and handing her her coat. "Goodnight, Miss Donovan. Go home and get a good sleep. We've got quite a journey ahead of us."

Out on the front stoop now, Marilyn and Lexa stared at each other, and then Marilyn's lips curved. "I'm staying, aren't I?"

"What do you think?"

Marilyn threw her arms up in a victory V, and Lexa blinked at the dark. Then she tipped her head up to the night sky, finding the moon. The slice of silver was bigger tonight. She twisted her ring, once, twice.

"That ring." Marilyn lowered her arms, slow and thoughtful. "The one you're always touching. It was your mama's, wasn't it?"

When Lexa nodded, Marilyn went on, "You know what? If your mama's able to see you right now, I'm sure she's real proud." She studied Lexa. "I don't get it, though. What made you want to—all of a sudden—do the play?"

"I *don't* want to," said Lexa.

"Then why?"

"I guess everything and everyone kind of smashed into me. And—and having to choose . . . I don't know, somehow choosing to quit seemed worse." She spied the moon again. "I—I couldn't say no."

"No," said Marilyn, "you just couldn't."

Blowing out a long breath, Lexa stepped off the stoop, huddling deep into her coat as she walked. "Did Mr. B really say 'quite a journey'?"

Invisible fingers cupped Lexa's chin. "He has no idea how right he is, sugar."

Chapter Eight

Monday morning came, bringing a call from Em. An instantly very confused Em. As soon as she could, Lexa ended the call.

"That was quite a performance you gave," said Marilyn, slow, breathy, and sarcastic as hell.

"Ha ha," Lexa said. Since she'd been too chicken to call Em the night before to tell her she was staying in Mr. B's workshop, she'd known talking to her this morning would be awkward. It *was* awkward, the more reasons and fibs Lexa'd piled on, the more questions Em asked.

"Awkward?" said Marilyn. "I'd say it was a little more than that. I don't think she bought that fake excuse for why you didn't want a ride this morning either."

"Sure, she did." Lexa stuffed her phone into her pocket. "Anyone can have a last-minute doctor's appointment. Besides." She shuffled along the sidewalk, the long trek to school now not nearly long enough. "By the time I see her at lunch, she will have so moved on. Probably."

"Why don't you tell her the truth? About me?"

"Oh, wouldn't that be perfect. For my best friend to be the first to think I've gone loco."

"Are you sure that's what would happen?"

"I have no idea what would happen." Lexa walked faster.

"What if I showed myself to her?"

That stopped Lexa. "*What* did you say?"

Marilyn leaned back in her chair. "You heard me."

"How—how would you do that? I mean—" Lexa's lips clamped shut as she looked around, all at once aware that she stood in the middle of the sidewalk, sputtering. She scurried to a nearby fence, grabbing the rails like she was taking in the view. "You could *do* that?"

"I'm sure I could figure out something. Wouldn't telling her make things easier?"

Staring ahead, Lexa's brain churned through scenarios of telling Em about Marilyn. Telling Dad, too. Dad and Em. Knowing all about Marilyn. Em and Dad and Marilyn. The scene beyond the fence came into focus: a cemetery of all places, snow-covered and full of headstones, bare trees at the far edge, and in the distance the frozen lake. The calm, peaceful, frozen lake. She exhaled a noisy stream. Frozen she could live without; she sure liked calm and peaceful, though.

"Why," murmured Marilyn, "you don't *want* to tell them about me."

"Some of me wants to." Letting go of the fence, Lexa returned to the sidewalk. "You're right, though, most of me doesn't. This is all totally weird. I mean, I've never kept anything important from Em or Dad. Never. Now it seems like that's all I'm doing. Keeping stuff from them. Being a big fat liar."

A dull *chuff* had her spinning around. Her phone had fallen out of her pocket. When she reached down, the red scarf slithered from her neck. She snatched up the phone and the scarf, and squeezed her eyes shut.

"That's right, slow down," crooned Marilyn. "Hey, you know what? Keeping something to yourself is not the same as lying, and you don't have to be in such a hurry to figure everything out."

That invisible hand, stroking Lexa's head. She wished she could grab that hand, hang on.

"I wish you could too," said Marilyn with a final pat.

Lexa's breath shuddered out, and she opened her eyes.

"You okay now, sugar?"

"Yeah."

They stood quiet a moment, the only sound the steady stream of high school traffic whizzing by on the road.

"Come on, let's get you to school." Marilyn gave her a bright smile. "After last night, I can't wait to see what goes on in that workshop."

Lexa trudged on, stashing her phone and tying the scarf around her neck.

"Don't walk too fast." Marilyn's voice was like happy bubbles. "Oh, I love being out here. Everything new and—and strange. And terribly fast. Like this morning. Why, you were on a tear."

"That's because I overslept."

Marilyn laughed, and Lexa's blood zinged hot, like her veins would overflow.

"Whew!" Lexa unbuttoned her coat. "The second I think I'm used to having you in there, it's like—*zap*! All of a sudden, my entire body feels like a hot air balloon with too much hot in it, and too much air. Why do you think that is?"

"I wish I knew," said Marilyn with a slight head shake. "I suppose spirits have to have *some* kind of presence. Maybe that presence you're feeling is about a spirit being here with the living?"

"Maybe. I sure got a jolt when you 'popped' in this morning . . ." Lexa trailed off, something prickling at her. "Hey. Where even *were* you this morning?"

"What do you mean?"

"When I woke up, it was like I was me again, and then you appeared. Where did you go? You know, while I was asleep?"

"Where did I go?" Marilyn touched her pinky to her lip—her lip that quivered.

Before she could ask again, the buzz in Lexa's blood zinged to boiling shocks. "Now what?" She fanned her overheated body with her open coat. "Why aren't you answering me? You wouldn't—"

Marilyn's eyes cut to Lexa's. "No, honey, I won't lie to you. Not *ever*."

"But." Lexa swallowed as the shocks faded. "But all this—heat. Is it because something's going on with you? You're keeping stuff from me, aren't you?"

Marilyn opened her mouth, only Lexa spoke first, parroting her, "Keeping something from someone's not the same as lying."

"You catch on fast."

"Maybe I can't read your mind the way you can read mine," Lexa said. "I guess I can't get too mad at you for doing exactly what I'm doing with Dad and Em. Keeping stuff to yourself."

"I don't want to scare you, and don't think I don't know what that rolling-your-eyes means. I was a teenager too, once upon a time." The tip of Marilyn's tongue touched her upper lip. "Oh, all right. Now don't go haywire on me. I can't help hearing your thoughts when you're awake. Most of them anyway. Sometimes those thoughts of yours come too many and too fast, like a million raindrops. And, being in you is even loonier at night with your dreams going all over the place, so . . . I find some quiet little part of your mind and stretch out." She smoothed her hair. "I need my beauty rest too, you know."

"You need beauty sleep?" Lexa almost laughed, then what Marilyn meant clicked. "Hold on. Some quiet little place? What does *that* mean?"

"There's a lot of unused real estate in that brain of yours." Marilyn grinned wide. "You should see your face. Much more horrified than when I pulled my zombie act the other day. Trust me. I'm not up to no good. Your head, well, it's like a big old house full of rooms. Loads of them. And some of those rooms are empty and waiting for some action. Last night, I spent the night right smack in the middle of your mind, in a big empty room that seemed to be begging for something to happen. Some lights to go on. Some *stage* lights."

"Ha," Lexa said. Brightness grew around Marilyn, and a room appeared—no, not a room, a cavernous empty stage with dark velvet curtains and a gleaming black floor.

"Stop that," Lexa whispered, walking faster.

"I'm not doing anything." The light around Marilyn dimmed, the stage fading away. "That's all you. Maybe you should pay attention to your own brain."

"What's that supposed to—?" Lexa stopped abruptly when she saw where they were. The turnoff to QueenHi. "Okay, heads up," she said, walking on. "Here we go." Her jitters grew at the sight of dozens of kids milling in front of the high school entrance. "Being at Mr. B's house was pretty controlled," her mind said. "This is like when we went to meet Em at Golden Oldies—except more. Remember. Do *not* talk to me when we're around other people, especially a bunch of random high school kids. I don't want to say something or do something by mistake."

Marilyn twisted her fingers in front of her closed mouth as if turning a key. "I'll be quiet as the grave."

That cracked them both up. "You're really funny sometimes," Lexa said. "Were you always?"

Marilyn smiled at being called funny, but Lexa's question made the smile drop. "You mean when I was alive? I barely remember," she murmured.

"I don't mean to hurt your feelings," said Lexa, "or ask dumb questions. But come on, *Spirit of Marilyn Monroe, now playing in Lexa's head for a limited time only*. You cannot blame me for wanting to know you. At least a little."

"Don't be sorry," Marilyn said, "I want you to feel like you can say anything to me. It's . . . being here with you this way is making me remember things. And remembering? That makes a strange sort of hurt, I guess. Right here." She rubbed the place between her breasts.

They walked on in silence, and it started to snow. Big lazy flakes.

Remembering their time outside Golden Oldies, Lexa tipped her head back, catching snowflakes on her tongue. They hit, feathery cold, and dissolved, the icy wet sliding down her throat.

After a moment, Marilyn spoke. "*Mmmmmm*. Who knew winter could be this swell?" She leaned her own head back and inhaled, long and deep. "Thanks, honey. I needed that."

The walk making her late, Lexa raced to Mr. B's classroom. Homeroom time had become their regular workshop time. She slipped into the first available seat, right next to Kevin. Before she could even get a breath, he bumped her shoulder with his, saying, "Hey, what happened to *you* last night?"

Why was *he* asking *her* a question like that? She didn't get a chance to ask, because Mr. B clapped his hands.

"People! Settle down, please." He looked around and, weirdly, as Lexa's eyes followed his, melty warmth flooded her. They were all there. Every one of them. Especially her.

"It is now the middle of January," Mr. B said. "Our immediate goal, and one that will be the full focus for the next month, is to get to know this play as intimately as possible. Within that framework we will then spend the rest of February—right up until official rehearsals begin in April—getting to know our characters, as well as each other. To do so," he paused to gather up a fat stack of papers and began handing them out, "each of you will be required to do the following."

As Lexa scanned over the pages, the list of acting exercises and assignments blurred. Whoa! This workshop was going to be some work.

Mr. B was talking again. "I always commence the work of this class by talking about why I began it." The room got very quiet. "Stories in any form, on the page, on the stage, are a large part of what connects us. What makes us *human*. This class is all about story, and I believe that when we act stories, they become part of us."

He lifted his gaze to the ceiling. "You have all read our play of choice, and each of you knows which role you will play. Thus, during the process of discovering your role, each of you will be tasked to discover not only the deeper story behind your character and this play, but also to become a cohesive acting troupe. Now then, creating a safe and respectful climate where actors feel comfortable taking emotional and physical risks is an essential element to any performing arts experience." He studied each face. "I don't believe we need to set a list of specific rules, because as seniors, I trust you all to be mature enough to understand the concepts of personal space and respectful touching."

Lexa's heart boomed at an all new level of *whathaveIgottenmyselfinto*? She tried to catch Marilyn's eye, but Marilyn sat forward in her chair, chin cupped in her hands, riveted by Mr. B.

And he was still talking. "We will start, as we will each meeting, with some warm-up exercises to help us transition to a more imaginary world."

A light groan to Lexa's left had her shifting. Right next to her, Graham and Dani-Marie sat as rapt as Marilyn. Not Brian, though. He sprawled back in his seat, chin dipped, unmoving except for his fingers drumming on his thigh. Another groan, deep and soft, a lion hiding in the brush. Yup. Him.

A jelly-like softness quivered along Lexa's limbs, settling into a swirl behind her belly button. She wished it was a real button she could push to make the quivery jelly-feeling stop. How she wished that would work. How she wished the sight of him didn't make her feel melty. Melty over every speck of his way-too-hotness.

At that instant, Brian crinkled his forehead, as if staring at his perfectly sculpted thigh would make the answers to his problems appear, and then he looked up. Right at Lexa. The quivery jelly sparked and boiled in her belly, and she jerked her head straight, slamming eyes with Jeremy. In a flash, the spark and boil turned to a stinging jolt that *zinged* up the back of Lexa's neck, right into her head. All at once the room was too bright, the lights painfully fluorescent. One side of Jeremy's mouth smirked.

Then everyone was moving. Not only moving, shoving chairs out of the way.

Marilyn's stage whisper made Lexa jump. "You're doing an exercise called 'Freeze,'" she said, "now stop mooning over those boys, and—"

"What? I am *not* mooning."

"You sure are. Now stand up. Everyone's waiting on you!"

Lexa lurched to her feet, her brain stuttering over Marilyn's continued instructions.

"Mr. B is going to tell you an emotion." Marilyn was on her feet too, hands clasped. "And you all are going to act it out until he says, 'freeze.'"

Lexa joined the others at the wall, and Mr. B called out, "Ready, set—*happy*."

For one beat no one did anything, and then Anton and Dani-Marie peeled from the wall. Dani-Marie began running in place, pumping her arms, and Anton, sweeping a hand high, flapped his mouth as though giving a speech.

Others joined rapid-fire. Clara sat cross-legged on the floor, her expression going dreamy as she pretended to cut something. Graham roved the room like a hungry wolf, holding one hand in a circle to his eye, while the other cranked around and around next to it, mimicking filming with an old-fashioned movie camera.

Kevin and Lexa goggled at each other, mirror images of panic. He shrugged and raised his hands to his face, making a small box with them, one finger clicking away, playing photographer.

Slow as a lazy cat, Jeremy wandered to his desk and sat, arranging his hands and knees to mime playing the cello. When his eyes slid closed and his lips parted, it was as if he could hear his imaginary music.

Brian in motion. Similar to Jeremy, he sat at his desk, only he stretched out his legs and crossed his arms. Even as Lexa wondered what he would do, he rested his chin on his chest and—*what the hell?*—closed his eyes.

Marilyn's voice buzzed. "What are *you* going to do?"

Lexa's brain went to white noise. Her gaze raced around the room, smashed into Mr. B. He was watching her.

"Oh, don't worry about him," Marilyn whispered. "Pick one thing. One little thing."

"I can't. I can't think of anything."

"Listen, sugar." Marilyn stared straight at Lexa, Lexa's chin pinching as though fingers grasped it. "Close your eyes and imagine the last time you were happy."

Lids slapping down, an image zapped into Lexa's head: Em sketching and Lexa watching her.

"Being with Em makes you happy," Marilyn whispered fast, "that's good. Only this is about *you*. About *you* doing something that makes *you* happy."

I'm always happy! That's what Lexa wanted to shout, along with, *Only no one's ever asked me to stop and think about it before, or yeah, act it out!*

Marilyn cocked her head. "You can do this."

Lexa squeezed her lids down so hard that black and orange and blue splattered and popped behind them. Air. She needed air. She inhaled, long and deep. Glittery specks of white whirled through her mind. Snowflakes. Falling. Feathery cold touching her cheeks, pepperminty fresh, filling her nose. She saw herself twirling and twirling; Marilyn appeared next to her doing the same. Then Marilyn fell into snow, her arms and legs moving up and down, making an angel. *An angel!*

Both of them laughed, and—and noise, slicing sharp noise, coming from far away.

"Freeze."

Lexa's eyes snapped open. To the ceiling. She was lying on the floor, arms and legs spread like a starfish.

And then Mr. B stood above her, peering down. Beyond his shoulders, the rest of the class gawked down at her. "Let me help you up," he said, holding out a hand. Lexa scrambled up on shaky legs, and he shifted away, continuing, "Excellent everyone. Let's go around. Miss Alvarez? Why don't you start?"

As Dani-Marie went off about how great running made her feel, Lexa slid back until she hit the wall. The cool, solid hardness was exactly what her trembling body needed. Little by little the trembling slowed to a bearable buzz.

Keeping her eyes on the floor in front of her feet, Lexa spoke to Marilyn. "What was I doing?"

Marilyn's answer was to do her mouth-key-twist and point to Mr. B.

"All but two of you," Mr. B said, rubbing his hands together in glee, "chose actions depicting a clear sense of happiness through a personally satisfying hobby." He circled to Brian. "Mr. McKinnon? Would you tell us about your choice?"

Brian sat up taller. "Napping's a hobby," he said. He smirked, but his lowered eyes made him look unsure.

Mr. B cocked a brow, then he wheeled to Lexa. "What of Miss Donovan. Your expression of happiness was quite unique. A dramatic inhale, followed by quiet with a hint of wonder, and then the whirl of a snow angel. Please, share with the group."

"I—I don't really know."

"Remember, you are safe here. Please share."

Exposed. Naked. Worse than naked. Lexa's arms crossed tight over her chest, her mind barking, "*Marilyn? A little help?*"

Marilyn raised her hands, palms open and pushing. *Go on*, they said, push, push, *you're part of this*, *so* be *part of this*.

"I was—I was out," Lexa spoke fast, "in the cold. Smelling the air. The snow. And I thought of angels." She braced for laughter.

None came, the room dead quiet enough that she began to wish someone *would* laugh.

"Intriguing," said Mr. B, "a full emotion conveyed through a moment of innocent exultation."

Brrrrring—the end-of-homeroom bell rang.

"Assignment two on the sheet is due Friday," called Mr. B. "Also, it's never too soon to learn your lines."

Relief swooped through Lexa. The second she sat at her desk, though, her hands began to shake. Then her whole body. Not with that outside-in-the-cold chill either. No, this was the super-tired kind of shaking, the suffering-through-a-killer-PE-class-where-the-teacher-forces-everyone-to-do-a-pull-up-marathon shaking. She reached under her chair for her pack, whispering to Marilyn, "This shaking have anything to do with your presence?"

"Sorry, honey. That's all you. Using those acting muscles is exhausting, isn't it?"

A voice poured down from above. "That was interesting. What you did back there."

Her chin popped up to Jeremy. Towering. His hair a wispy, electrified halo. He was still talking. "Did it have anything to do with what you were working on last night?" Those almond-shaped blue eyes trapped Lexa in her seat.

"Huh?"

"At Mr. B's." He was smiling now. "In the bathroom?"

Brian stopped next to Jeremy. "What were you two doing in Mr. B's bathroom?"

Jeremy's smile thinned. "What a typical thing to say." He nodded at Lexa and moved on.

Brian called after him, "Take a joke much?" He let out an amused *pfft*, muttering, "What's that guy's glitch?" and dropped into the seat next to Lexa. "Hey, can I ask you something?" He leaned closer, the mix of boy and soap and a hint of the apple he must've eaten before class making Lexa even tremblier, but in the good way. The *very* good way.

"You seem, uh, not totally sure about doing this. Last night I even thought you might bail. I was thinking of doing that, except . . ." The first block warning bell rang, and Brian cast his eyes toward the door. "Look, I gotta go, but I wanted to tell you I'm glad there's at least one other person in here who's not totally revved up about all this acting schlacka." He stood. "Catch you later, *Lex*."

Lexa looked after him. Looked after Brian. Brian. Who thought they had an actual something in common.

"That boy will make a perfect Bo." Marilyn's chuckle came low, whispery, and from far, far away. "He thinks he's got everything all figured out. Except he's simply a big, confused softie. And did he really call you 'Lex' rhymes with . . . ?"

Lexa couldn't keep her lips from grinning big. "*Lex*," she murmured under her breath.

Marilyn's voice still bubbling in her head, Lexa hoisted her pack and floated out the door.

Chapter Nine

Lunch came too soon.

Marilyn waved a hand in front of her face. "What is that awful smell?"

"Welcome to the caf," Lexa said, picking up a tray and joining the lunch line. "What are you in the mood for?"

"Nothing in here."

Ditching past the hot food, Lexa grabbed a yogurt and an apple. "Okay," she said, pressing her mouth into her bravest smile. "Let's go talk to Em."

Marilyn mirrored the smile, saying, "Break a leg, kid."

Em sat at their usual table, only she was not alone. Kevin sat right next to her, and they were looking at something together, deeply involved.

The question Kevin asked in class clicked for Lexa, the way he'd emphasized the "you."

"Awww." Marilyn's whisper tickled. "They look sweet together, don't they?"

Too dazed to speak, Lexa nodded. Kevin had asked her that question because he knew she'd stayed behind at the dinner to talk to Mr. B. There was only one person who could've shared that piece of info. Em. Obvious as it had been from the start that Kevin liked Em, what Lexa had totally missed was that Em seemed—maybe? Possibly?—to like him back.

Now Em laughed at something he said, throwing her head back. She caught sight of Lexa and popped up, waving.

"Maybe this is better," said Marilyn. "She won't be nearly as interested in you."

"Thanks a lot."

When Lexa reached the table, Em said, "What took you so long?" Her and Kevin's expressions were identical. Clearly, they'd been discussing Lexa "taking so long."

"Uh . . . Spanish was intense today," Lexa mumbled, sitting opposite them, "I had to ask Señora a couple of questions after class."

She busied herself with ripping off the foil cover of her yogurt, only not before seeing both of them give her first the chin-lift nod, then a couple of synchronized eye blinks. Lexa almost cracked up. She'd barely noticed that they maybe had a "thing" going on, and already they behaved as if they'd been together for ages.

Kevin and Em turned their attention back to what they'd been doing when Lexa spotted them. Photos on phones. Kevin held his up, swiping the screen, he and Em studying the images, murmuring to each other, something about what colors would help Anton interpret the brainy loneliness of the Dr. Lyman character. Next, they discussed vintage bus driver uniforms for Graham.

Lexa thrust her spoon into the yogurt. She should be glad, right? She took a big mouthful and almost spat it out, grabbing up the carton, grimacing at the prune on the label. Man, she wasn't noticing anything anymore.

"Take it easy, sugar. Being a little left out isn't the end of the world. Trust me, I know all about that."

"When have you ever been left out?" Lexa mixed her

yogurt hard. "You were like the biggest star of the century. You must've had a million people around you all the time. Falling all over themselves."

Marilyn froze, and Lexa did, too, her whole body going prickly and tight, as if both of them truly were stuffed inside her skin. Then Marilyn's head did one slow side to side, her lids squeezing down. "I always loved my fans," she said, her lips trembling, "let me tell you, though, having a million people around has nothing, *nothing*, to do with feeling like you belong somewhere."

"I'm sorry," Lexa said. She scrubbed the back of her hand over her quivery lips, her gaze flicking to Kevin and Em. "You're right. I do feel left out, because . . ." Then she knew. "Because Em and I tell each other everything, and she didn't tell me about this."

"Well, gee. Now you have an idea of why she was a little miffed with you this morning."

Across the table, a chair scraping snapped Lexa out of her head.

"Hey, Lexa," Kevin stood now, "want some water?"

"Um, sure."

The instant he moved off, Em leaned forward. "Okay," she said, elbows planted. "Tell me the real. What is going on with you?"

"*Me?*" Lexa dropped her spoon into the yogurt container. "I could ask the same about you. Or should I say, you two?"

Em barked out a breath, halfway between a cough and a laugh. "*What?* Kevin is . . . really helpful."

Marilyn mouthed, "Classic denial."

Em kept talking, "He's been doing some photo research, you know, for the costumes, and," her shoulders did a fast up and down, "he's fun to hang with."

"Are you . . . ?" Lexa wiggled her eyebrows.

"What? No! We're *buds*. Why are we talking about him anyway? What about you?" Em's eyes were hot points of searching light. "You've been acting strange since like—like *Saturday*. Back then you were totally determined to tell Mr. B you were out of the play. What happened to that? And don't give me any more of that, you just," she snapped her fingers, "saw the light and you don't want Hilary to win and you changed your mind."

More explanation scenarios careened through Lexa's head, all sounding like a load of exactly what Brian said in class—*schlacka*.

"Okay, okay. The truth is." She grabbed her apple, watched it roll between her palms. "The truth is, since we watched all those Marilyn movies? I've been having long talks with her. She convinced me that I should stick with the play."

"You've had long talks." Em's expression went wrinkly and confused. "With—with Marilyn Monroe. What? Like in your head?"

"Yup. Exactly," Lexa said. Marilyn stared at her, eyes excited-huge. "In my head."

"*Really?*" Em drew the word out.

She's a spirit. Lexa wanted to spit it all out, only . . . She glanced around at the loud, jarring crowd. Not here.

Before Lexa could move, Em let out a bray of laughter that had heads from the nearest tables turning. "You are too much. *Talking to Marilyn*. That's beautiful. And you're being so serious, like—like I don't know what! See?" She reached across the table, batting Lexa's arm. "I told you you could act."

Lexa shook her head, staring at her friend. Look at her, smiling, beaming. Em was *so* proud of her. Her, alone. The same way Dad was when he learned she'd put her name in Mr. B's jar. All at once Lexa understood that the true reason she didn't want to tell Em about Marilyn—or Dad either—had everything to do with not wanting them to be disappointed in her. Not wanting them to know just how scared she was.

"So," Em said, "what does," she made air quotes, "*Marilyn* say to you?"

"All kinds of things," Lexa mumbled. She pushed her yogurt carton around on the tray, rolled the apple. "You know, mostly being *rah-rah*. She's a lot like you."

"Cool. Thank you, Marilyn Monroe!" said Em to the air. "Tell me you're happy about it now. The play, I mean."

"That would be pushing it," Lexa said.

Chapter Ten

"You guys go ahead." Lexa kept her eyes on the contents of her locker, the thought of more fibbing to Em making her mouth dry and hot. "I completely forgot about this, uh . . . Spanish project, yeah. I'm going back to check something with Señora."

"We could wait," said Em, "right, Kevin?"

Sneaking a look, Lexa caught Kevin nodding. She banged her locker shut, speaking fast. "Don't bother. I-I'm pretty sure Dad said he had, you know, something to do out this way, so my ride home's covered."

"Are you sure?" Em did not look convinced.

"Oh, yeah," Lexa said, "totally sure."

As Em and Kevin headed away, Marilyn let out a breath. "You covering your behind with that Em is wearing me out. Honestly, I don't really get why you figure you have to work that hard. She is your best friend, after all."

"I know." Lexa blew out her own breath. "It's just really difficult to be with her right now. I mean, usually I skip telling her stuff that I think will worry her or make her mad. But now that I'm hiding *you*? Well, it's easier to, I don't know, step back a little. Besides, good old Kevin seems like he needs the boost, you know? I guess we better get home." She hoisted her pack onto her back, and thoughts of the day surfaced. Of Mr. B's workshop. Of what Brian had said at the end.

"I wonder what *he* does after school," said Marilyn.

Lexa shot her a look, and Marilyn's brows arched. "I can't help it. Your head is full of that boy."

"He's got a girlfriend."

"Does that mean he can't have any *friends* who are girls?"

"No."

"You *are* in a play together." Marilyn brushed invisible dust from her skirt. "Come on, sugar. What would it hurt to simply," her lids dipped low and dreamy, "walk by his locker?"

The second Lexa hit the corridor where Brian's locker lived, she saw him clang the door shut and head down the hall fast and away from her.

She slowed to a shuffle. "Too late," she said.

"Gosh, do I have to think of everything? Follow that boy."

Heart knocking, Lexa shifted to fast-walk mode after Brian. He rounded a corner and went into the library of all places. Head buzzing with what she would say when they "bumped" into each other, Lexa skulked in after him. The library's carpeted hush surrounded her with a quiet thick enough to taste. Ms. Hughes, the librarian, stood behind the checkout desk thumbing through papers. On the opposite side of the room, a couple of kids sat hunched at computer stations, clicking away. No sign of Brian.

Ms. Hughes looked over at Lexa, whispering, "Something I can help you find?"

"Oh," Lexa whispered back, "no."

Marilyn's voice jabbed fast. "Since we're here, ask her if she has any books on acting."

"Uh, actually?" Lexa said.

"Yes?"

"Do you have any books on, um, acting?"

"Why yes," said Ms. Hughes, instantly scooting to her computer and clicking happily. "The stack against the back wall, starting at 792.02."

Lexa trekked to the seven hundreds and ducked into the stacks.

"Look for something by Lee Strasberg," Marilyn said.

"Who?" Lexa's fingers ran across book spines. "Lou, what?"

"Lee! Lee Strasberg!"

Marilyn's whispery shout had Lexa jumping. "Relax," Lexa muttered.

"Do not tell me you've never heard of Lee Strasberg," Marilyn said, full-on pouting. "Why, he was one of the greatest acting teachers ever."

Lexa was about to say that she didn't know squat about acting at all, much less acting teachers, when she heard the dusty hiss of whispering. One of the voices belonged to Brian.

"C'mon, Hils." His whisper sizzled with frustration. "Don't be like that."

Hilary said something too low for Lexa to make out anything other than unhappiness.

Lexa inched to the end of the stack. Around the edge, she saw an open door to one of the study rooms. Inside, Brian's and Hilary's backs. They sat at a long table, laptops open and books and papers piled on either side of them. Brian was talking again.

"I don't know why you're pissed at me. You're the one who got me into this."

Glancing at Marilyn, Lexa whispered, "They're talking about the play."

Hilary now, sniffing hard. "I'm not pissed at *you*. I'm only—I'm only bummed we're not doing the play together. That was my plan. I was sure we'd both get it."

"Well." Brian blew out a sigh. "I don't know why you were sure of your 'plan' since Mr. B was pulling random names out of jars. Now I'm the one who has to be in this play. The least you could do is, I don't know, be supportive."

"I *am* supportive. That's why I'm writing that article, so I can be around a little. It's not the same. I wish . . ." Hilary's voice lowered, forcing Lexa to slink closer. "I wish you'd drop out. Then we could forget the whole thing."

Huge silence.

"I can't *believe* you," said Brian at last. "First you bug the effing crap out of me to put my name in the damn jar, and now you want me to drop it? Well"—the sound of a hand smacking the table made Lexa jump—"hell no! I am not gonna be a dick. Even for you."

"I'm not asking you to be a dick." Hilary took in a long wet-sounding breath. "It's only—you're already busy helping your dad with farm stuff. If you do Mr. B's play and I do the spring choral, we won't even see each other until, like, finals."

Brian said something else, low enough that the next thing Lexa knew she stood right outside the door, crammed tight to the wall to stay out of sight. Hilary's only response was another hard sniff.

"How about this?" Brian spoke slowly now. "Maybe you could blow off the choral and help us out. Do costumes. Or backstage, or something."

"But—but," Hilary began. Brian's loud, impatient breath cut her off.

"Okay already," she said, fake-cheerful. "Maybe that is a

good idea." Her voice turned fierce. "It's only . . . I was positive we'd both be picked to do Mr. B's workshop. I had a *feeling*, you know? Now it's like I'm missing out. That makes me, you know, miss us."

They were both silent. Then *not* silent.

In the same second Lexa understood Brian and Hilary were making out, Lexa found herself actually feeling bad for the girl. As well as crappy for listening in on them. She backed away, Hilary's low, throaty voice following her.

"Mmmmm. And I am really sorry I set you up to kiss that—that—"

"No," Lexa mouthed, "don't. Not that. Don't—"

"*Bovinian*," Hilary finished.

The word slammed Lexa to a halt and, from faraway she caught Brian's annoyed huff, his, "Jesus, Hil, I—"

No! She couldn't bear to hear his response. Swinging around, Lexa stopped short of bashing right into Ms. Hughes.

"Did you find what you were looking for, dear?"

"What?" Lexa croaked. Behind her, the sound of chairs moving, creaking.

"The books on acting?" said Ms. Hughes.

"*Shuuuush*," said Lexa. Desperately, she darted a look over her shoulder. *Please let Brian and Hilary stay put in make-out-ville*. "I mean—I mean this is a library, right?"

Ms. Hughes looked at her with total confusion. "Well, I know that—"

"Here it is." Lexa grabbed the first book off the nearest shelf and bolted from the stacks.

At the front desk, Lexa kept her gaze fixed to Ms. Hughes, who took a lifetime to check out her book. The second the book was in her hand, Lexa dashed out of the library, not stopping until she'd banged out of the school.

The cold slapped Lexa breathless, and she couldn't move.

Simply stood there on the walk. *Bovinian. Bovinian.* One by one, the events of that sixth-grade dance paraded through Lexa's mind. From the itchy feeling of Em convincing her to try one of her "designs," to the stares of the kids in the gym, to the girls' room. And Hilary. Ever gorgeous Hilary and the mean little slice of her mouth opening and calling Lexa that name. That awful name that sounded more like a rabid dog jumping out to bite than a cow.

Marilyn's voice was quiet, like it came from the end of a tunnel. "That girl—"

"Don't." Lexa took in a long, noisy breath, exhausted. She scrubbed a hand over her mouth. "Don't say anything to me right now."

Eyes big, Marilyn nodded.

Looking down at the book in her hand, Lexa read, "*The Idiot's Guide to Acting*. Perfect." Bitter as it came out, she had to laugh. Marilyn's laugh was a sad echo.

They trudged up the hill in silence and, at the bus shelter, Lexa tilted her head to the sky. Only around 4:00 p.m., the afternoon light was already that drab shadowy January gray that meant early dark. And the temperature was dropping. She dug her free hand into her pocket, and her fingers found the papery crinkle of the red scarf. Even though she shivered, she didn't pull it out. Peering down the road, she hoped maybe she'd luck out and spot an oncoming bus. Nope. One lone person heading her way on—of all things—a bicycle.

Marilyn perked up, her gaze fixed on the biker. "Get a load of this."

Wrapped from head to toe in winter gear, the biker cranked along like mid-winter was the best possible time to be on a bike. A bike with two bulging saddlebags.

Marilyn's fingers covered her mouth. "Now I've seen everything," she whispered.

The biker reached the bus shelter and stopped. In two quick moves, goggles went up and neck warmer pushed down. “Hey.”

Lexa almost choked.

Jeremy Leith.

Mortification level spiking, she said, “What are *you* doing here?”

Jeremy’s long blue gaze made her squirm, until one side of his mouth lifted. “I’m not ‘doing’ anything here.” He waved at a sign for the condo complex on the other side of the road. “This is where I live.”

“Oh,” she said, wishing he’d take off.

He didn’t.

“There won’t be another bus for a while,” he said.

Lexa shrugged, watching the toe of her boot kick the pavement.

“It’s pretty cold,” he said. “Do you want to come in for a cup of tea?”

Her head shot up. Before she could say a word, the rev of a pickup truck and the toot of a horn had her almost swallowing her tongue. Brian. Window down. “Hey, Lex?” His eyes were intense on hers, cheeks blazing. “Need a ride?”

Hilary sat beside him, her smile more frozen than the day.

“No thanks, I’m good,” Lexa heard herself call, and out of nowhere follow up with, “Jeremy and I are about to have tea. C’mon, Jeremy.” She waved blindly in the direction of Brian and Hilary and crossed the road, glaring at Marilyn, her thoughts fiercely, *This is* all *your fault!* Marilyn only lifted and dropped a shoulder.

Lexa kept walking, except something about Jeremy’s bike creaking behind her was like a finger drilling into her spine, making her imagine his expression. No, making her *remember* his expression. The smirk he’d worn when he’d caught her staring at Brian in class that very morning—*Busted!*

Chapter Eleven

There had to be an easy, painless way out of this. *Gee, look at the time*. Lexa's brain begged and begged. *Wow. I have got to get home*. Her mouth refused to follow orders, though, her feet following after Jeremy as he wheeled his bike into his garage and then led the way into his family's condo.

Trailing after him from the mudroom to his kitchen, Lexa couldn't help noticing again how tall he was. Tall, but not really skinny. She studied the muscles of his back, easy to see now that he'd stripped off his winter layers and was down to a stretchy, dark blue long john top. Like her thoughts tapped him, he looked over his shoulder: that one-sided smile again.

"Have a seat," he said, gesturing to a booth-like eating nook.

Lexa watched him put the groceries he'd taken out of the saddlebags on the counter and then lift a kettle off the stove.

"You're serious," she said.

"What?"

"About the—the tea."

Raising one brow, he shifted the kettle to his other hand. "Did you think I invited you in here to—what?—burn one?"

"Ummm." Lexa had a mad urge to laugh. "I have no idea."

Jeremy gestured to the nook again. "Why don't you have that seat."

She slid onto the padded bench and looked out the window. Beyond the edges and angles of the next unit, a field stretched, surrounded by bare-limbed trees and gray sky. She shivered, one quick twitch, the lateness of the afternoon sinking into her bones. Part of her wished she could go back in time, take that ride with Em and Kevin; keeping secrets and shoving into their cozy twosome sounded pretty damn good about now.

The muted thud of cupboards opening and closing drew her back to Jeremy. He held up two canisters.

"Earl Grey or jasmine?" he said.

"Ummm. Doesn't matter to me. You choose."

"Somehow I get the feeling you don't drink a lot of tea."

A quick huff of laughter escaped Lexa. "Good call."

"I think Earl Grey," he said, checking the window. "Fits the day."

He opened another cupboard, pulling out first a delicate-looking green china teapot and then two small matching cups with no handles.

The kettle whistled on the stove, and then Lexa could do nothing but gawk as he made tea, literally, the whole loose leaves spooned out of the canister and into the teapot, followed by the boiling water. He put the entire shebang on a tray and brought it over to the table. Then he slid in across from Lexa and sat there, calm and sort of waiting, his usually wispy hair flattened down a bit, his eyes even longer, even bluer. *Bang*—the whole thing set Lexa off.

"Who *are* you?" she sputtered. "I mean, you ride a bike in winter? Now you're making tea like—like some kind of professional tea guy?"

"What's wrong with riding a bike in winter?" He sounded genuinely confused. "I have the right gear, and my bike is fixed with studded tires. And I'm not a 'professional tea guy.'

My dad is British, and we lived in Beijing for a while. We made tea every day. Real tea." He lifted the top off the teapot and replaced it. "Not ready yet."

"Oh," Lexa puffed out, quiet and small. Small as she now felt.

He grinned. Not that one-sided mouth lift: a real grin. Surprisingly, a grin that unknotted her.

Grinning back, she sat up taller. "You're not exactly—you're different."

"Unexpected," he said, checking the tea again. "Good, it's ready."

He poured dark golden tea into their cups, then raised his, saying something in what she assumed was Chinese.

Lexa blew on her tea and took a sip. Light, tasty, with only a hint of sweet. "This is good," she said. "Thanks."

He nodded, sipping from his own cup.

"What did you mean?" she said.

"Oh. That was a Chinese toast I like to say. 'Savor it slowly' is about the closest translation I can think of."

She shook her head. "No. I mean before. When you said 'unexpected.'" While she waited for his reply, she remembered him using that very word when he saw her new hairstyle.

He regarded his tea, his hands loosely circling his cup. "I like things that are unexpected. Riding a bike in winter. Drinking tea from leaves instead of from a bag. Doing a play because I put my name in a jar." His eyes lifted to hers. "Wondering about a girl who looks one way on one day, and completely different the next. Inviting her to tea."

His last words caught Lexa in the middle of a sip, and she almost swallowed the wrong way.

They stared at each other, one long beat. A beat that had prickles sparking in Lexa, starting at her fingertips, and threading fast and electric up her arms to her neck. Her brain churning with confusion, she whirled to the window. The scene outside came at her sharp and clear. Like someone had added some kind of filter. All spiky bare trees against heavy clouds. Biting her bottom lip, she took a breath and then another and said, "Looks like it's going to snow again."

She hoped Marilyn would offer a sign—*something*—to help her out, and she almost choked again. Marilyn sat curled in her chair, nibbling from a bag of popcorn, her expression as though she was watching the most intense movie ever, starring, yeah, Lexa and Jeremy.

"Where did you go?"

Jeremy's question snapped Lexa back. "W-what?" she stuttered.

His forehead crinkled as he continued watching her. "Your face kind of rippled, and for a second you weren't here anymore."

Lexa wanted to bolt; those Jeremy-eyes pinned her, though. "I—I don't even know what you're talking about." She drained her cup. "Thanks for the tea, but I'd better get going."

She stood, and two things happened. Jeremy stood too, saying, "Hold up," and a door out in the mudroom shut hard. An instant later a taller, older version of Jeremy appeared in the kitchen archway.

"How do you like that?" murmured Marilyn before popping another kernel of corn between her lips. "The dad's as dreamy as the son."

"Well, hullo there," the guy who had to be Jeremy's father said, his British accent clipping into the room.

"Hey, Dad," said Jeremy, "this is Lexa. She's in the workshop with me."

"Lexa," said Mr. Leith, drawing her name out, "Is that short for—?"

"A-Alexandria," said Lexa.

"Ah, the Greek. Nice to meet you, Alexandria." He offered her a red-cheeked smile that was full of, *Smashing! I'm so glad to find my boy here with a girl*, and moved out of sight. Soon the sounds of him taking off his coat and boots floated into the kitchen.

"I really should go," Lexa whispered.

"Now that my dad's home, I can drive you."

Much as Lexa would've rather escaped on her own, another peek out the window, at the growing dark, had her nodding. "Okay," she mumbled.

Mr. Leith came into the kitchen, rubbing his hands together, a few folders stuffed under one arm. "It's a cold one out there." He pointed to the teapot. "Any of that left?"

"Sure." Jeremy took their empty cups to the sink and grabbed a clean one for his dad, saying, "I'm going to give Lexa a ride home."

"Right." Mr. Leith tucked himself into the booth and spread out his folders. Then like he'd had a brilliant idea, he glanced up at Jeremy. "She *could* stay for dinner, though." He smiled at Lexa, hopeful, and as quickly frowned. "I expect I should ask, what *is* for dinner?"

"That is so super nice," Lexa said fast. "I've got to get home."

"Good to meet you, then. Don't be a stranger." He gave them both a wave, his attention on the teapot now.

Jeremy and Lexa trooped into the mudroom and, while he put on his coat and snagged keys, she gathered her things. All at once her eyes cut to his back, and she didn't know how she knew this was true, only she did.

"It's you and your dad."

Jeremy faced her, slowly, carefully. "That's right," he said, two spots of color high on his cheeks.

"It's the same with me," Lexa said. When Jeremy didn't answer or move, Lexa lurched toward the door out to the garage.

Then they were driving. Driving, and not talking.

The silence got weird fast. Even weirder was that after her "Dad" comment, Lexa had a bizarre need to give something to Jeremy. She rubbed the back of her neck. "Before? When you were talking about what you liked? I—I've never thought much about what I like and don't like." She was babbling. "Being in Mr. B's play is my 'totally unexpected' thing." Her head fell back against the seat. "I don't know what I was thinking putting my name in that jar. I must've been nuts."

Jeremy shot her a narrow look, but he didn't say anything, only steered them out of the condo complex entrance.

Silence again, this one stranger than the last. Lexa stared out the car window. Man. Jeremy had no idea what he was getting into inviting her, the girl of strange silences, for tea. Now he could add the girl of complete psycho-loserness. She tried to catch Marilyn's attention, except Marilyn wouldn't turn to her, her stiff shoulders telling Lexa she was trying to give Lexa and her true confessions some privacy.

They stopped at a light.

"Why nuts?" Jeremy's voice was low, curious.

"Just . . ." Lexa peeked at him, "just totally not like me."

As the light changed and the car moved forward, Jeremy said, "What *is* like you?"

His question made Lexa's skin do that prickling thing again. She pressed her lips together and then said, "I wish I knew. I mean, I don't know. I wasn't trying to start a whole conversation." She plucked at the scarf in her pocket, pulled it out. "It's only, you were talking about all that 'unexpected' stuff, and I wanted to . . . I guess, show you I got what you were saying? That's all." She ran the scarf through her hands, a trace of Chanel wafting up. She took a deep breath.

He glanced over again and took in the scarf, and for a second Lexa had a desperate urge to stuff it back in her pocket.

"What's that smell?" he said.

"Chanel No. 5," she whispered, the place behind her breastbone tightening, as if merely the sight of the scarf, the name of the scent, was giving too much away.

"Smells good."

The way he said it—simple, easy—told her he had no idea whose signature scent it was. Slowly, she looped the scarf around her neck, the tightness in her chest easing.

Up ahead Lexa could see the intersection leading to Film Buzz. Marilyn sat up tall, her wide-open eyes full of wanting to talk to Lexa. They pulled into the parking lot, and Lexa had her seatbelt off before Jeremy even stopped the car.

"Hold up," he said, "answer me one last thing. If you don't want to do the play, why don't you drop out?"

She studied Jeremy's quiet, waiting face. He'd given her tea and yes, saved her from riding in the truck with Brian and Hilary. Shared some little bit of himself with her.

"I don't know," she said at last. Except she did know. Sort of. "I guess . . . because now that I'm into it, the whole being-in-a-play thing still scares the crap out of me, but somehow the thought of *not* doing it is worse. I guess that's making me stick with it."

Jeremy nodded slowly. "Right," he said. A smile swept over his face. "In case you were wondering, stage fright is my middle name, too. See you tomorrow."

Lexa watched him drive off. Watched until his car disappeared.

Chapter Twelve

Marilyn and Lexa didn't say a word until they were in the apartment. Then they both exhaled, big enough that if they'd been blow-up dolls they would've deflated all over the floor.

"Oh, honey," Marilyn said, "I've been wanting to tell you this all afternoon. I am terribly sorry! Of course, Brian was meeting that Hilary after school." She slapped her palm against her chest. "From that dinner I could tell that girl was ambitious, but who knew what a backstabbing—" She shook her head. "My, what an after*noon* you've had."

Lexa almost laughed. God, she'd practically forgotten about Hilary, only Marilyn hadn't. A strange guilty heat—not generated by her—flushed over Lexa's skin, making her want to pat Marilyn's hand.

"Don't worry about it," Lexa said. *Patpat* went her brain. "I guess I was pretty pissed before."

An acid taste filled her mouth as she remembered bitch Hilary calling her a "bovinian." Again! And Brian, well, she still didn't want to know what he'd said to that.

"I wanted it to be your fault," Lexa said, dumping her backpack and coat. "It wasn't."

Marilyn's teeth worried her lower lip.

"Really," Lexa went on, heading for the kitchen. "I'm the one who decided to follow Brian into the library, and I'm the one who told Jeremy I'd have tea with him. Now we're back here and, oh look, I survived. Life can go on." She yanked open a drawer. "Dad and I usually fix sandwiches or something for dinner, but tonight," she pulled out a menu, "I think we deserve pizza."

Marilyn continued nibbling her lip, even when Lexa waved the pizza menu right up close to her head.

"You are something," Marilyn said at last, "and I'm sure pizza would be swell. You know what would truly fix me up, though?"

Lexa shook her head, unable to help a small quiver of *what now?*

"I feel like." Marilyn popped out of her chair. "Cooking." An apron—white with a lacy frill—appeared around her waist. "What do you say?"

The next thing Lexa knew, she stood at the stove, a dish towel apron stuffed into the waist of her jeans, swishing a sizzling pile of chopped garlic and onions mixed with freezer bag carrots and peas in a large flat pan.

"This stuff is strong," Lexa said. She wrinkled her nose against the onion-garlicky burn. "What are we making again?"

"Mmmmmmm." Eyelids low, Marilyn inhaled big. "That smells like heaven. And we're not making any kind of official recipe," she said. "Those ingredients should make up a nice pasta, though." She pointed to the pan. "Give that another stir and then turn the heat down. Perfect. Now that's simmering, and that big old pot of water is just about boiling." She clapped her hands. "Let's grate some cheese. Mmmm. I'm dreaming of freshly grated parmesan."

All Lexa could find in the refrigerator was a dried-up hunk of cheddar. Marilyn told her to go ahead and grate it up, her mouth puckering a little, amused. Yeah, Lexa got it. What could be more ridiculous to a spirit than worrying about having the right kind of cheese?

Shoulders loosening as she grated cheddar into a frothy pile, a warm sensation spread through Lexa. This was nice. Being in a cozy kitchen, cooking. Delicious smells all around. Sweet onion. Tangy cheese. She opened her mouth to say as much, only Marilyn's voice—super low—murmured in her head. No. Not murmuring, humming.

"What's that song?" Lexa said.

"Don't you recognize it?"

While she listened to Marilyn hum again, the grater and cheese stilled in her hands. "That's the song from *Bus Stop*. What's it called? Something about black magic?"

"That's right. Want me to teach you the lyrics? You're going to have to sing it in the play, you know."

Fingers of ice sliding through her insides now, Lexa grated more cheese, muttering, "Thanks for reminding me."

Marilyn tapped her lip. "I know you didn't forget about that."

"No, I didn't forget. Since we haven't practiced anything about the play in class . . ." Lexa pressed the cheese harder. "I've pretty much decided to put the whole thing—singing included—out of my mind until we do."

"I see how that kind of thinking might chase off your fear about being in the play." Marilyn touched a pinky to her bottom lip. "What is it doing for that other feeling you mentioned? Something about dropping out feeling worse?"

Startled, Lexa said, "That—that was private. You shouldn't listen—" Her hand grazed the grater's razor-sharp edge. "*Ow!*" She shoved her stinging finger into her mouth.

"You okay, sugar?"

"Yeah," Lexa said, pulling out her finger. She'd tasted the metallic salt of blood, but only a tiny, jagged flap of skin stood up under her nail, the sting already fading.

Marilyn seemed to study Lexa's finger, and then she shrugged. "Now, where were we?"

"We were talking about, um, fear," Lexa said, picking up the grater again. "The only fear *I* want to talk about right now is stage fright." There was something about the calm way Marilyn sat there watching her. Something strange. Shaking it off, Lexa went on, "How about you? Did you ever get nervous about a part?"

"Sure, I did," Marilyn said, "oh, and I tried all sorts of ways to get rid of those nerves."

"Like what?"

"Why." Marilyn lowered her head, brushing at her skirt. "I did lots of things." She lifted her chin, a small smile blooming. "You know what? Cooking would've worked."

"Ha ha," Lexa said. She lifted the top off the saucepan and hesitated. Marilyn was right. Through the chopping and mixing, she hadn't thought of the play or Brian or Hilary or anything. Her phone beeped with an incoming text. Dad, wondering about dinner.

"In my day, there was nothing a man liked more than a plate of home-cooked," said Marilyn.

Lexa wiped a hand on her dish-towel apron, and a thought popped into her head. Before she could squash it, Marilyn nodded.

"Me, too. Jeepers, the minute that Jeremy boy's dad invited you, I wondered what they'd have for dinner."

"I wasn't *wondering* that." Lexa yanked the dish towel from her jeans. "The thought kind of—kind of came into my head. And now it's gone."

"Whatever you say." Marilyn held up her hands. "I don't want to do anything to get you riled up again. Only I'm here if you want to talk. About anything. Like, I don't know, the play, stage fright, fright in general." She gave Lexa a bright smile. "How you feel about Jeremy."

Lexa's whole face scrunched up. "I don't have any 'feelings' for him."

Marilyn's brows lifted.

"I barely know the guy."

The brows went higher.

Lexa tossed the dish towel on the table, and Marilyn tilted her head, her patience infuriating.

"Fine." Lexa licked her grated finger again. "I don't know why, but he's always sort of—sort of intimidated me. And now . . ."

"Now?"

"I don't know. It's like we're friends all of a sudden. It's kind of confusing."

"I wish I had answers for you. I was never exactly an expert on men."

"If you're not an expert, who is?"

Marilyn's expression flickered, a cloud moving over the sun. "You mean because a million men looked at my pictures? Watched my movies? Wanted me?" Her voice sank to a whisper. "Because I was married three times?"

Lexa swallowed hard and, after a moment, nodded.

"Experience, honey, does not always equal expertise." Marilyn's lids dipped. "I liked watching you and that Jeremy today. It made me feel . . . different. Different than any feeling I ever remember having." She chuckled as though she'd made a joke, a joke only she would think was funny. "I guess my feeling anything now is neither here nor there, but there you go. Watching you two having your tea was like wrapping up in the softest blanket on a cold day."

While Marilyn spoke, a strange heat swelled inside Lexa, like a fevered hand rubbing her heart. She pressed at her chest, trying to push the heat away even as she wanted to ask Marilyn what she meant. A desperate rattling had her head whirling. The pasta water boiled hard, the whole pot shaking and steaming, ready to explode. She lunged to turn the burner down. The pot settled, and she tried to focus on the simple job of opening the bag of spaghetti. The fevered hand fisted tightly around her heart now, giving a painful squeeze, and then let go. Let go, but left Lexa trembling, especially her hands clutching the bag. She faced Marilyn.

"What was that all about?"

"What do you mean? Did you burn yourself on the pot?" Innocent confusion radiated.

"No." Lexa studied her quivering hands. Focused on her cut finger. Again, she saw Marilyn's face: how it looked then; how it was the same now. Calm, easy.

"You don't feel this," Lexa said.

"Don't feel what?"

"My hands shaking right now. And before, when I cut my finger. I thought you felt *everything* I felt. Why not now?"

"I—I have no idea."

"You *have* to know."

Marilyn looked at her, a long stretched-out look, saying at last, "Only I don't."

Slowly Lexa picked up the knife, cut open the spaghetti package, and dropped the pasta into the pot. Together they watched the water bubble, cloud.

Thoughts and images tumbled through Lexa. Tumbled and churned. All of them adding up to one fact: The spirit of Marilyn Monroe lived in her body.

"I—I invited you to stay like I knew what it would mean to have you here. To have you in me," Lexa whispered, a hollow cold sweeping through her. "Like I believed *you* knew."

Still watching the pasta boil, Marilyn whispered back, "From the first moment I was in you, I knew this was every kind of strange. Every kind of complicated. I knew it. Except I wanted to be here. I wanted to be with you so much, I—I put those thoughts away, telling myself I wouldn't have been able to come if it wasn't all right."

"I . . ." Lexa paused. "I guess I figured it would be like some movie."

"Oh, the movies." Marilyn's smile was small and blue. "No, sweetie. I don't think this is going to be like any movie either of us has ever seen."

Chapter Thirteen

Over the next few weeks, Lexa's time with Marilyn blurred by, a crazy cross between an endless sleepover and a . . . Lexa had no idea. Seriously. She did her best to forget the trembly heat and the shivery cold of that day in the kitchen, when she'd realized that neither of them understood truly what having—or being—a spirit inside a living girl could mean. It was like they were both tiptoeing, being extra nice to each other. Extra gentle. The easiest times were when they cuddled up on Lexa's bed or during a slow shift at Film Buzz, surfing the internet for recipes or clothes or makeup.

The acting book Lexa'd grabbed had actually turned out to have some good advice. Even some of the famous Lee Strasberg's advice. "That's right," Marilyn would coo, "listen to Lee. You have to use your imagination, your senses, your emotions, your memories. All of it to become the character." Lexa would smile and nod, wondering what any of her imagination or senses or emotions or memories had to do with being a super-hot showgirl kidnapped by a lovesick cowboy. "Oh, honey," was Marilyn's usual response. Then she'd shake her head and let Lexa distract her by clicking to photos of Marilyn. They swiped through dozens and dozens, even watching some of the old vid clips. Marilyn liked that.

What Marilyn liked more, though, was the cooking. When they cooked together, Lexa could practically taste how Marilyn yearned to chop and stir herself, the yearning a deep, physical itch pushing at Lexa. Marilyn never asked for that, though, both of them remembering the dangerous craziness of that first day.

Working on the play held its own dangers and confusions, the two biggest factors: Brian and Jeremy.

Jeremy. Complete weirdness there. The way he'd talk to her after school sometimes, walk with her to the bus stop. He didn't invite her for tea again though, and when they were in class, it was like he'd put up a Do Not Disturb sign. Or maybe she had. All Lexa knew there was that sometimes she'd catch him looking at her and then at Brian.

Brian? Total confusion there. Since that miserable day in the library, she'd tried to stay out of his way. He didn't get it, though. He'd come into Mr. B's classroom, give her the old chin-lift, saying, "Hey, Lex," or simply, "Lex." Sometimes he'd sit next to her. Too close. Too nice. Or maybe simply too guilty. Lexa hated how she couldn't help her body going fluttery and weak when he was near. Disturbing.

More disturbing was thinking about why she was there at all. About what was coming. When Mr. B would tell them that they were done with reading and writing about the play, and it was time to start rehearsing *Bus Stop*. That it was time for Bo and Cherie to get up close and personal.

Then the first Monday in March came.

Lexa pulled open her shade that morning, and sunlight poured over her, making her whole body stretch into the warm and bright. The snow on the ground sparkled.

"Mmmmmm." Marilyn reached her arms over her head. "Creamy."

"Definitely," Lexa said. Rolling out of bed, she opened her closet, and Marilyn crossed her arms, wanting to make a suggestion, the pressure of that want firm as a nudge. She didn't say anything, though, only huffed out a breath when Lexa reached for one of her flannel shirts.

"Wait, please," Lexa said, taking out the shirt, and then skipping her fingers to hangers holding a swishy black skirt and a lacy white vintage camisole, both of which she'd found on a recent outing to Golden Oldies. Marilyn dutifully put her hands over her face as Lexa dressed and, after, applauded as Lexa tied the unbuttoned flannel shirt at her waist. "You're really learning, sweetie. That looks perfect."

"Perfect," said Lexa, "for me."

On the whole walk to school, Lexa's steps were light. Blue, blue sky with wisps of puffy cottonball clouds. The air crisp, clear, and peppermint fresh.

Once inside QueenHi, her mood dulled, though, dropping to dirt when she spotted Brian and Hilary outside Mr. B's classroom. They leaned against the wall, wrapped around each other in a deep, suction-cup kiss. As Hilary pulled back, she offered Brian a mini cupcake, saying, "I have an SASA meeting after school, but don't you worry, we'll really celebrate later, birthday boy."

Birthday boy? Before Lexa could block the kind of celebration Hilary had in mind for Brian, images strobed of the two of them naked and rolling on Hilary's probably pink cupcake of a bed.

"Put a leash on that imagination," Marilyn whispered. "It is his birthday after all."

Determined to avoid an actual Hilary encounter, Lexa ducked back into the stairwell. She still stung from Hilary's famous article in the school paper. That experience was bad from the get-go, beginning with Hilary's interview of the class. How she'd whipped to Lexa, those brown eyes like bullets, saying, "What about the star? Cherie is the starring part, after all. How do you feel about carrying the whole show on your shoulders?" Lexa'd about swallowed her tongue, sputtering an incoherent, "I don't know," instead of parroting any of the clever replies Marilyn offered.

The bad got worse when the article came out, and Hilary, in her syrup-nasty way, had focused on how it was "wicked awesome" that QueenHi could afford to devote the resources of the entire high school auditorium and an ace teacher to a group of mostly untested—read "pathetic"—actors, putting on a show for a traditionally intimate—read "nonexistent"—audience.

As Marilyn was telling her once again to "Forget about that darn article," the bell rang. Lexa dashed to class, her spirits lifting that Hilary was no longer in sight, and even more when she scored a seat far away from Brian.

Mr. B dove right in. "I have some news." He clasped his hands behind his back. "It seems that an unusual circumstance has arisen. Yesterday afternoon I was told that SASA, that's Students Against Substance Abuse to the uninformed, has scheduled an event for the end of the year that conflicts with our use of the auditorium." He paused. "The only option is to do our show in the gym, or," his expression went dreamy, "take advantage of the opportunity of a lifetime. I'm sure you have all been to Queen City's one and only Marquee Theater. Well, my wife does quite a bit of volunteering there, and she called the executive director, and they have generously offered us the use of the theater for our show." He paused. "The only caveat is that we must move up our show, and be ready to perform one month from this coming Friday."

The classroom was quiet as a held breath. A suffocated breath.

"Of course, I spoke to the powers that be," Mr. B went on like eight pairs of eyes weren't boring into him. "And they, meaning the principal and even the school board, are 100 percent behind us taking that opportunity if we can be ready. So, I put it to you. Could we be ready?"

The class erupted in a flurry of "This is crazy" and "Could we really be ready?" and "This is the coolest" with two exceptions—Brian and Lexa. They looked at each other so long and so silent that Lexa almost didn't feel Marilyn poking at her, her whisper hot. "Why I've never heard of anything like this," *poke*, *poke*, "aren't you going to add your two cents?"

Her two cents? Lexa slouched down, forcing herself to speak. "Maybe we should use the gym," she said. "I—I mean, it's not like we're professionals or anything."

"Yeah," Brian chimed in, faster and louder. "This play . . . It's supposed to be like not a big deal."

Silence roared again. This one a strangled choke, everyone in the class, Mr. B included, gaping from Brian to Lexa as though both of them had turned traitor.

"Performing on a true stage, especially one as grand as the Marquee's," Mr. B said at last, "would be an experience like no other. Transformative is the only word I am able to think of that describes the feeling. I would hate for you all to miss it and, not to be too presumptuous, I am confident you all could be ready in one month." He raised a hand to hold the silence. "That said, to make this change would require a significantly higher level of work and flexibility that I feel we must agree on unanimously." He rose, striding to the door. "I will give you a few minutes to discuss amongst yourselves."

The click of the door had Anton standing, his gaze roving around the circle. "What the actual *eff*? The Marquee, people, the Marquee!"

"Really," said Dani-Marie, ponytail bouncing, "this is like winning the lottery times ten." Her face went fierce. "A month is plenty of time. Let's do this." She raised her hand, "All in favor?"

One after another, hands went up around the circle, until all had voted except Brian, Lexa, Jeremy, and Kevin. After a moment, Jeremy laughed out loud and raised his hand. "This keeps getting more and more unexpected. What do you say, Lexa?" He turned those blue eyes to her and then to Brian and Kevin. "How about you two?"

Kevin groaned and, with a darting look at Lexa that told her he was really thinking of Em, he raised his hand.

Glaring at his desktop, Brian shifted his feet, his boots making a heavy *thump*. "Did Mr. B say that we're screwed out of the auditorium for an SASA thing?"

When he looked up and saw heads nodding, he blew out a fiery breath. "Damn." Cheeks blazing red, he lifted his arm, saying, "Whatever. I'm in."

Now everyone focused on Lexa, including Marilyn. "Stop looking at me like that," she said to Marilyn. To the others, her appeal was a low, unhappy, desperate moan. "A month? For the Marquee? That's not even close to enough time!" She buried her head in her arms. "I can't. It's too much. Too big. There's just no way."

"Please, Lexa. Think of how great this would be for Em. Her costumes on the Marquee stage," Kevin began soft and persuasive, but when Lexa didn't lift her head, Dani-Marie called out, her tone a frustrated snap, "Well then, *you'll* have to tell him."

"Fine." Lexa lurched up, stumbled for the door.

Mr. B was at the end of the hall, peering out the window, his shoulders, his nose, even his hair lifted as if in a rosy dream.

"Jeepers," Marilyn murmured, "the idea of the Marquee has that man on cloud nine."

"Fine, fine, fine!" Lexa shouted in her head as she marched to Mr. B. "We're all in," she said and, angry as she was, the pure joy on his face was what almost tore her into pieces.

Back in the classroom, Mr. B clapped his hands together, settling the surprised and freshly noisy group down to the task required by their new venue and performance schedule.

As Lexa retook her seat, avoiding meeting anyone's eyes, Marilyn whispered, "You're not the only one who's unhappy."

Ignoring the shoulder pats and whispers of encouragement from Clara and Graham, who sat on either side of her, Lexa stole a look at Brian. Sure enough, he looked as unhappy as she felt: mottled red cheeks on a stone-cold face.

"Think of it this way, honey," Marilyn went on, "the play will be over that much sooner. Everything will be peachy. You'll see."

Lexa gave her a quick, unconvinced inward eye roll and turned her attention to what Mr. B was saying.

"Now that we're all agreed, we will shift our focus from study of the play to preparing for the stage." His gaze swept from face to face. "To date you've all worked hard to understand the play, the characters, and I have every faith each and every one of you will be able to be ready. As I'd hoped you would choose as you have, I prepared a special exercise for today, focusing on taking risks. Personal risks."

Lexa and Marilyn caught eyes and, before she could stop it, a nervous laugh bubbled from Lexa's mouth.

"Miss Donovan?" Mr. B's booming delight had Lexa jumping. "Why don't you start. With Mr. McKinnon. What I'd like you to do is *connect* with him. Only in an unusual way. A way that takes a risk. A risk that Cherie might take. Spend a moment thinking of what you'd like to do."

Lexa stared down at her desk, wishing she could carve an idea into her brain the way someone had carved the tiny shape of a duck into the wood.

"You can do this." Marilyn sounded exactly like Mr. B.

"I don't think so," Lexa's mind returned, "no, I—I can't." She closed her eyes, hearing Mr. B say again that they'd do the play in four weeks. *Four weeks*. And he wanted her to act. This minute. Like Cherie? With Brian? She sucked in a breath, the air strangling in her throat. Now her brain took her to the library, hearing Hilary calling her a bovinian. Before she could think, she snapped at Marilyn, "You. You do it!"

Marilyn's brows shot up. "No, honey. You made me promise not to do that. Ever."

"I don't care what I said! You said you wanted to help me. So, help me. I'm desperate! Please!"

Marilyn worried her lip, her cheeks pinking. Then—*Whoosh!* Like a brick wall of wind, blinding white energy slammed into Lexa. From somewhere far away she heard herself gasp and then—*thud*—Marilyn and she had changed places. Not the same as way back when Marilyn first arrived. No. Bigger, deeper, more. Lexa was herself, only now she sat in her own head, in Marilyn's director's chair, Marilyn's bag of popcorn on her lap. Dazed, Lexa touched the chair. Wood. The popcorn bag. Paper. What was strangest of all was how not strange being in her own head was.

Then it started. Lexa, shimmying the coat off her shoulders, everything about her locked on to Brian.

More electricity sparked through Lexa, only this time like magic. Like getting the best present ever. A haze of Chanel No. 5 swam through her senses, roses and talcum, fresh line-dried laundry. Lexa inhaled deep, every part of her pulsing hot and sweet. So sweet. Except—except what was Marilyn *doing*?

Lexa raised her hands, cupping them below her chin as if she held a microphone. She smiled at Brian, lids half-lowering ready to taste deliciousness, and placed the tip of her tongue on her upper lip like that taste was a secret only she and Brian could share. And then she sang.

"Happy Birthday. To you . . ."

The bag of popcorn slid from Lexa's lap. Only days ago, she and Marilyn had been watching Marilyn clips online, and Lexa'd seen this. A clip of Marilyn from the 1960s, in a dress as sparkly as a lit birthday candle, standing on a stage in front of thousands. In front of the President of the United States. Singing this.

"Happy Birthday . . . to you."

That voice. Lexa couldn't sit still. That whispery voice.

"Happy Birthday . . . dear Brian."

Brian leaned way back, lips parted, expression glazed. Any second cartoon stars and birds would appear, circling over his head.

"Happy Birthday. To . . . you."

Lexa sat down and—*whoosh*—the inside-Lexa flew high, like swinging on an out-of-control swing and—*bam*—slammed back into her sitting body. Shaking, she gasped, like the wind had been knocked out of her.

Everyone in the circle stared at her, Mr. B most of all, his expression stricken like he'd seen a ghost.

Hold up. Hold up. Mr. B wasn't staring at her most of all. Brian was. Brian. Looking at Lexa as though she'd become a person he'd never seen before.

Still struggling to quiet her breathing, Lexa glared at Marilyn. Tucked on her chair, Marilyn lifted and dropped a shoulder, red-red lips pouting. "That got his attention."

Chapter Fourteen

The applause in the classroom was so loud that Lexa almost didn't hear Marilyn say, "Now don't get mad at me. You know you asked for it, honey."

"Why did you do that?" Lexa's brain mumbled at Marilyn.

Marilyn shrugged. "I hardly know how to answer that. I guess I wanted you to knock his socks off."

"Mission accomplished." Lexa's whole body wanted to whimper, only she had to stay silent and unmoving: stuck in her seat in Mr. B's classroom, surrounded. Longingly, she imagined herself as she used to be, only now—as if a movie flickered away in her head—she saw her old self differently. The old Lexa in baggy flannel shirts and jeans drifting through QueenHi like a tall smudgy shadow, always quiet and always at the very edges.

Sitting forward, Marilyn said, "Tell me that is *not* who you'd rather be?"

"I don't know." Lexa took a shallow breath. "At least—at least no one stared at me back then."

Marilyn blew out a sad-sounding breath, saying, "I suppose that's one way to live."

✦

The class dragged by—*dripdripdrip*. Then Jeremy's turn came. Mr. B paired him with Clara. When Jeremy stood, he flicked Lexa a quick glance before focusing on his hands. He mimed spooning something, then pouring that something into his cupped hand and offering it to Clara.

Tea. Crazy how thinking of that one little three-letter word started a slow burn at the base of Lexa's neck.

Before she could even think about what Jeremy meant, Mr. B said, "Mr. McKinnon? You're up. You'll be with—"

Of course. Lexa's eyes slammed to the floor.

The room went eerily silent. Then the sound of paper ripping from a notebook and a pen scribbling. From under her lashes, Lexa watched Brian cross the room, the paper folded into a small square in one hand and the pen in the other. Heat blooming in every part of her, she could hardly breathe. He knelt beside her chair, fumbling her backpack out of his way, the nape of his neck pink and bare, smelling of soap and apples and boy.

When he took her arm, she jumped. Her skin flinched and burned when he turned her wrist to write on the inside over her pulse. He returned to his seat, and Lexa read what he wrote on her skin. A question mark.

"Intriguing," Mr. B said, then opened to the group. "Wonderful work, everyone. I see it already, each of you finding the core of your character." He handed out papers. "I'll have an updated schedule for you tomorrow. After-school rehearsals will start at the end of the week, and until we are told to be out of the auditorium, we will use that space as planned for rehearsal as well as for after school. Oh dear, I'll have to figure something out for when our backstage helpers join us, since we'll have to move everything to the Marquee."

Dani-Marie's hand shot up. "When are we supposed to be off book?"

"As soon as possible." Mr. B regarded the group. "Some of you know this, but for those unfamiliar—running lines with each other is an excellent way to prepare." The end-of-homeroom bell rang. "Ah, perfect punctuation to a very inspiring meeting." He shifted to Lexa. "Miss Donovan? A moment of your time."

He didn't say anything more until the others filed out. "Miss Donovan." He pursed his lips, his brows beetling. "I know a while back we had an exploratory conversation about Miss Monroe as a performer. As a star. Today's exercise makes me wonder if perhaps you are taking what I said back then a bit too much to heart. I take this workshop very, very seriously, and I wouldn't want any one of my performers to get . . . lost." He peered at her over his glasses. "Do you know what I mean when I say lost?"

Lexa nodded. Of course, he meant the song; too bad his idea of lost had nothing to do with having a rogue spirit in the head.

"Emulation," he continued, "is the sincerest form of flattery, only don't get too carried away."

"Got it," Lexa managed.

"Good," he said, "because clearly you've been studying Miss Monroe's work."

"That's one way to put it."

"What?"

"Nothing," she said, fingers plucking at her ring, "I—I have to get to my next class."

Lexa was almost out the door when he called out. "I will admit, though, that was quite a good impression. Spooky how you captured that famous performance. Gave me goosebumps."

Marilyn smiled big and sparkly.

Yup. Lexa'd asked for it all right. She slid into the mass of clomping high schoolers in the hall. Loud chatter surrounded her, echoing off the walls, then something else, something more specific, closer—a hissing giggle, a whisper. "Can you *believe* her? Yeah, check this . . . *wishwishwish* . . ." Lexa listened, straining, the thud of her heart telling her what her insides knew: that the voices talked about her. Almost stumbling, she walked faster. At the door of her next class, she glanced up and down the hallway. A few kids wandered by in both directions, one, then two of them clicking away on their phones and then sneaking looks at her in that way that meant someone in the workshop had told another someone about her singing to Brian, and that probably another someone had spread the word. Ah, the wildfire power of gossip.

"I am so screwed," she muttered.

Marilyn put her fingers to her lips; she didn't even pretend to tell Lexa otherwise or to hide a small, satisfied smile.

Creeping to her Spanish class, Lexa slipped in and took a seat in the back. Immediately the inside of her wrist tickled, Brian's question mark.

She was screwed all right, only—she ran a finger over the question mark on her skin and thought of Brian. And of doors opening. Looked like Marilyn's song had done something else, too.

The end of Spanish class came too soon. Lexa dawdled at her seat. It was lunchtime, and the last place she wanted to go was to the caf.

"But we're hungry, honey," Marilyn said, "even for whatever nasty business they're serving."

Ignoring her, Lexa peeked down the hall, a thief trying to make a getaway. One empty hallway and one dark stairway later, she was outside the front door. Her stomach growled, and she put a hand on her belly.

"What about eating?" Marilyn rubbed her belly, too. "You need to keep up your strength. Take care of your instrument."

"I think I have a granola bar." Lexa slipped off her pack, crouching with it on the walk.

A shadow fell over her, even as a familiar voice said, "Another acting exercise?"

Lexa squeezed her eyes shut. "Hi, Jeremy."

"Or maybe this time you *are* just talking to yourself."

"Maybe I am," she said as she rose, making the words come out even and unhurried.

He studied her and she knew—practically hearing the words coming out of his mouth—that he wanted to ask her about her "performance" in the workshop. He did ask her a question, not that one, though.

"Skipping lunch?"

"Uh, yeah," she said, "I wanted a little fresh air."

He let out a small huff of, *Sure, that's the reason you're out here*, and smiled.

"What's your excuse?" she said.

"Pardon?"

"What's your excuse for being out here instead of in the caf?"

"Maybe I have an earlier lunch."

"This *is* early lunch."

His smile grew. "Maybe since I live basically across the road, I like to go home for lunch. And maybe today I was looking for you. Want to join me?"

"Join you?"

His grin became amused. "For lunch," he said, enunciating both words.

"Um, I'm not really sure." Lexa trailed off, and she sent out a plea to Marilyn to come up with an excuse. Marilyn offered her a slow shrug. Sometimes Lexa hated it when Marilyn left things up to her. Face it, sometimes she hated it when Marilyn sat there in her head in that same spot on that same damn director's chair!

Lexa's stomach rumbled again, and Jeremy's gaze lowered, noticing.

Mirroring Marilyn's shrug, Lexa said, "Why not?"

Chapter Fifteen

Walking to Jeremy's this time seemed almost normal. Easier. Like they'd planned it. Like they were friends.

Lexa figured now was the time Jeremy would say something about what happened in the workshop. He did. Not about the birthday song, though. No. He talked about the Marquee and the schedule change. About how soon they would be rocketing into rehearsals, about the risks others picked.

"I think Clara's was the simplest. The most direct," he said as they strolled into his kitchen. "Sit, and I'll see what we've got."

"Okay."

Sun poured through the big window, making the whole room more welcoming than that other day. More cheerful. Probably because of the light-catcher. Lexa hadn't noticed it on her first visit, the light that day much too late-afternoon dark and gray. Now bright sun caught the star-shaped crystal, scattering dreamy pink, blue, and orange spangles everywhere.

Jeremy stood in front of the open refrigerator, talking more about Clara. "What she chose shows she understands Elma, you know? Bloody brilliant of her to take off her scarf and wrap it around Anton's neck. Showing that even though her character's young, she knows people need to be taken care of."

He leaned way into the refrigerator and bent over.

Now there's a dreamy view. Those words came into Lexa's head fast enough that she wasn't sure who thought them. Jeremy was still talking.

"Elma wants to take care of all the other characters. She pays attention. Like knowing that lonely Dr. Lyman needs comfort." Jeremy turned, a take-out carton in each hand. "Do you like Vietnamese?"

Lexa'd never had Vietnamese but, even as Marilyn's eyes went wide and quizzical, she nodded furiously. Guess they needed to try it. "Sure."

Jeremy grabbed a casserole dish from the top shelf of a cupboard and . . . *Man, he was tall.* His shoulders were pretty wide too, the thin fabric of his dark brown sweater stretching tight. He dumped the contents of the cartons into the casserole and, while he reached again to slide it into the microwave, Lexa's gaze traveled to where the bottom of his sweater lifted, exposing the bare skin of his hip. She jerked her face to the window.

"Nothing wrong with looking." Marilyn mouthed the words, and Lexa cringed as if she'd yelled. She shouldn't be looking at Jeremy that way. She frowned, Jeremy's kitcheny clattering making her want to watch him again. She stared out the window harder. *Lunch*. He was offering her lunch. That's all.

A hot, perfumy-spicy scent wafted. Lunch that smelled amazing! And different. She traced the spot on the sunny window where her frowning face should've been reflected. How was it that Jeremy was always comfortable doing something totally different?

Drawers opening snapped her back. "God, what is wrong with me?" She stood up fast. "Need help?"

"Um, yes." Jeremy was already by the table, his hands full of two steaming bowls with chopsticks poking high. He pointed his chin over his shoulder. "You could grab those two glasses of water."

Both of them sitting now, Lexa took a good look at what was in her bowl. The green and brown and sauce definitely looked familiar, sort of. She prodded at some yellow strands with the tip of her chopstick.

"Lemongrass," mumbled Jeremy, his mouth full.

She nibbled and then took a whole bite. "This is really good," she said, "different."

"Not much like the real thing," he said, "still pretty tasty, though."

"You sound like you've been to Vietnam," she said, not even trying to keep the wonder out of her voice.

"A long time ago," he said with a shrug, "my dad was there for one of his conferences."

"That's so cool," she said, "and you used to live in Beijing? Man, sounds like you and your dad have been to a lot of different places."

"I suppose we have," he said. "How about you?"

Lexa shrugged. "I've never been out of Vermont."

Jeremy's brows went up, and the way he didn't say anything made Lexa's face go hot, like she'd admitted she still slept in a onesie or something. They ate in silence for a while and, whenever their eyes met, both would turn to the window.

Marilyn slumped against the canvas back of her chair. "This silent treatment is killing me. Any way to fast-forward this scene to more actual conversation?"

Letting out a strangled choke, Lexa covered by grabbing up her glass and gulping water.

"You okay?" Jeremy said. When she nodded, he continued with, "I wanted to ask you about the risk *you* chose today . . . I know you were acting." One finger traced the rim of his glass. "It seemed—you seemed—bought into it. Beyond bought into it."

She put her glass down with a snap. "What—what do you mean 'beyond'?"

"I'm not sure. It *could* all be acting. Or it could be . . ."

Somehow Lexa knew they'd gone back to that January afternoon a few weeks earlier, when she'd accepted his tea invitation.

"That you have a thing for Brian. Do you?"

Those blue-blue eyes held her. Long-lidded and clear. The kind that made lying impossible. No, that simply asked for the truth. The truth that now came out of her mouth. "Sort of, I guess."

The words hung there, while Lexa picked at her food. She couldn't look at Marilyn, and definitely not at Jeremy. Jeremy. She could still see his eyes opening to big round circles at her honesty.

"What kind of 'sort of thing'?" he said.

Her head jerked up. "What?"

"What kind of 'sort of thing' do you have for Brian?" His brows lifted as though he actually expected her to tell him that she thought Brian was the hottest guy at QueenHi.

"I—I don't really know," she managed finally. Marilyn was doing exactly what Lexa thought she'd be doing: watching, with her good old popcorn bag.

Lexa shoveled food onto her chopsticks and hesitated. The thought of putting anything into her mouth, well, it wasn't happening. "What is it about you?" she said, her eyes now hot on his. "That makes me—makes me tell you stuff?"

Jeremy shrugged, a slow one-shouldered up and down that paid no attention to her outburst. "Maybe it's the workshop," he said, "the talk about taking risks."

He took a bite of food, smiling at her as he chewed and, all at once, being here didn't feel risky to Lexa. Being in this kitchen, with the sun gleaming and the crystally star shooting warm light.

"I don't even know Brian," she said, the words coming low, "I mean, sure I *know* Brian. We've been in school together since forever, but we don't exactly hang with the same people. Now we're in this play together, and we have to be this couple, and he has a girlfriend."

Jeremy cocked his head. "You didn't seem to have a problem with that today."

"That was Marilyn." Lexa's involuntary murmur had her clamping her lips tight.

"So." Jeremy looked out the window now, frowning as if searching for what he wanted to say in the air and trees. "Sounds to me like who Brian is and his having a girlfriend are making you nervous about working with him."

"That would be 100 percent true."

"Only you *have* to work with him." He faced her again. "Is your nervousness what's making you act the way you do in class?"

"Yes." Man, it was good to be able to tell the truth, especially the part where she didn't actually have to explain anything.

"Huh." He took another bite, chewed a moment. "It must be working," he went on, "because, you know, singing the way you did? Is exactly a risk Cherie would take."

"Really?" shot out of both Lexa and Marilyn, in stereo.

Jeremy nodded. "Hopefully you can keep it up once you guys are doing scenes together."

"Scenes? Together?" Lexa shook her head.

Jeremy's forehead creased. "What do you mean 'no'?"

"I—I'm not sure I can do those scenes."

"Sure, you can. Just keep taking the same kind of risk you took today."

"That wasn't—" She pressed her lips together.

"That wasn't . . . ?" He turned those *can't-lie-to-me* eyes on her again.

"The play," she said, "the exercises aren't the play. I'm not sure I can bring the same risk to the play."

"And I'm sure you can. What are you most afraid of? In the play."

She blinked at him. Wasn't it obvious? *The whole thing*.

"I'll go first." He paused, then leaned forward as though telling her a secret. "I'm most afraid of the scene where Virgil has to play the guitar and sing."

"Don't you play an instrument, though? I—I mean, you did that cello thing that first time."

"Doesn't matter," he said, "I play cello for myself. Only for myself. The thought of playing guitar and singing in front of an audience?" He fake-shivered. "Now you."

"I have to sing too, and I'm definitely afraid of that. But I'm most afraid of . . ." She had to take a sip of water. Another. God, her mouth was still dry as dirt. "The kissing scene."

Jeremy's brows shot up, then lowered. "I've got an idea that would help us both. Yes." He nodded, a slow grin spreading. "You and me. We should follow Mr. B's advice and run scenes together."

Lexa bobbled her glass and spilled water all over her lap. Both of them jumped up, her yipping at the icy cold and him offering up his napkin.

"Wow," he said, "you really soaked yourself good."

She mopped at the water, seeming only to make the spot bigger, colder, and wetter.

Staring at her crotch, he said, "We could throw your skirt in the dryer. Or I could loan you some—"

"No, no. That's okay." She squeezed the bunched wet spot into a wrinkled wad.

"Go for the pants, honey."

Dropping her skirt, she snarled at Marilyn, "They probably wouldn't fit." Then she snatched up her dishes, saying too loudly to Jeremy, "It's fine. I—I've got some sweats in my locker."

"You do not," shot Marilyn.

"I do too."

"Do too, what?" asked Jeremy.

Lexa stopped cold, snapping her mouth—the one that had let out those actual swords—shut. She put a hand to her cheek and took in a long breath as she scrambled for a response. "Uh, I think we should run lines together. Yeah, that's what I meant. We should do that."

Chapter Sixteen

Back in the high school building, Lexa held her wet skirt under the hand dryer and scowled at the bathroom wall.

Running lines with Jeremy?

She scowled harder, and Marilyn giggled.

"What's so funny?" Lexa said.

"Funny?" She gave Lexa her trademark innocent face: big blinking eyes and soft, slightly parted lips. "Why nothing at all, sugar. You should relax."

"Tell me why you were laughing," Lexa whispered. "It's about Jeremy, right?"

Marilyn's eyes crinkled, delighted. "Sometimes you're the mind reader."

"Yeah, I should have my own psychic show. Look, I need your help on this." Lexa shook out her skirt—still wet—and hit the hand dryer button again. "How nuts is it for me to try practicing with him?"

"That's the thing. I don't think practicing with him is nuts at all."

"Really?"

"Really. Something else, too." Marilyn's tongue darted to her upper lip. "I think he's interested in more than rehearsing. That boy wants to get to know you better."

Shaking her head, Lexa tried to ignore the prickly rushing feeling filling her chest. It was like she'd run to catch a bus, only she wasn't even sure there was a bus. "I don't know. It's more like I'm a—like a project to him. It's all this." She plucked at her hair. "And the stuff in class. He's trying to figure me out. Except, oh look, it's not me. It's—"

"Don't say it!" Marilyn's smile was gone. "I won't listen to you cutting yourself short that way. All I'm saying is rehearsing with Jeremy is a good idea."

The main bathroom door squeaked open, and Lexa froze, putting every bit of *Shush!* and *We're not done with this* in the look she threw at Marilyn. Dropping her skirt, she turned. Only to stop. Smacked by a hot glare and the cool voice that followed.

"There you are!"

Hilary Poss.

What next? went through Lexa's head even as she barreled desperately to the door mumbling an idiotic, "Hey, Hilary."

"Not so fast," Hilary said, blocking her escape, "you and I need to have a little talk."

"A little talk?" Lexa said, stepping back. "Uh, how did you find me anyway?"

Hilary smirked. "I have my ways. And every one of them told me *all* about that birthday song."

Lexa stole a peek at Marilyn. *Enjoying the show?* Marilyn nodded hard as she nibbled popcorn, murmuring, "Forget politics. That girl should be a spy."

Raking Lexa up and down, Hilary said, "*New* look. *New* hair. Singing to Brian like you think you're what—Marilyn Monroe? You think you're so smart, but you know what?" Letting out an unamused *huff*, Hilary whirled to the mirror and took out a lip gloss. "Nobody cares." The words twisted as she twisted the cap off her gloss. "That's right. I'm here to tell you that nothing you're doing changes anything."

Changes. *Anything*. Hilary's snide comment was like a trigger, sending Lexa right back to—

"Stop thinking about that old middle school dance!" Marilyn's concerned voice filled Lexa's mind, almost physically trying to shove away twelve-year-old Hilary's sneering jibes back in that middle school girls' room. "What you need to do is get a load of Hilary and her lipstick," Marilyn went on, "it's the surest sign that *she's* the one who's scared to death here."

Jangled by the clash of that old memory and this reality, Lexa wanted to demand that Marilyn explain what she meant, only Hilary was still talking.

"Do you really think changing up your look replaces years—*years*—of being onstage? Uh, get real." Hilary slicked gloss over her upper lip. "No way are you gonna fool Mr. B—or Brian—or anyone, with some new clothes and a new haircut." She swiped gloss onto her lower lip now. "And doing the play at the Marquee? *The Marquee?*" She shook her head, rubbing her lips together so hard that Lexa thought she'd take off a layer of lip. "It's all too insane and pathetic, and that's what everyone is going to see." She snapped the cap on the gloss. "And when it's all done? They are so going to wish someone who *really* knew how to act had jumped in and saved your sorry-ass play. That's right . . ."

Lexa brain-whispered to Marilyn, "What should I do?"

"Good question, sugar. Wait her out, I guess. There, she looks about done."

Hilary was done, but she wasn't finished. "Well?" she said, smoothing her hair back from her face as she turned back to Lexa.

"Well, what?"

"What do you mean, 'well, what'? Say something."

Biting her lip, Lexa said, "What do you *want* me to say?"

"Oh, stop pretending to be thick." Hilary crossed her arms. "We are not done until you admit I'm right."

"The only thing I'll admit," said Lexa, knowledge blooming, "is that somehow you think you have a say in what I do. And that right now my whole life revolves around screwing up your life." She pushed by Hilary. "It's always about you, isn't it?"

Chapter Seventeen

What an exit! Feet barely touching the floor, Lexa sailed to her next class. It wasn't until she took her seat in French that she realized Marilyn had been talking to her all along.

"Don't you agree?"

"Agree with what?"

Marilyn pouted. "Why . . . why, you didn't hear a word I said."

"Sorry." Lexa couldn't help a tiny smile. "I keep seeing Hilary's face at the end there. That was awesome. I mean, you are totally right. *She's* scared of *me*."

"That's what I've been telling you, sugar. No. It's not *you* she's scared of."

"What?" Lexa sat up fast, too fast because the kid next to her startled. He frowned at her but looked away when Madame called out, "*S'il vous plaît, prenez vos livres et passez a la page . . .*"

In her head, Lexa pinned Marilyn with a hot stare. "What are you talking about?"

"If you'd been listening to me," Marilyn said, looking up from examining her fingernails, "instead of patting yourself on the back for leaving that poor girl in a puddle, you'd already know and," she pointed to the kid in the next seat, "if you want *him* to mind his own beeswax, you should open your book."

"Mind your own beeswax," Lexa said to the kid and dragged her book onto her desk.

"I'm not much for French," said Marilyn, "I think she said page—"

"Yeah, got it. Sixty-two." Flipping pages, Lexa said, "Isn't leaving Hilary in a puddle a good thing?"

"That's one way to look at it," Marilyn muttered, "she probably deserves it after how she's treated you and, honestly, I have a feeling her fingerprints are all over that auditorium-schedule change. That's neither here nor there. What's done is done. Besides, I am only interested in you. Is *that* who you want to be? Someone who leaves people in puddles?"

Lexa squirmed in her seat.

"I didn't think so," Marilyn said. "Now, don't you want to know why Hilary's scared?"

When Lexa nodded, Marilyn tapped a smooth cheek. "I'll give you a hint. Think of . . . think of our performance in the workshop and then think of who else was there."

Staring down at her book, the type blurred as Lexa brought up the memory. There she was singing in that whispery, torchy, sexy way and—*oh*.

"You're terribly quick when you want to be." Marilyn's chin lifted. "Let me add that since I've been back here with the living, I've had plenty of time to think on how everyone always gave me too much credit for my magical power over the opposite sex. It takes two, honey, and I figure that was the part that made women green. Maybe even some men, too." Her eyes widened, bright and clear now. "The part where *I* performed, and *the audience* responded."

"You're saying that what happened with Hilary is all about Brian?"

"Of course, it's about Brian, only not completely," said Marilyn. "First I want you to think of what is important to that Hilary."

Answers came to Lexa like gunshots. "Being popular. Being in charge. Being the center of attention. Getting Mr. B to notice her."

"Bingo on all counts, but let's think about Mr. B," said Marilyn. "She must've heard how much you impressed him, and it doesn't take a genius to know she wouldn't like that. Now think about Brian. You could have jumped up on a table and sang that song buck naked, and Hilary wouldn't have given a rat's behind except for Brian and," her lids lowered, "his response."

Brian's face came to Lexa again, how hypnotized he'd been during the song, dazed, actually. That moment had to have stayed with him, maybe all the way to sharing it with Hilary.

The skin on Lexa's wrist prickled like she'd been pinched. She turned her arm over, staring at Brian's question mark. "What do you think it means?"

"I don't know exactly, except you'd better watch out. Before today, that Hilary was just angry about the play. Now she's angry about her beau."

The end of the school day couldn't come fast enough. Shoving out the front door, Lexa pulled the red scarf from her jacket pocket and twined it around her neck. The faintest hint of rose and powder made her breathe in, long and slow.

"Mmmmmm." Marilyn inhaled too. "That's nice after that mess of other smells. Thank you again for splurging on that little bottle of spray perfume. I always loved that about my Chanel. How it lingered on my clothes. On my skin. That wintry air feels nice too." She hugged herself. "Walking home is exactly what we need to clear our heads, right sweetie?"

Before Lexa could answer, an arm linked with hers.

"Hah! Caught you." Em grinned up at her. "Hey, your eyes are *huge*. I really startled you, didn't I?"

"Yeah," Lexa said, her breath hitching. "Where's . . . ?"

"Kevin? He had to stay late for a photography project." Em tugged her toward the parking lot. When Lexa pulled away, Em clung tighter. "Uh-uh. We haven't spent time together in like—forever, and we have got to get going on your costumes! I can't believe the news about the Marquee! We only have a month! Say you can come over for a while."

Movement over Em's shoulder caught Lexa's eye. Brian. Heading her way.

Throwing her arm around Em's shoulders, Lexa hurried them to the parking lot, saying, "You're right. We've got loads of work to do."

In a snap, she and Em were in the car, speeding away. Peeking out the window, Lexa searched the masses of students for Brian. No sign of him. She couldn't help wondering what he wanted.

"I'm near dying to find out," whispered Marilyn. She winked and settled into her watching-out-the-window mode.

"Okay." Em sucked in a noisy breath. "I'm assuming what happened just now—you running away from Brian back there—has to do with what Kevin told me." She threw Lexa a grinning glance. "The whole 'happy birthday' thing?"

"W-what?" Lexa's brain whirled. "Why would I be running away from Brian McKinnon? But oh, yeah. That was a pretty whack exercise we did in class this morning. Totally nuts." She trailed off, desperate to change the subject. "What about the new schedule? How about *that*?"

Em's grin faded. "You got that right. Man, we need to . . ." And she was off.

"Nice going, honey." Marilyn smiled, and warmth hit Lexa's shoulder, like a pat on the back.

All too soon they pulled into Em's driveway.

"Come on," Em said, "I can't wait to show you what I've come up with, especially now that it needs to be done yesterday!" She grabbed her bulging satchel along with a huge plastic bag.

Lexa followed her into the house and, as she and Em took off their jackets, Ann called from the kitchen. "Halloooo! Is that Alexandria with you, lovey? I hope so, because it's been too long. And you're in luck, I have fresh fruit smoothies."

Lexa didn't have to look to know Em had to be rolling her eyes. That made her smile. Ann gushing about smoothies. Em eye-rolling. Man, she'd missed that. Missed every familiar bit. Loose and easy now, she stepped into the kitchen. The second Ann spotted her, her whole face going buggy, all easiness evaporated.

"Why, that can't be Alexandria Donovan!" Ann said, marching over to put her hands on Lexa's shoulders. "Only it is. I barely recognize you. What have you *done* to yourself?"

Lexa ran a hand over her head. "I—I got a haircut," she said. "I've seen you since then. Haven't I?" She looked at Em. *Help!*

"Lexa cut her hair like over a month ago." Em frowned, came to Lexa's side. "You know," she said, studying Lexa as she thrust a glass of bright purple smoothie into her hand. "Ann's got a point. You do look different."

"Of course, I've seen Alexandria's hair," Ann said. "I'm talking about how she's trimmed down. Why she looks positively svelte."

"You're joking," said Lexa.

Invisible hands smoothed over her hips. "No joke, honey," crooned Marilyn.

"Seriously," Em said, "I guess I haven't seen you without a coat on lately. So *that's* what you've been up to." She shook her head. "Here I thought you were mad at—" Em's mouth snapped shut, her eyes darting to Ann. "You do look awesome," she added fast, busying herself with a long sip of smoothie.

Ann peered at Lexa over her glasses. "Yes," she said, considering, "yes, she does. Now then. Come visit for a few minutes. I want to hear what prompted this makeover. Is it because of a boy?"

"What?" From weight to boys? Lexa's head spun. "I mean, no. *No*! It—it's for the play. Yeah. I'm doing the play now. Tell her." She flicked another silent plea to Em for help. "And I'm, I mean, *we're* trying out some new looks. That's what we're working on today, right?"

Em's gaze was sharper than Ann's. "Right," she said at last.

"And," Lexa went on, "we've got a ton of work to do."

"You girls," said Ann. She smiled, her eyes going soft and teary. "You are *both* such hard workers. I cannot wait to see this play."

Lexa moved to put her glass in the sink and saw that she hadn't even taken a sip. She glugged the smoothie down. "Wow, that was delish." She turned to Em. "Ready?"

"Sure." With a too sweet smile, Em took the glass from Lexa's hand and then put it in the sink with hers. "Let's go . . . *work*."

They headed out of the kitchen, and Marilyn hummed a quiet little *hmmm*, saying, "Brace yourself, this one wants some answers."

Chapter Eighteen

Closing her bedroom door, Em leaned against it, saying, "All right. What is going on with you?"

Lexa tried a laugh. "Why do you keep asking me that?"

Em's brows went up.

"*Nothing's* going on," Lexa said. When Em only looked at her, Lexa bounced her butt down on the bed. She had to come up with some explanation. "Okay, okay. There's a *lot* going on. Not to mention Mr. B's latest with the new schedule. This whole play thing gets more and more intense."

"Is that why you've been MIA?" Em nibbled her lower lip. "Because I was beginning to think you were . . . you were mad at me."

"What?" Not what Lexa expected. "Why would I be mad at you?"

"Because, um, because of Kevin."

Really not what Lexa expected. She sputtered, "I'm glad you have a boyfriend."

"He's . . ." Em looked everywhere but at Lexa. "He's not my boyfriend."

"But you're into him, right?" When Em didn't answer, Lexa repeated, "Right?"

"I don't know," Em said, "we've been hanging a lot. Working on play crap, and we're interested in tons of the same things, except . . ." She threw up her hands. "At first, I thought, *here we go*, another guy pretending to be my friend and then trying to hook up with me. Wonder when he'll sit me down for"—she made air quotes—"'the talk.' You know, *blah blah* about how we need to be *more* than friends? Except that didn't happen. And then we *were* friends and," she trailed off.

"Why don't you have 'the talk' with him?"

Em's eyes got horrified-huge. "No way. Besides." She crossed her arms, stuffing her hands under her armpits. "I mean, what's the point? We're about to graduate, and everyone will be going all over the place. I'm not sure I want that kind of change before *everything* changes."

The weight of all that everything settled between them, touchable as a pile of rocks.

"Maybe everything's already changing." Lexa was talking to Em, even as her attention drifted to Marilyn, sitting silent in her director's chair, nodding. "I mean, isn't that what's always happening? All the time? Maybe you should, you know, give him a chance."

"I don't know." Em stared down at her feet, and all at once she looked different. Breakable, fragile. Then Em pushed off the door, all full-steam-ahead again, and the sense of her fragility evaporated. "Hey," Em said, plopping down next to Lexa. "Can we forget about Kevin right now? I want to talk about us." She shook Lexa's knee. "I feel like I haven't seen you in—in years."

"I know, only you've got to believe me." She shook Em's knee back. "Nothing I've been doing lately is me being mad at you."

"Okay. Want to talk about what went on with Brian?" The words weren't even out of Em's mouth before she half-smiled.

"The look on your face tells me no." She fake-shuddered. "Damn, who knew this acting thing would get so serious! Tell me this at least—have you really been trying to lose weight?"

"Um." Here was something about Lexa that could make sense. "Maybe a *little*?" She rose, crossing to the dresser mirror. Svelte was a stretch, except she did look . . . sharper. She pushed her fingers against her cheek, her chin. Sharper and different. She tried to remember how she looked, how she felt before Marilyn came, and couldn't. She only knew how she felt now: warm and full, like she had more blood running through her veins.

"Your body's working hard," Marilyn said. "I guess having a spirit inside is like living for two."

Em's voice cut in. "Why didn't you tell me you were trying to drop some pounds?" Watching Em in the mirror, plucking at her quilt, Lexa scrambled for an explanation. "Because—because I wanted it to be a surprise. And I was afraid I wouldn't be able to do it. That it wouldn't work."

"Why would you think that? If you're doing it, of course it's going to work." Em studied her. "What are you doing anyway?"

"What?"

"To lose the weight."

"I'm, uh . . ." Lexa looked to Marilyn, and Marilyn popped up, walking in place, pumping her arms, the lacy apron around her waist. "Oh, yeah. I'm doing this walking thing. And this cooking thing. Dad loves the cooking thing."

"Sounds pretty cool," said Em with a nod. "You really do look fantastic." A smile appeared. "Not that you didn't before. Now you look, I don't know, more like you. Wait. I've got to do some new sketches. Where's my bag? I must've left it in the mudroom." All but out the door, Em looked over her shoulder. "I've really missed this," she said, her expression warm and bright and totally focused on Lexa.

"Being with you. Talking to you. Even when everything seems confusing."

The second Em was out of sight, Lexa said, "I never thought she got confused about anything." Then she sagged against the dresser. "I feel like a dick, keeping so much from her."

"I know," Marilyn said, "you did great, though."

"I guess I'm finally figuring this acting thing out," Lexa added, "except, a lot of what I told her was kind of the truth, too."

Marilyn chuckled. "Drama lesson number one."

The next couple of hours were not confusing, and that was a relief. Being with Em. In her room. Em sitting on the floor, surrounded by loose drawings while sketching away in yet another book with one hand, and holding up fabric samples with the other. Lexa going through a separate sketchbook full of makeup ideas, actually trying some of the designs for Cherie.

Stroking a dab of bright green shadow over each eyelid, Lexa said, "What do you think?"

Em glanced up, eyes narrowing. "Too much and too green. I kind of figured full-on Vegas showgirl wouldn't work. Still, it seemed like what Cherie would be going for. Try the next page."

Lexa grabbed the makeup remover.

"Hold up," Em said, "come check this out first."

Both sketchbook pages were covered with finger-sized drawings of Lexa in various Cherie-like outfits and positions.

Lexa shook her head. "Would Cherie really wear white?"

"That's exactly it," Em said, her voice sure. "Bo keeps calling her his 'angel,' and I get that a blonde actress like a Marilyn Monroe could pull off that glowy, tainted angel look no matter what she wore. I don't want to stick a blonde wig on you, though. I want something different. Something more about you." She tapped the page with the end of her pencil. "No matter what Cherie's done, she has this innocence that's all about what she hopes for. Sure, Bo's hot for her, only it's her kind of 'pure hope' that he's in love with. That's what gives them a chance. I want to capture that in her look."

"Wow," Marilyn whispered, "she's the genuine article, isn't she?"

Gazing at the sketches, all Lexa could see was Em—almost like keeping away from her so much over the past few weeks made it possible for her truly to see her friend now. She put her hand on Em's shoulder. "You really get this," she said, and Em's forehead creased. "No," Lexa went on, "I know how important designing is to you, but I never actually got it before this second. You're like—*born* to do this."

Em's lips curved, but only slightly, as if to tell Lexa she thought she was acting nutty. "I sure hope Fashion and Design sees that."

"Of course, you're going to get in," Lexa said.

"No," shot out of Em's mouth, "not 'of course.' They get tons of applications, and I've been on their social media." As she spoke, Em snapped her sketchbook closed and began to snatch up her loose drawings into a stack. "And," she went on, knocking the stack against the carpet to straighten the edges, "since it's rolling admissions, people are totally posting about being accepted."

"Well," said Lexa, "good for them." She watched Em, fully expecting her to crack a joke. When Em didn't, Lexa's forehead wrinkled with confusion.

"Did you honestly have no idea your friend was thinking this way?" said Marilyn.

Lexa blinked, and Marilyn blew out a breath. "I would love to talk to you about this, sugar, but this is not the time. Your friend needs you right now."

Shifting back to Em, Lexa cleared her throat. "Listen to me," she said, "even if by some freak chance you don't get accepted, you're going to do this. You're going to be a costume designer. That's all."

"Thanks," said Em. She tried a smile, only her lips trembled a little.

"Are you," Lexa whispered, "are you really scared about it?"

"Uh, yeah!" said Em.

"But—" Lexa began, stopping when Em blew out a loud breath.

"I know. I know," said Em. She put the pile of drawings on top of her sketchbook. "I mean, I don't even like thinking about it. How important going to Fashion and Design is to me. How scared I am that I won't get in. That I won't make it to New York. That's why I'm working my butt off here." She threw her hands in the air. "All right, enough."

Lexa watched her friend give herself a shake and then start picking through the loose drawings she'd just stacked, studying each one, brows in a V of concentration. Lexa wanted to ask Em more about how she felt, about her fears, only she wasn't sure what to say. And right now, it didn't look like Em wanted to talk about it more. Still . . . *Em, her Em, scared.*

"I've never seen her like this," Lexa murmured to Marilyn.

"Well, I guess she really cares about that school," said Marilyn, "and goodness, will you look at all those drawings? She really is working her behind off."

Scared and working harder than ever. Lexa studied Em a moment more and then leaned forward to look at the drawings, too. All at once there was the muted squawk of her cell coming from her pack.

"Bet it's your dad," said Em. As she was closer, she grabbed the pack, unzipping the bleating pocket. A piece of folded paper fell out; everything in Lexa froze. Mr. B's classroom. Paper ripping. Brian. Kneeling by her. No. Kneeling by *her pack.*

Stunned, she took the cell from Em's hand. Even as she put it to her ear, she stared at Em picking up the paper and stuffing it back into the pack. That made her totally miss what her dad said.

"What?" she said.

With exaggerated patience, Dad said, "I asked when you would be home?"

"Golly, tell him 'soon,'" said Marilyn, "that paper needs your attention pronto."

Chapter Nineteen

As Em drove her home, Lexa could almost feel the burn of the folded paper glowing and pulsing from where it sat stashed in her pack. She didn't take it out in the car, though. And not the second Em dropped her off either. Not even hurrying across the parking lot or blowing by Film Buzz.

Alonealonealone. She needed to be alone.

As Lexa hammered up the stairs to the apartment, Marilyn leaned forward on her chair. "Slow down. There is no need to be so dramatic."

"How do you know?" Lexa jammed her key into the lock. "Maybe there's every need to be dramatic!" She pushed open the door. "You can't fool me either. I know you're dying to know what he wrote and—*wait*." She threw Marilyn a narrow glance. "Do you already know what he wrote? Is that one of your spirit powers?"

"What a thing to say." Marilyn mirrored Lexa's narrow look. "I am in your head, and as far as I know I'm only able to see what you see, do what you do and, well, all of that. Whether I can or not, I would never move to a different body. That would be . . . that would be plain *rude*."

"Fine," Lexa said, "let's go see what Brian wrote."

"Yes. Let's."

In her room, Lexa sank down on her bed.

"Good luck, honey," said Marilyn.

Drawing out the paper, Lexa unfolded it. Printed in dark blue ink in tiny square lettering was the letter "B" followed by three numbers, a dash, and another four numbers. A phone number. In one long swoop Lexa's insides dove, and then those same insides rushed high.

"His number." The tip of Marilyn's tongue touched her upper lip. "He wants you to call him."

Lexa swallowed, pressing the phone to her swooping, rushing belly. Then, slowly she tapped the numbers. Her thumb hovered over the send button.

After a second, Marilyn whispered, "What are you waiting for?"

"What if this is a joke?" Lexa's eyes cut to Marilyn's. "I mean, he left a number. He didn't write, 'call me,' or anything."

Her gaze going soft, Marilyn said, "Leaving you his number is as good as writing 'call me.' It's up to you, though."

"Take a chance," Lexa whispered, "that's what you think I should do."

"I can't help myself, sweetie. Here's another bit of advice—there's no time like now."

Lexa moved the phone from one clammy hand to the other. "Oh, fine," she said. She cuddled back on her pillows. "Might as well be comfortable while I embarrass myself to death." She grimaced at Marilyn. "No offense."

With a bubbly half-laugh, Marilyn waved her hand in that *get-to-it* motion, and Lexa tapped "send."

Brian's phone went right to voicemail, the message *beep* coming too fast. "Hi, um, Brian." God, she could barely breathe! "I found your note and . . ." She blinked at Marilyn with desperation. Marilyn mouthed some words and Lexa repeated them. "Thought I should call." *Aaaaah!* She sounded like a robot! "Okay, uh, see you tomorrow."

She ended the call and, as if it had burst into flames, threw her phone to the foot of the bed.

"Well," Marilyn said with a pout, "that was terribly disappointing."

"I guess," Lexa mumbled, hating that her voice was on Brian's voicemail.

"Jeepers, you didn't say anything compromising."

"Let's forget about it." Lexa dragged her pack close and took out books and notebooks. "That's probably what Brian did the second after he stuffed that paper into my pack." Her hands froze on the paperback of *Bus Stop*. "Oh, no! What if 'B' was for Bo? What if the whole thing was—was only part of that acting exercise?"

Marilyn shrugged again. "How are you supposed to know that?"

"I'm not," Lexa muttered, "but I still feel like an ass."

"I can tell."

"'*I can tell*,'" Lexa parroted, and then her sarcasm drained away as she studied Marilyn. "How does that even feel? Me feeling like an ass?"

Marilyn smiled, not in a way that reached her eyes, though. "Better than nothing."

Nodding, Lexa caught another glimpse of her phone. Cold and plastic and lying at the end of the bed, a tossed grenade.

With a moan, she grabbed both her French and her Spanish books.

A knock on her door had Lexa jerking awake, opening heavy lids. The bright light of the nightstand lamp burned them closed again.

Her locked door rattled, then a muted voice. "Lexa?"

Worried-sounding Dad. The door rattled again. "Why's the door locked?"

"Hey, Dad," Lexa croaked out and rose, her Spanish book sliding to the floor. "Wait a sec." She stumbled over to the door.

"There you are," he said when she opened up. "Why didn't you come down to the shop? Didn't you get my text? About a late dinner?"

"Oh, no." Lexa hugged her arms over her chest. "I fell asleep."

"Well, I was going to grab some leftovers," he said. "Want to join me?"

"No, I'm good." She yawned big.

"Good and tired," he joked, ruffling her hair. Then his gaze shifted, focusing on something high over her shoulder.

She glanced behind, too, at the window near her bed, at the wall, the couple of travel posters. "What are you looking at?"

He shook his head with a quiet laugh. "Never mind. How's the play going? Full speed ahead, I bet."

"Yeah." She tried to smile, only her lips seemed to stick to her teeth as everything that had happened that day crowded into her mind.

"Boy, you're really doing it all," Dad went on, "and I know I've been saying this a lot lately, but I'll say it again—I'm very proud of you, love."

"Thanks," she said. His whole face beamed at her, and she had to turn away, all her secrets seeming to smack her sideways. She pointed to her Spanish book on the floor. "I—I guess I'd better get back to my homework. I've got French, too."

"I know it's only 8:30," he said, checking his watch, "but try not to stay up too late."

"Sure. 'Night, Dad."

He didn't move, only kept looking at her.

"Dad?" she said.

He tugged his beard. "All right, I'm going to say something, and I—I really hope you won't take this the wrong way. It's just you getting picked for this play's had me thinking about a few things and . . ." He cleared his throat. "There have been many times over the years when I wished for your mom, but now, with you working so hard on the play, putting yourself out there. I wish she could see it. That's all."

He reached out his arms and, as Lexa went into them, she whispered, "Maybe . . . maybe she will."

When he drew back, she rushed on. "I mean, why can't we, I don't know, *imagine* she's up there? You know, her spirit. Watching."

"I like that," he said, his expression going soft. "I really, really like that." He hugged her again, hard. "Okay, I'm going to get some food. Sure you won't join me?"

"No thanks."

Closing her door after him, Lexa leaned her forehead against it, then glanced to Marilyn. She wasn't in her chair. The second Lexa wondered which part of her brain Marilyn'd tucked herself into, her phone pinged. She snatched it from the end of the bed, the calling number flashing on the screen. Everything in her went liquid. "Hel—hello?"

"Lex?"

"Um, hi, Brian."

Marilyn *poofed* into Lexa's head, hair tousled, tying the sash of a white satiny robe.

"Hey," Brian was whispering, "I'm glad you called. Hold up a sec." Scrambling noises on his end cut into her ear. "I'll be right out." His voice had that faraway, calling-to-someone-else distance. Then he was back. "I can't really talk now because I'm at Hilary's."

Images of her bathroom encounter with Hilary strobed behind Lexa's eyes. Wait. What was he saying? "Your voice is breaking up," she fibbed, "what?"

"I said," he spoke louder, "could you—could you meet me tomorrow?"

This couldn't be happening. Except it was. Even now Lexa could hear Brian breathing fast.

"Lex? You still there?"

"Yes," she mumbled, "sorry. What did you say?"

"I want to talk to you about something." He was really in a hurry now, his words tripping over each other. "Can you meet me?"

Chapter Twenty

When: before school. Where: the stone bench near Queen-Hi's entrance.

Eleven hours after Brian's call, that's where Lexa was headed.

"What do you think he wants?" She'd asked Marilyn that question about a thousand times.

"What else?" Marilyn looked at Lexa with wide eyes, her reddened lips impossibly full. "To declare his undying love, of course."

"Hah!" Lexa said, both out loud and in her head.

Marilyn shifted to watching-mode. "I suppose we'll find out soon enough. This is the quickest we've walked to school yet."

Rounding the bus shelter, Lexa scanned down the hill. Instantly the place behind her chest squeezed. A body, wearing a familiar ball cap and bundled into an oversized gray hoodie, sprawled on the stone bench.

"Ease up, girl," Lexa said to herself under her breath, "you have no idea what he wants. No idea. No clue. It's probably nothing."

Spotting her, Brian sat up, lifting a hand.

Marilyn faced Lexa.

"Don't say anything," Lexa spoke fast, "please—don't. I'm nervous enough as it is."

Marilyn did her lock and key.

Walk, walk, walk, and then Lexa stood in front of Brian.

"Hey," he said.

"Hey." Lexa sat on the bench and held her breath. She didn't think the world could get quieter, only it did. She peeked at him. He'd taken his cap off and was tapping it against the bench. In profile his buzz cut bristled, fuzzy and damp from his morning shower. A muscle in his neck worked like he had to keep swallowing. *He* was nervous. She almost wanted to laugh and could see that Marilyn already had her hand over her laughing mouth.

In a rush, Brian spun to her. "How did you do it? What you did yesterday? Where did that—where did that *song* come from?"

Lexa didn't know what she'd expected. Not this. "I—I'm not sure what you mean." She backed up on the bench as she spoke, her whole body going wobbly.

"You seem like you've *found* something," he said, "some way into this play. Into your character, I mean. I want to know how you're doing it."

The way he stared at her, his brows rumpled, made Lexa wish she could tell him the truth.

"That's a great question," she began, then dropped her fake-jokey tone. "It's kind of—kind of a feel thing, I guess." She shot a glance at Marilyn. "You know. In the moment."

Engines revving had all three of them gazing up the hill. Cars rolling down to the school lot.

"You know," Brian spoke fast and low, "I had zero interest in putting my name into Mr. B's workshop jar. Hilary *convinced* me to do it because *she* was doing it. Only I got picked and, now that I am in it up to my neck, I want to do a good job. I kind of thought you were pretty much in the same boat. That you didn't want to do the play, but now something changed and you do." He scrubbed his palm over his head. "Yesterday made me wonder if I should ask you to help me."

"Me? Help you? What about Hilary?" The questions shot out of Lexa's mouth. She pressed her lips together, her cheeks on fire. "I mean, she's done tons of plays."

"She *has* been helping me, except it's not working. She's always ragging on—" He shot her a hot glance. "On the workshop, on Mr. B. And now that the Marquee is in the mix? Damn. Basically, she's pissed I'm still in the play. That I'm—never mind." He searched Lexa's face. "What you did yesterday? I didn't even recognize you when you were singing. You became a different person, and that other person? She was amazing."

Their eyes riveted together, molten metal, and Lexa's throat tightened to the point where she couldn't even swallow.

"Well, now," Marilyn whispered, soft as satin, "isn't *this* something."

Brian's lips slid into a smile. "That's what I want to do with Bo." His fingers trailed over the bench, plucked at the cuff of her coat. "Maybe we could help each other."

"Wouldn't that get Hilary even more pissed?"

"That's kind of her problem." He shrugged. "Besides, how I practice isn't really any of her biz. Plus, we'd only be doing what Mr. B said. Running scenes. We could—"

A brisk voice. "Lexa? McKinnon?"

Goofy as cartoon characters, Brian and Lexa swiveled.

Jeremy, strolling closer, said, "You two are here pretty early."

"Yeah," "Uh," Brian's and Lexa's mumbles mixed.

"What's up?" Jeremy's question was for both of them; he watched only Lexa, though, his expression smooth.

"Nothing," she managed, "Brian and I were . . ."

"Talking about the play," Brian said, standing and eyeing her in a way that asked her to remember what he'd asked. "I'll catch you later," he said and turned, all ready to go.

"Yeah," Lexa said, clutching her pack strap, all ready to go, too.

"Because I thought . . ." Jeremy's voice stopped both Lexa and Brian. "Because I thought," he repeated softer now, "I heard McKinnon here ask you to rehearse with him."

Brian rounded. "What if I did?"

"Nothing," Jeremy said, "except Lexa and I already have a plan to run scenes today." His cool blue eyes splashed her. "Are we still on for this afternoon?"

Choking on the sudden and intense drama factor, Lexa glanced at Marilyn, who only cocked her head, nibbling at a kernel of popcorn. *Oh, perfect!*

"Sure, fine," Lexa mumbled, peeking at Brian. "Sorry."

Cheeks slashed red, Brian nodded fast and walked off.

Neither Jeremy nor Lexa moved. One beat. Two. Then he said, "I didn't make a mistake, did I? We do have plans for this afternoon, right?"

"Um, yes."

"Except maybe you'd rather rehearse with him?"

Lexa clutched her pack strap tighter. The way Jeremy talked was like he was really asking about what she'd told him over their lunch at his condo. About how nervous she was about kissing Brian in the play. That maybe now he was wondering just how much Lexa thought about Brian *outside* of the play.

"No, no." She made a dismissive sound, even though on the surface her rehearsing with Brian did make sense. He was Cherie's Bo after all. Still, doing so would be dangerously beyond nuts, because she'd be dead. The second after Hilary found out.

Jeremy studied her a moment more. "So," he said, pointing from him to her, "us. Running scenes? Today?"

While her entire body wanted to catch one more look at Brian, she stayed focused on Jeremy. Jeremy Leith who wanted only to help her.

"Sure," she said. "When and where?"

They met after school at Jeremy's, spreading out on his living room couch. Mostly they sat there, reading from their playbooks, but when they came to the part where his character—good old cowboy Virgil Blessing—had to sing and play the guitar, he reached over the arm of the couch and brought out a battered ukulele.

"That is one tiny guitar," Lexa said, amused.

"Ha ha," he shot back, plucking the strings.

Both their faces puckered at the sour twang, and Jeremy fiddled with the tuning knobs. When his strumming sounded good, he cleared his throat and sang, "Oh, Su-*sannah*."

"Oh, my God." She put her hands over her ears, laughter bubbling at his rough, jokey imitation of a cowboy. "Stop."

"What, you don't like my singing?"

They both cracked up hard, and then Jeremy strummed again and began singing the song from the play. Deep and mellow, his voice brushed along Lexa's skin like gentle, tickly fingertips. That song. "That Old Black Magic." Her insides shivered. She'd have to sing it onstage. In front of people. She shivered again, frowning and shaking her head when he gestured for her to join in.

"No time like the present, sugar," said Marilyn, nudging as well. "That's why they call it rehearsal."

With a sigh, Lexa sang, her voice crinkly and whispery in her ear. Jeremy nodded at her, his expression soft and, somehow, the quiet of the room and Jeremy's relaxed strum on the ukulele settled her. She sang louder. Stronger.

At the end of the verse, he put down the ukulele. "Coming along, Donovan," he said, stretching his arms over his head. "Want to take a break?"

"Sure."

"I'm going to go find food."

Alone, Lexa sank back into her corner of the couch.

"You know something?" Marilyn sat in the corner of a couch too, hers what looked like worn brown leather. "You two work well together."

"Yeah." Lexa pushed away the memory of the two of them singing, glancing down to her playbook. "I know most of my lines, too."

"That Mr. B of yours is good," Marilyn said. "All that writing he's making you do? About the play and Cherie? Why I bet you've read *Bus Stop* a dozen times."

"Good point," Lexa said, half-laughing.

"What's funny?" Jeremy asked, all at once in the room again.

Sitting up fast, Lexa dropped her book on the floor. "N-nothing," she said. Face burning, she leaned down for the book.

Jeremy plopped down on the couch, a bag of cookies in one hand and a bowl of grapes in the other. He put both on the coffee table. "Ready to move on?"

"Sure," she said. Marilyn poked her, pointing at the grapes until Lexa snagged a small bunch.

Jeremy flipped through his book. "Cherie's next big scene is . . ." He paused, frowning. They both knew exactly what Cherie's next big scene was. Fingers trembling, Lexa put her grapes on the table.

"Looks like it's where Bo says 'goodbye' to Cherie." His voice stayed easy-breezy, as if it wasn't only the day before that she'd told him this was the scene she was most afraid to do.

"Got it," she mumbled.

Jeremy's gaze met hers and, probably a trick of the light, his eyes seemed darker, bluer.

"Why don't you try a little of the method acting I was telling you about," whispered Marilyn. "Stand up and follow the stage directions. You know, really try to live inside your character."

Lexa hesitated, a jittery skip in a song, and repeated Marilyn's suggestion to Jeremy.

They stood, Jeremy close enough that the top of his book touched hers. Lexa's breathing sped up—tiny, choppy, too fast puffs.

"Ready?" he said.

She nodded and he began, his voice raspy and whispery. "'Cherry?'"

"'Hi, Bo!'"

Jeremy said Bo's next line, and when he smiled Bo's big face-cracking smile, he grabbed her arm, following what the stage directions described as Bo's rough embrace attempt.

Insides jumping, Lexa squared her shoulders and slapped a hand on his chest—exactly like Marilyn did in the movie—and said her line about how this embrace had to be different.

Jeremy's face changed, the Bo-look of bewilderment so perfect that a bubbling fizz of glee surfaced in Lexa. This acting thing? It wasn't about how insane it was for anyone to believe that a Brian McKinnon could be obsessed with a Lexa Donovan. It was all about these characters. Being these characters. Marilyn gave her a double thumbs-up.

His hand gentling on her arm, Jeremy said his line, Lexa said hers and—

"Go on," whispered Marilyn, "you can do it. Finish the scene."

Ignoring her pounding heart, Lexa reached up and pecked Jeremy on the mouth. There. She stood down, smiling up at his shocked face. His shocked face that rippled and warmed. Then her cheek was in his palm. *Not a stage direction!* And he kissed her.

A loud "Hullo?" sang out from the mudroom.

Lexa and Jeremy jerked apart. Blinked at each other.

The voice called again. "Jerz? Are you home?"

Without taking his huge eyes from her face, Jeremy answered. "In the living room."

Lexa touched her vibrating lips, and as soon as she realized what she was doing, snatched her fingers away.

Marilyn's mouth was popped wide enough to swallow Lexa whole.

Mr. Leith came into view. "Well, hullo there," he said.

"We were . . ." Jeremy cleared his throat. "We were rehearsing."

Looking from Jeremy to Lexa and back to Jeremy, Mr. Leith said, "Ah."

That *ah* kicked Lexa into panicked escape-mode.

"We're done, though," she managed. She moved to slap her book closed, only—where was her book?

On the floor. Where she'd dropped it when Jeremy . . . when they . . . She scooped up her book.

"Yeah," she heard Jeremy say. "We're done. I mean, we're . . ."

Lexa could not look at his face. She grabbed her pack, shoved the play into a side pocket.

Jeremy was still talking, "Done for *now*, that is."

She peeked at him. He wasn't smiling. As a matter of fact,

she had no idea what his face was doing. Wide and open and still. Not even close to a mirror of the absolute-clanging-fire-engine-brick-red her face had to be. Except for his eyes. His dark, dark blue eyes.

His lips parted, drawing her gaze to them. Soft. Lexa's tongue touched her own bottom lip. She swallowed hard, felt her mouth move to form the words, "I've got to go," only she couldn't say them. She couldn't because she couldn't run away like every part of her wanted to. It was already late, and the plan was for Jeremy to drive her home when his dad got home. She swallowed again.

Like her thoughts pricked him, Jeremy said, "I—I should drive you home. I—"

"Blast it all," Mr. Leith said, his words making Lexa jump. "I've left my briefcase at the university. Ah, well, I'll have to go fetch it. I suppose I can drop Alexandria on my way."

"That'd be great," said Lexa, and then in Jeremy's direction, "okay, see you."

"Yeah," she heard him say to her back as she followed Mr. Leith, "see you."

"If that isn't saved by the bell, sweetie," Marilyn said on a long breath, "then I don't know what is."

Chapter Twenty-One

The end of this bizarre blur of a day couldn't come fast enough. Right before Lexa went to bed, two texts came in. The first was from Brian: "Think about practicing together." The second, Jeremy: "That was . . . unexpected."

She read them both over and over.

"Aren't you going to answer those boys, sugar?" Marilyn lay draped on a cushioned lounge chair, wrapped in a full-length black chiffony-looking robe, her face buried in a book Lexa had to read freshman year called *Of Mice and Men*.

Glancing down at her own oversized T-shirt and flannel PJ pants, Lexa sighed. "Did you really sleep in stuff like that?"

Marilyn lowered the book. "You are avoiding my question."

"It's only . . ." She read the two messages again. "It's only I can't seem to figure out what the hell happened today."

"Let me see." In a series of slow, almost dancer-like movements, Marilyn put her book aside and swung her legs off the lounge. "Brian seems to want your help," she said, "and Jeremy seems to want to help you, among other things."

Lexa slumped down on her bed, mumble-moaning, "Help." Two flashes burst behind her eyes: sitting with Brian on the bench, followed by kissing Jeremy. She groaned, dumping the phone on her bedside table. "This is impossible. Brian

McKinnon—the hottest guy ever—is noticing me, and I feel like a lame-o because he has a girlfriend. Let's not forget that probably the only reason he's noticing me at all right now is because of you. And Jeremy? That kiss? Well, maybe I've messed around a little, but I've never kissed any boy like *that*. Never like that."

Marilyn put a hand to her chest. "Never?"

"Never."

"Oh, dear," said Marilyn, her perfectly manicured fingers now fanning her face. "Oh, dear, oh dear."

"'Oh, dear' is right, and I have no idea if he was rehearsing or—or . . . You didn't." Lexa swallowed an invisible lump. "You didn't influence things when Jeremy . . . ?"

"Why, no! Even if I hadn't already promised not to do that, I would never simply jump in. I will say, though . . ." Her fanning slowed, her smile silky. "That kind of kissing is the most."

"Just the *thought* of kissing Brian makes everything go shaky. But kissing Jeremy was . . . I don't even know. Why is this so confusing?"

"I have no idea. Maybe you'll find out when you kiss Brian."

Lexa fell back on her mattress.

Marilyn continued talking. "That's got to happen soon, right? Tomorrow even. Isn't that what Mr. B said? That you'd start rehearsing tomorrow?"

Dizzy, Lexa nodded.

"Well then," Marilyn said, "you better get some rest."

Play practice was first thing the next morning, because to start getting them used to a stage, Mr. B had snagged as many openings in the school's auditorium schedule as possible. Most of those times were early in the morning or late in the afternoon. When Lexa walked in, the hush and dim of the large room full of empty seats surrounded her. Down by the stage, brighter light bled from under the closed curtain. Behind the fabric came muffled voices and shuffling feet, making the folds of the curtain ripple and billow.

"Here we go," Lexa whispered.

Marilyn blew her a kiss. "Break a leg, honey."

Taking a firmer hold on her backpack, Lexa headed to the stage, slipping behind the curtain. Here was noise and light and action, the air heavy with a dusty, painty smell. Blocky set pieces from dozens of school plays piled against the back wall, the black stage floor scuffed and spattered with paint and strips of ancient duct tape. At the center stood Mr. B bent over a clipboard. Behind him, Anton, Dani-Marie, and Graham sprawled on one raised flat talking at top volume. Clara and Kevin slumped near each other on another flat, Clara staring off into space, and Kevin, thumbs flying, texting madly. Probably with Em. Lexa's gaze traveled past him. Brian sat off to the side on a lone metal folding chair.

Feet stomped up the stage steps behind her and, as the curtain rustled, she looked over her shoulder. Jeremy. She turned away fast, squeezing her lids shut for a beat, then faced him. "Hi."

"Hi." He wasn't quite looking at her, and she bristled with a need for things to be normal and friendish.

"I—I'm sorry I didn't get back to you last night," she began, "I . . ." *was what? Afraid? Confused? All of the above?*

Before her muddled brain could choose, he cut her off. "Don't worry about it." He didn't meet her eyes. "I think we got a little carried away."

"Um, yeah, sure," she said, slapped down.

Mr. B called out, "Miss Donovan. Mr. Leith. Join us, please."

Jeremy gestured for her to go ahead, and they trooped in, her suddenly trembly legs making her drop down on the first flat. He strode by fast, and she caught a whiff of his lemony-warm scent. Her heart twinged, sharp and quick as a stab.

"Here we are," Mr. B said with a sweep of his arm. "In four weeks you will be on a stage much like this one, performing *Bus Stop*. From this moment until then, we will be in full production mode." His eyes roved their faces. "All of our work until now has been to create a foundation for that interpretation. With the heightened timeline, we must speed up. So. This morning I will meet with each of you in turn to discuss your individual parts." He glanced at his clipboard. "Mr. Leith, you will meet with me first." Jeremy stood, and Mr. B pointed him to two chairs at the far edge of the backstage. Before he followed Jeremy, he said, "The rest of you will start in the following groupings, and I will trust you to choose which scenes to rehearse." He read off names, but Lexa knew whom she'd be working with.

Everyone began talking and moving about, and Brian strolled over, his playbook in his hand.

"Hey," he said, smooth and blank, like yesterday morning hadn't happened.

"Hey," Lexa mumbled. Should she say something about yesterday? Marilyn's only answer to that thought was to lift her shoulders in an exaggerated shrug and touch her pinky to her upper lip.

"Where do you want to be?" asked Brian, glancing around.

Nerves jangling, Lexa looked around too. The others took up each end of the stage flats, their noise and clamor grating in her ears.

Brian cleared his throat. "How about?" He gestured with his book toward a quiet spot way over in the wings.

"Sure. I—I need my book." Before "book" was out of her mouth, he marched off, everything about the way he moved jagged and jerky.

She unzipped her pack fast. Too fast. The zipper snagged.

"Slow down." The concern in Marilyn's whisper made Lexa scowl.

"I don't want to slow down." She yanked the zipper hard, stole a quick peek in Jeremy's direction, then over to where Brian had disappeared behind the wing curtain. "Why're they being such dicks?"

"Honey!" Marilyn's finger went to her lips. "*Shh!*"

"I will not '*shh*,'" Lexa began, but then another voice piped up.

"Who are you calling a dick?"

Barely an arm's length away, Kevin, Graham, and Dani-Marie stared at her. Dani-Marie repeated her question.

Before Lexa could stutter out a response, invisible fingers pinched her butt hard, and she lurched up, saying, "My zipper. I said it, uh, sticks." Moving fast, she stumbled toward the wings. "You didn't have to pinch that hard," she whispered to Marilyn.

"Apparently, I did."

Behind the wing curtain, Lexa paused, her eyes adjusting to the dim. There was Brian, waiting. As she approached, she took him in. His overly pink cheeks. How he slapped his book, *slapslap*, against his thigh.

"My—my zipper got stuck," she told him. He took her pack and *rip*, unzipped the zipper.

"Oh, thanks."

She fished for her book and somehow Brian's pink cheeks, his slapping book, his helping her took her back to the confused Brian of the stone bench: the one anxious about doing a good job in the play.

"Where do you want to start?" he said, and now Lexa could hear the nerves tightening his voice.

"I don't know. Where do you want to start?"

"Well." Their eyes caught, held, the pause like a big gulp. "Why don't we do the scene where Bo and Cherie have to, you know, kiss?" he whispered. "We should. To get it over with." His eyes went horrified-wide. "Not that I want to get it *over* with, or anything. I—I think we should get that scene behind us. Then we won't have to worry about it. Not that we're worried about it. *Man.* I really sound like a douche."

"No. No," she said, a smile wobbling at the amazing fact that he'd joined her in nervous-mutant-ville. "That's probably a—good idea."

"Good." His head craned around. "I don't really want the others to know I've been stressing about this." He raised his brows at Lexa and opened his book. As she opened hers, Marilyn raised her hands, fingers crossed, and mouthed, "Find your Cherie."

Right. Find Cherie. *Her* Cherie.

"Can we take a second? To—to get into character?" she asked.

He nodded. "Good idea."

Closing her eyes, she inhaled, long and slow. Cherie. Her Cherie. Images of Marilyn playing Cherie unspooled in her mind, followed by Em's drawings, the two Cheries mixing, merging, blurring. *Stand still,* she wanted to shout, *let me see you.*

Marilyn shook her head, pointed at Lexa, and then put her hands together as though holding a book. Lexa's fingers tightened on her book. By this scene Cherie'd been on the road, trying to live her singing dream, had had some man troubles, had hooked up with Bo for a night, only then to deal with the whole bus-kidnapping thing. Shadows played against Lexa's closed lids. Cherie'd also watched Bo in the diner, trying super hard to get her to like him, and had noticed that he really believed he loved her. So, by now? By now she'd be . . . a little charmed by him. Yeah. A little willing to give him a chance.

Lexa sucked in another fortifying breath, opened her eyes, and began, "'Hi, Bo!'"

Brian swallowed, his fingers kneading the edge of his playbook as though it was the brim of a cowboy hat, his nervousness thick and touchable. Then he said his line. And—as Lexa said her next line—a scratchy tickle crept up her spine, the friction making her think of a match dragging across the rough strip on a matchbox. Everything in her sparking with what would come next, she shuddered, the lit fuse of a firework. She was about to kiss Brian McKinnon. Brian *hottie* McKinnon! Her lips on his. Any second now.

He leaned forward and her lashes swept down and—Brian McKinnon. Lips on hers. Kissing her. *Her!*

They stood there, lips pressing.

Pressing.

Lexa waited to ignite. Waited.

Lips still pressing. Marshmallowy-spongey now. Cool. Like when she was younger, and she and Em practiced kissing on the backs of their hands.

Lexa had to squash her eyelids to keep them down. Why was she thinking about her eyelids? And about fireworks fizzling?

Brian's lips left hers and her eyes shot open, watching his mouth moving away. Her stomach dropped, and the moment passed.

"Hey, that wasn't so hard," he said. The words came out light with relief.

"Yeah." She had to clutch her book to keep from wiping her mouth.

His gaze dove to his book. "The stage directions say the kiss should last a bit." He cleared his throat, now looking at her mouth with interest. "Maybe we should practice again." He leaned toward her and, as she stepped back, the wing curtain swished aside, and Mr. B marched toward them, Jeremy on his heels.

"There you are." Mr. B glanced from Lexa to Brian. Jeremy glanced at both of them too, lingering on her, on her mouth, and she could swear the color in his face, his eyes, everything went a shade darker.

"Miss Donovan?"

She snapped to Mr. B. "Huh? What?"

"I said that you will meet with me next." He shifted to Brian. "You and Mr. Leith will work together."

Jeremy brushed by, and Lexa grabbed her pack, hugging it to her chest as she hurried after Mr. B.

"That was a good start, Lex." Brian's cheery voice followed her. "Real good."

Her brain churning with confusion, she marched as fast as her noodly legs would go. Then a long, slow "Mmmmmmmm" purred in her head.

"Well now." Marilyn's lashes fluttered, her mouth spreading with pleasure. "That Brian is full of potential."

Dreamy. That was the word floating in Lexa's mind. That was the sensation pouring off of Marilyn in waves. But wasn't Lexa the one who was supposed to be full of dreamy?

Chapter Twenty-Two

Lexa tiptoed through the rest of the school day. Something was different. Marilyn was different. Except she was still right there, even now sitting on her chair, staring out the window, legs crossed and one bare foot swinging. It was as if Lexa saw her through glass, or she was a movie, or . . . Lexa didn't know. Then they were walking home, alone as usual, and Lexa knew she couldn't wait any longer.

"Marilyn?"

When Marilyn turned to her, Lexa said, "What happened this morning," she walked faster, "you know. With Brian?"

Marilyn's big eyes drank her in. "I've been thinking on it, and I honestly don't know how to answer that. All I know is that kissing Brian felt creamy to me. It didn't to you, did it?"

"No," Lexa said, "I mean, it didn't feel bad, or anything. It was like I was watching myself doing it, instead of—of feeling myself doing it." She stared at her feet hitting the sidewalk, then murmured, "You sure felt it. But how? Aren't you only supposed to feel what I feel?"

"Up until this morning that's what I thought, too."

With a quick shiver, Lexa went back to that day in the kitchen, when the grater sliced her finger.

"I sort of get how you might not feel every single thing I feel. What I don't get is how you could feel something I *didn't* feel."

"I don't know either." Marilyn's voice, low and mournful, stopped Lexa cold.

Slow and measured, Lexa stepped away from the sidewalk, grabbing onto a fence.

"How can you *not* know?"

"I suppose, well, being dead—a spirit, I mean—is not exactly a science, honey."

The not-exactly-a-science of spiritishness sinking in deeper than ever, Lexa leaned her forehead against the cool iron fence and stared through the slats at the—*seriously, again?*—cemetery beyond. A ways off a landscape guy trimmed a pine tree, the rasp of his saw grating. Above, a lone bird chirped one long note.

Marilyn had to hear that chirp, smell the tang of pine, only—only was that because of Lexa, or was there some mysterious something else? Breathing in deep, Lexa focused on her body, searching through the warmth, the fullness, the pulse of blood for some part of the change that would offer up an explanation. Everything was different and, at the same time, nothing was different. Marilyn had been in her—she did a quick calculation—almost exactly six whole weeks. *Gulp!* Lexa could barely remember the before.

"Do you think," Lexa whispered, "you being inside me for this long is maybe not the best idea in the world?"

"Maybe not. After all." Marilyn's smile was a sad little smudge. "We both know I shouldn't be here in the first place."

Everything beginning to swirl in her head, Lexa looked up at the sky, at the blue, at the clouds, at the nothing.

"There's something I've been wondering awhile," Marilyn said after a bit. "I didn't say anything, because I kept hoping I'd figure it out. I haven't." She tugged at the ends of a blonde curl. "What if I'm not here to help you with the play? What if my being here is about something else? Something I'm supposed to do for—for me?"

Lexa pressed her lips together. "I never thought of that."

"I want my being here to be about you." Marilyn let out a heaving sob, quickly covering her mouth with the back of her hand. "I want it to be about the play. Only—only what if it's not?"

Pushing herself off the fence, Lexa tried to smile. "Like you said a long time ago, isn't that the $64,000 question?"

Later Lexa sat on the floor of her room munching popcorn. Salt and butter and quiet. Little by little, the peace of simply being in her room slipped around her, soft and easy as a worn quilt. Marilyn seemed peaceful too. She lay on her side on her long cushy leather couch, palms together under her cheek.

"I guess I should do homework," Lexa said.

Marilyn's eyelids lowered. "How about a little music?"

"Sure." Lexa scrolled through her playlists and queued up something mellow.

After a few beats, Marilyn cleared her throat. "This is nice, and it's been a kick hearing lots of your new music. But how about a change? Have you ever heard of Frank Sinatra?"

"Heard of? Sure. Wanted to listen to? No."

Marilyn's *pleaseohplease* expression was loud and insistent.

"Fine." A second later, Frank crooned out, singing about flying to the moon.

Marilyn sighed. "Isn't he the creamiest?"

"Yeah," Lexa said, cracking up, "totally the creamiest."

"You're making fun of me, aren't you?"

"You yourself have shown me pictures of him." Lexa pulled out her French book. "He looked like a boney-faced troll."

"A—a *troll*?" Marilyn's whisper was hot with disbelief. "Well listen and learn, sugar, looks aren't everything. And a million women can't be wrong."

"Whatever you say. Now can you be quiet for a bit? I'm gonna . . ." She flipped open her book.

Marilyn huffed out a pouty *pfft* and shoved a pillow under her head.

Lexa tried to ignore Marilyn, wanting only to be a girl doing homework. Translating was slow and plodding, though, her brain trudging like it had grown a shell and become a turtle. The music and that voice wouldn't leave her alone either. Giving up reading, she leaned against her bed.

Smoky blue and chocolate. That was Frank singing. Melty dark chocolate.

"See?" Marilyn's whisper tickled.

Lexa smiled but didn't move and, when the song finished, said, "Okay, troll-face aside, the guy had it going on."

Marilyn grinned. Then she looked around. "You know, I've been paying so much attention to the play, I haven't had a chance to ask you about all these pictures on your walls. I'm confused. Didn't you tell that Jeremy you've never left Vermont?"

Even as Lexa said, "No, I—I haven't," she looked at the posters: Spain, France, Greece, Ireland.

"Is that why you're studying all that Spanish and French, honey? To travel?"

Nodding, Lexa plucked at her ring. "Yeah," she said, "doesn't everyone want to travel?"

"I'm not talking about 'everyone.'" Marilyn wrinkled her nose. "I'm talking about you. You don't talk much about what *you* want."

"I thought you could read my mind."

"Mostly I can, only the longer I'm here, the more your

mind's like a storm. All those thoughts whipping around like snow in a blizzard. Wanting to survive *Bus Stop*," Marilyn said, "wishing for your mama. Worrying about your dad. About Brian. About Em. No, I'm talking about before the play. Before I came on the scene. What did *that* Alexandria Donovan want?"

Lexa sat up straighter, lips pursed. "That Alexandria Donovan had no idea either," she said finally. "In a couple of months I'm going to graduate from high school, and I'm all set to go to State right here in good old Queen City, except sometimes I feel like going to college is a joke, because I don't know what I want to do, so it seems kind of like a waste of money. Money we don't have a lot of." She hugged her knees. "Even though I know Dad would be happy supporting whatever I do, I know he needs me at Film Buzz. We can't afford to hire someone else. If I stay here, I could go to college and keep helping him, only that seems so—so like what I've been doing forever." She paused, let out a tired breath. "Why would I do anything else, though? I've got nothing burning a hole in me. Nothing like what Em has with her designing. Or what you had to have had in you to become the biggest star in the world."

Lexa dropped her forehead to her knees, her voice going even lower, quieter. "Sometimes I dream about going to the places in those posters, like backpacking around Europe, or maybe teaching English somewhere. About doing something completely different, *being* someone completely different. Except leaving my dad for that? It seems selfish as hell, and not really like a job. I don't know. I can't even think about any of that now. The play." She looked up. The posters crowded in on her, almost accusing. For a second, she didn't realize Marilyn was talking, and then she heard what Marilyn said.

"No one's saying you have to know what you want to do for the rest of your life, sugar, and I think traveling the world sounds like a wonderful plan. A wonderful way to open you to new things. I am sure your daddy and—and everyone—would agree with me when I tell you being open to things is half the way to finding out what you want in this life."

"Open to things?" A laugh barked out of Lexa. "I've invited a spirit to live in my *body*! And, if you'll remember from earlier, neither of us—me or said spirit—is 100 percent sure that's turning out to be such a good idea. How much more open can I be?"

Marilyn's mouth spread slowly into a smile. "Touché."

"Which brings me back to what happened with Brian," Lexa said. "Any thoughts on why my lame kiss with him was not lame for you?"

"I've been thinking on that." Marilyn tapped her cheek. "I could feel how anxious you were right before he puckered up. Maybe that caused some kind of block. Yes. Like a mental block, against your feelings."

"So . . . what you're saying is that a mental block could have blocked me from my true feelings, but didn't block you?"

"It's possible." Marilyn's shoulder sliced up and down. "After all, *I* wasn't nervous, and you have to admit, deep down you've been thinking about that kiss for ages. You look pretty when you blush."

Rubbing at her cheeks, Lexa's hands all at once went still, her eyes widening. "You're right. I've been thinking about Brian—worrying to be honest—ever since I found out he was playing Bo. Do you think my—my mixed-up feelings about him have anything to do with why you came?"

Marilyn's fingers went to her lips. "I never thought of that."

"They might." Butterfly nerves made Lexa's voice rise. "Maybe we'll see the next time Brian and I . . ."

"Kiss," Marilyn finished.

Chapter Twenty-Three

Over the next few days, what Marilyn said about needing to be "open" kept creeping into Lexa's head. Had she not been open to new things before Marilyn? She wanted to ask Dad, Em, even Ann if they thought she was closed off. Take a poll. Then, like an electric jolt, the play would *zap* into her head and she'd *zing* with everything she had to do in the right now.

Using the auditorium made every meeting an onstage rehearsal, and Lexa worked to "find her Cherie": to get past the faraway, watching sensation that happened when she and Brian practiced The Kissing Scene. Brian had no problems there, his lips only getting softer and warmer. Hers? Not so much. The more she tried to follow Marilyn's advice about using her senses, her emotions, her memories to become Cherie, to relax mystically into the part, the more her robot-girl brain clicked and whirred.

Marilyn seemed to have no problem following her own advice. Every time Brian lifted his head, she purred, content as a kitten.

And every time they did the kiss and Lexa went cold, she promised herself that the next time the scene would go differently. That by the next time for sure she'd have done it enough to relax. Relax into what half the girls at QueenHi—more likely *all*—would love to do: kiss one of the hottest boys ever. That had to happen. Had to. Look at the other scenes! Sometimes Lexa was so into her lines, into the scene, that she even forgot what she was doing. Didn't that mean she was finding Cherie? That she was relaxing about the play? Wouldn't that happen with The Brian Kiss? Next time?

The next time would come and . . . she'd start thinking about the time after that. Today was no different. Brian lifted his mouth and, following the script to the letter, charged off to confer with Bo's cowboy buddy, Jeremy/Virgil.

As Cherie, Lexa was supposed to sink back onto the diner counter stool and look stunned. She started sinking, and Mr. B called out, "Stop. Please, stop."

Everyone froze as he trudged up the stage steps. When he headed for Lexa, she swallowed hard, deflating as if her whole body had known this moment was coming.

"Miss Donovan," he said, gesturing for her to follow him, "if you please."

She shuffled after him behind the wings, and Marilyn shot her a deer-ready-to-bolt face, probably mirroring her own.

"Have a seat," Mr. B said, sitting and waving to the chair across from his. "First, let me say that you are doing a wonderful job with Cherie." He hesitated. "In most of the scenes, that is."

Lexa's insides caved.

"I'm wondering," he went on, "about the scene we just did. What exactly is going on there?"

"I—I'm not sure," she said, hating how miserable she sounded. "I'm trying."

"I can see that. Oh, yes. That's part of the problem. I can *see* how hard you're trying, and that makes Cherie's kiss with Bo seem . . ."

"Lame?"

He smiled. "That's not the adjective I would've chosen, but yes. Now then." Leaning toward her, he rested his palms on his thighs. "Mr. McKinnon seems to have no problem with the kiss. That's why I'm talking to you. Tell me, is there a problem?"

"No!" The word shot out, and the second Mr. B's brows lifted, she wished she'd kept her mouth shut.

"Miss Donovan." His tone oozed patience. "I know having to kiss someone for a play can be awkward. At first. We've been working on this scene for over a week now, however, and I am certain you are mature enough to handle a stage kiss." He pursed his lips. "Unless there's something else going on of which I am not aware."

"No. There's nothing going on." She stared at the floor. "You're right. I should be able to kiss him. It's . . . I thought it would be *different*."

"Different?"

"Yeah."

"This is a play," Mr. B said, "a work of theater. You don't need to concern yourself with what you think of the kiss. It's *Cherie* we are interested in at this pivotal moment. What *she* thinks of the kiss. What would that be?"

Lexa blinked, blinked again. "That she . . ." A memory of standing with Jeremy, thinking of Cherie in this scene. Then what happened after. Her skin went hot and then frozen cold. She pushed the image away. "That—that she wanted to give Bo a chance," she managed, "to be different."

Already nodding, Mr. B said, "That's right. Use that. For the actual kissing part, try to draw from your own experience. Think of how you kiss a boy you really like. Don't go too wild. Do put some honest *oomph* into it, though." He stood. "Let's go give it another try, shall we?"

"Sure," she said. He motored off and, limbs dragging, she rose. "What am I going to do?" she whispered, creeping back toward the stage.

Marilyn's shoulder lifted a fraction. "What he said."

"I don't have any of that kind of kissing experience to draw on."

"Why, of course you do."

"No," Lexa insisted, "I don't. I mean, sure I've kissed boys. Who hasn't? Only—only not with anyone I gave a damn about—"

"What about Jeremy?"

"I—" Lexa's whole body jolted. She shuddered. "I—I can't. Everything's weird with him now."

"So, what are you going to do?"

One step short of the stage, Lexa stopped. She was letting them down: Mr. B, Cherie, the play, the others.

Movement in the audience caught her eye. Hilary, settling into the first row.

"Why is she here?" Lexa hissed. "Now what am I going to do?"

"Any chance the prospect of getting *that* girl's goat would inspire a little more kissing oomph?"

"Ha. More like the exact opposite," Lexa began, then trailed off. One choice surfaced. "Could you . . ." she wetted her lips, "could you, you know, do it for me? The kiss, I mean?"

Marilyn's eyes grew huge, her mouth a perfect O. "You can't be serious," she said.

Mr. B called, "Miss Donovan? We're waiting."

"Just a sec," Lexa answered, then muttered to Marilyn, hot and fast, "I *am* serious."

"Gosh. Seems a little risky, don't you think?"

"I know. I know." Lexa bit her lip now. This step was risky, except between her wooden lips and now Hilary watching, she had to do something. "Maybe—maybe if I watch you do it, it'll help. Besides this could be like a—like a little experiment."

"Okay, I'm not sure what you're getting at." As Marilyn spoke, her lips seemed to grow redder and riper, hugging her small teeth. "If you think it will help you."

Hurrying onto the stage, Lexa's face burned and tingled as everyone's attention shifted to her. Mr. B waved her to her mark.

Brian was already in position. "Mr. B says we're doing the kissing scene again," he whispered. His eyes flicked to the front row.

Lexa managed a short nod. She shifted on her mark, and there was Jeremy, only a few feet away. Their eyes caught, and he looked down. A space inside her chilled, broke off.

Mr. B clapped his hands. "Places, people."

Lowering her lids, Lexa took a few deep breaths. Inside she spoke to Marilyn. "Ready?"

Marilyn saluted her as Mr. B called out directions. "From Cherie greeting Bo, please. Ready when you are, Miss Donovan."

Exhaling a shaky stream, Lexa opened her eyes. "'Hi, Bo.'"

The instant she said "Bo," her brain and body geysered, flooding with warmth, the smell of Chanel No. 5 filling her nose. Flung into the Marilyn chair, she watched herself now—her Marilyn-self—go into action.

Brian said his line, the one about how terrifying serious kissing is, and Lexa said hers, a breathy, whispered agreement. Then here came Brian's mouth.

She watched her own lashes sweep down in slo-mo, her trembling lips rising to meet Brian's. Heat and more heat, and right in front of her, a private movie, as hot in her head as on her Marilyn-possessed mouth. Brian off into new territory, too, his hands sliding off her biceps, clutching around her back, the kiss going deeper and deeper, her own body leaning back in his arms, her own lips parting under his.

Lexa gripped the sides of Marilyn's chair. This was too much. Too much! Marilyn wasn't here with her anymore. She was there, in Brian's arms, lost in his kiss. *Lost*. "Stop," Lexa yelled. "Marilyn! You have to stop!"

All at once everything in and around her swung high and leaped, flying, flying—and she thudded hard into her own body. She blinked up at Brian and, as Bo, he was supposed to look dazed. His expression, slack-mouthed and blurry, gave new meaning to the word.

Lexa sank, slowly and achingly, into her seat.

"And," Mr. B's voice came from miles away. "Cut."

Silence. Roaring and echoing. Over the stage. Over the auditorium. Over the world.

Then the crack of a single clap, more following until everyone clapped, some hooting and hollering. Lexa stole a peek at Mr. B.

"Bravo," he mouthed.

Next to her, Brian's mumbled, "Oh, man," had Lexa shifting Hilary's way. Her seat was empty.

Catching eyes with Marilyn, she couldn't think of a thing to say. Marilyn could, though.

"I think—I think we stepped out of bounds, honey."

Chapter Twenty-Four

"What was that?" Marilyn's question came out as a low, spooked moan. "What is going on?"

Still in the middle of rehearsal, all Lexa could do was give her a look that she hoped told her she wondered the same thing. All Marilyn could do was sit on her chair, staring straight ahead, one pinky resting on her lower lip.

At last rehearsal came to an end, and Lexa slunk down into the auditorium seats, where she'd left her backpack.

"Let's just chill," Lexa said, taking out everything in the pack, pretending to reorganize. "You're here to help me with the play. Let's focus on that."

"Honestly, there's nothing I want more," said Marilyn, "only—"

"The kiss is part of the play," Lexa interrupted, shoving her pencil case into a side pocket. "We're trying to figure out why I'm making such a mess of that. For the play."

Marilyn gave her a tiny nod and shivered. That shiver ran right through Lexa, the ice of it all about edges: dangerous-feeling edges.

"I simply wish I knew what to do, sugar."

Before Lexa could answer, Mr. B was calling for everyone's attention and holding up a sign-up sheet for costuming.

Costuming! Lexa signed up for the first slot—right after school that very afternoon—her instincts reaching for a person she knew she could count on: Em.

The last block bell ringing in her ears, Lexa bolted for the QueenHi costume closet: a dank room in the bowels of the school. Bright lights buzzed above in that fluorescent way, the air smelling thick and damp as a cave. Creeped out, she skulked around one corner, then another, the whole place getting quieter and quieter. Quiet enough that she imagined she could hear Marilyn breathing in her head.

Lexa almost started humming, if only to hear some noise, and she had no idea why she didn't. Then there before her was the half-closed door of the costume closet, and the very familiar sound of Em's low chuckle. Another voice piped up. The second she realized it was Kevin in there with Em, all talking, noise, whatever, inside the closet went quiet. Even as a tiny part of Lexa told her to walk away, she was already peeking in the door.

Em and Kevin crushed in a fevered kiss, his hands under her shirt, hers gripping his butt.

Marilyn and Lexa stared at each other hard, and Lexa did the only possible thing: crept back one, two quick steps. Smack into a moving body. Her "Aack!" jumbled with a loud "What the hell!" a split second before her body and the other stumbled and reeled. Then she was eye to blinking, flustered eye with Hilary Poss.

"What's going on?" This from Em, now standing in the doorway straightening her shirt. Kevin hovered over her shoulder, all four of their cheeks blazing, fresh and hot and pink.

"Lexa crashed into me," said Hilary, glaring at Lexa. "At least she didn't trash the couple of possibilities for diner curtains," she said, holding up a lump of fabric. "And these two round tablecloths."

"Let's take a look," Em said slowly.

Hilary swished by, and Em raised her brows at Lexa, saying, "Hey."

"Hey," Lexa answered.

Kevin, his face redder than before, sidled by Em, his hands shoved into the kangaroo pocket of his sweatshirt. "So, we'll finish talking about the . . . the *thing* later. Okay?"

"Yeah, later," Em echoed and, even though Em crooked her finger for Lexa to follow, her blurry smile made it obvious that her attention wasn't exactly focused on costume-fitting.

Inside, Hilary spread fabric out on a table. "What do you think?" she said, her mouth tight, her gaze razored to Em.

"In case you're wondering," Marilyn murmured, "it's terribly clear she saw that kiss with Brian."

"You think?" Lexa edged to the farthest possible corner, listening in while pretending high interest in a rack of men's tuxedo jackets.

Oblivious, Em fingered a cottony piece of fabric with a green and white check pattern. "This looks perfect for the curtains," she said, "really perfect." She moved on to the tablecloths. "These are too lacy. We need something that says 'diner,' like maybe plain white or cream. Maybe with a green trim?"

"I didn't see anything like that," Hilary said. "There were a couple of bins I didn't go through yet. I'll check them out." She strode out the door, boot heels clicking.

"Thanks," Em called after her.

"Are you kidding me?" Lexa managed, "Hilary Poss as your assistant?"

"Not with the costumes," Em said, "but with our tight schedule, Mr. B put out the word for emergency help with stage and props and, well," she shrugged, "Hilary stepped up. The crazy thing is, she's serious and she's not doing a bad job."

Uneasiness flaring like a struck match, Lexa muttered, "Well, don't let her work on anything to do with me."

With a snort, Em said, "As if. Forget her." She plucked up her measuring tape. "Let's get going on you. I need final measurements."

Obediently, Lexa held out her arms and, for the next few minutes, the sole sound was the slip of Em's tape.

"Well, go on," crooned Marilyn. "You know you want to ask her for help and, after what we just saw, she's going to have lots to say about kissing."

"I know, I know," Lexa whispered back, "I'm waiting for the right moment."

Marilyn's only response was to pinch Lexa's butt.

"Hey," Em said, chin coming up fast, "stand still." She frowned. "Why are you staring at me?"

"*You* know."

Em's brows rose in confusion.

"Don't make me pinch you again," whispered Marilyn, "this is no time to be shy."

"You and Kevin," Lexa sputtered. "The—the door was open and I saw you."

Em's gaze skittered away, her cheeks pinking again.

"I couldn't help it," Lexa mumbled.

"That's okay." Em stayed quiet a beat before saying, "Since you're obviously dying to know, newsflash—Kevin and I have taken our relationship to the next level." Her smile made Lexa think of sweet, happy little girls. "He is the best kisser."

Lexa blurted, "Because it was a surprise, right?"

"A surprise? I—I don't know what you're asking me, Lexa. It was kind of a private moment."

"You think I'm being a creep." Lexa almost laughed. "Wait. I *am* being a creep. I'm kind of desperate here."

"What's going on *now*?"

"I . . ." Lexa looked over her shoulder, making sure the door was still closed. "I don't get this kissing crap." When Em frowned, she rushed on, "I mean, Brian has to kiss me in the play, and I go stiff as a board. I'm thinking it's because I'm expecting it, and I tense up."

"C'mon, Lexa, kissing for a play is totally diff—" Em pursed her lips, studying her. "Is something up with you and Brian?"

When Lexa didn't answer, Em said, "Oh, my God! You have the hots for Brian McKinnon."

"No, I don't. Really. Okay, maybe a little?" Lexa trailed off, putting her hands over her face. "This is so super weird." She dropped her hands and faced Em again. "What I mean is, doesn't everyone have the hots for Brian McKinnon because he's totally hot? And shouldn't that make me glad to kiss him? Be all swoony, or something? That's why I thought maybe me 'expecting it,' you know, for the play, was screwing everything up, because I'm supposed to be all swoony. For the play."

"I guess that could be a reason." Em went back to measuring. "Only that means you think me kissing Kevin was great because it was a big surprise."

"Well, wasn't it?"

"Actually, I kind of planned it."

"Planned it?"

"Not *planned* planned it. Like that it would happen at that particular moment." Em shoved to her feet. "I thought about doing it. A lot. And when he still didn't go for it, I thought about what you and I talked about and decided *I* was going to. And," she shrugged, "I, you know, went for it."

They blinked at each other.

"Huh," said Lexa.

Em pressed her lips together, moving her mouth side to side. "I'm guessing I blew your theory. About you kissing Brian."

"Yeah."

"Well," Em went on, "when it's right, it's right."

"And then it's magic," whispered Marilyn.

Something rushed into Lexa, like it had been waiting. Jeremy. Planned, not planned. Probably a mistake. Still, kissing him had been . . . Lexa swallowed a gasp.

"Are you okay?" Em put her hand on Lexa's arm. "Your face went pale as a ghost, and now it's on fire."

"I'm fine," she croaked, her gaze shooting to Marilyn, who stared right back, eyes huge, fanning herself with both hands. "I think I need something to drink, or some air. I'm going to get going."

"Damn, I want to keep talking about this," Em said. "I'm stuck here for a while, though. I've got three more measuring sessions to do. Are you sure you're okay?"

"I'm fine," Lexa said, hurrying to the door.

"Text me later."

Lexa yanked open the door. Brian and Hilary stood out in the hall, both of their cheeks splotchy red—not in the smoochie, just-had-a-massive-make-out way. No. Unhappiness poured off of them.

They spun to her, and at the same instant Brian's face brightened to sunny-smiley, Hilary's darkened to even stormier.

"Hey," Lexa said, barely getting the greeting out before Hilary stalked into the costume closet, slamming the door.

Brian rubbed his palm over his head, his smile now full of *sorry you had to see that*. When she moved to slip by him, he murmured, "Lex?"

The softness of his voice stopped her.

"Yeah?"

"You still rehearsing with Leith?"

Before she could muster an answer, he held up his hand. "Never mind. Doesn't matter. Look, there's a cool-sounding film festival at the Waterfront Theater this weekend and I was wondering . . ." he stepped closer and her insides did a noodly dropping thing, "if you wanted to check it out with me. On Friday night?"

Friday night? With Brian? *What?* Her head buzzed. "What about—what about Hilary?"

"That's what you saw." Brian lowered his lashes. "Me telling her—*again*—that I think we should take some time. Hang with other people."

Other . . . whoa! "Brian," Lexa began but had to stop, her mouth too dry to let out any words.

"Will you think about it?"

Man, he looked as full of serious and yearning as when he was playing Bo.

"I think we should spend some time together," he went on, reaching out, lightly touching her arm, "so think about Friday, okay? You've got my number."

He sauntered over to the costume closet door, disappearing inside.

As Lexa scurried away, Marilyn prattled on about how it was high time Em got up the gumption to go after Kevin, and how it was even higher time Brian gave Hilary the old heave-ho. Lexa couldn't really listen to any of that. No. What she wanted was quiet. Wrong! What she wanted was to stop feeling like she was stuck in the middle of all this drama.

She stole a look at Marilyn as she hoofed it to the bus stop. Talked out, Marilyn sat on her chair, hugged up in a buttery cream-colored sweater, the twin of Lexa's red scarf knotted around her throat. Lexa touched her own scarf, the crinkly fabric prickling against her fingers, the faintest hint of Chanel No. 5 wafting.

Everything Marilyn said was true, only none of that was what was eating at Lexa at this particular moment.

Marilyn's chin lifted as if she waited for Lexa's thoughts to catch up.

"Fine!" Lexa hissed. "I *am* mad. Burning mad. Ready to kick things mad. And as much as I want to be mad at you, or—or anyone else, what I'm pissed about is that now I can't stop thinking about Jeremy. About our kiss. About how he's not even talking to me anymore."

"We'll get to him in a minute," Marilyn said, "but first, we've got a situation to deal with. Are you going to go out with Brian?"

"G*o out with Brian?!?*" Lexa made a desperate *pffing* sound. "That would be nuts."

"Why nuts?"

"Hilary," Lexa began. Marilyn was already shaking her head.

"I was there too, honey. I heard what he said about her. So? Are you going out with him?"

Shocked, Lexa's whole body jerked. There it was. That face. From their first day together. That expression. From when Marilyn asked her for that favor. Raw, naked hope.

"Wait," Lexa said, "you sound like you *want* me to go out with Brian."

Marilyn's eyes flicked away, and another bolt hit Lexa. "Do—do *you* want to go out with him?"

"Lord, I don't know," Marilyn said, leaping out of her chair. "I did like the look of him. Right from the first time I saw him." Hands fisted at her sides, she paced now. "And when he'd talk to you sometimes? Well, he looked so terribly confused, like he was really trying to figure out the play, figure out what he wanted. Kind of earnest and tender. I like that. Then when you kissed him that first time . . ." She whirled to Lexa, pressing her fists to her chest. "Feelings kind of burned through me. Not like when I'm feeling things through you, though. Different." She was whispering now, her eyes shiny with unshed tears. "As if they could be *mine*. As if they were mine."

Lexa could only stare at Marilyn. What she'd said every kind of . . .

"Wrong." Marilyn threw herself into her seat. "Every single kind of wrong, except I can't seem to help it, and it's not about any of my memories. This is how I feel right now." Wonder touched her voice. "I am able to feel actual living feelings. And they're mine. Isn't that a kicker?"

"Do you want to go out with Brian?"

"We both know that's impossible, only . . . if I was young and alive and had the choice?" Marilyn's expression went dreamy. "Why, I'd give almost anything to have one night out with a boy who has no idea about Marilyn Monroe."

A place deep inside Lexa's chest tightened and pulled, as if she had just watched the saddest part of the saddest movie. Digging out her phone, she fired off a text.

Marilyn blinked once, whispering, "I can't believe you did that."

Lexa's phone beeped. "Well, believe it," she said, reading the text, "because Friday night, we're hanging with Brian McKinnon."

"Oh, my. Is that really a good idea?"

"Who knows?" Lexa let out a slow exhale. "Only it sure seems like part of why *you're* here has something to do with what's going on with you and Brian. Maybe we need to spend time with him. And if we're going to do that, I'd rather it be off the stage."

"I—I honestly don't know what to say."

Lexa walked on. She'd set up a date with a boy who thought he would be going out with her, except it was possible he really wanted to go out with the spirit in her head. Marilyn Monroe. An icy chill slithered across her shoulders. "It's only one night," she whispered, as much to herself as to Marilyn. "No matter what. It's only one night."

"One night."

They walked on in silence, until she sensed the heat of Marilyn studying her hard.

"What?" Lexa said.

The tip of Marilyn's tongue touched her upper lip. "What about Jeremy?"

"What does any of this have to do with him?"

"Why, only everything," said Marilyn. "Maybe the honest-to-goodness reason kissing Brian isn't working for you is because there's another boy you'd rather be kissing."

"Oh, God!" The words sprayed out of Lexa's mouth and into the air, surrounding her. Head down, she walked faster. "I cannot think about that right now. I mean, he's not even talking to me anymore."

"Who's not talking to you anymore?"

That voice—no! Her chin shot up and she jerked to a halt a split-second before bashing into Jeremy. She stared at him, mouth open.

"Whoa. Forget I asked," he said, hands up in mock defense. "I *have* been waiting for you, though."

"You—you have?"

"Yeah, I wanted to talk to you." He hesitated, his lips pressed together so tight that they looked cemented. "Okay," he went on at last, "you wanted to talk to her, Jeremy, so—talk. I'm sorry I've been such a dick lately. What happened that day at my place surprised me." He stepped closer, his voice lowering. "Can we try something?"

"What?" she said.

"I think we should do something totally expected." A smile lit his face. "Like make a plan."

"Make a plan?" She could barely move her lips. His eyes, clear and focused on her face, were like laser beams.

"Yeah. Like how about we hang out on Friday night?"

"Friday?" She couldn't help a desperate little laugh. "*This* Friday?"

Nodding, his forehead puckered, as if beginning to think talking to her was a mistake.

She gulped in air. She should say *No*, only . . . "I can't do Friday," she said fast, "how about . . . Saturday?"

"Sure," he said, the word coming out completely unsure. "There *was* something on Friday. Never mind, Saturday works. Hold up. I promised my dad we'd cook dinner together on Saturday. Hey," he smiled a little, "maybe you could have dinner with us this time."

"Okay," she managed.

"Cool." He backed away. "I'll check with my dad about timing and let you know Saturday morning."

"Sounds great." Tossing him a small wave, she watched him cross the road, disappear down the entrance to the condos. Then her mind mumbled, "Did that happen for real?"

"It sure did, sweetie," said a dazed Marilyn. "It sure did."

"He—he probably just feels bad," Lexa said, "because of, you know, what happened at the condo."

"That's not what I think," said Marilyn, "but we'll sure find out on Saturday."

Chapter Twenty-Five

By Friday night, Lexa was a wreck. Brian would be picking her up soon, and she couldn't even decide what to wear.

"How about that one?" Marilyn said, "the green silk shirt?"

"Nah." Lexa slapped the hanger holding the green shirt along the rod in her closet. Next was a snug fuzzy black sweater. "Definitely not," she mumbled.

Marilyn opened her mouth; before she could speak Lexa said, "Too hot."

Pouting, Marilyn crossed her arms over her chest. "It's not hot. It's winter.

"I meant sexy," Lexa muttered. "It's too sexy."

"What's wrong with sexy?"

Fingering the sweater, Lexa said, "This is weird. I feel like it's important for us to spend some time with Brian, but it's kind of confusing." She glanced at Marilyn. "I mean, maybe it'll help me do better in the play. Maybe it'll help you. Maybe we're just sticking it to Hilary." Her hand dropped from the sweater. "I wish any of those things felt real."

"Real's kind of a slippery word, sugar."

"Tell me about it," Lexa said. "One thing I know for sure is that he only asked me out because of you."

"That's not true, well, not completely." Marilyn uncrossed

her arms. "Maybe I've suggested a few things to you along the way, and maybe he's responded to those times I took over, but it's you he sees in that workshop."

"Partly me," whispered Lexa, "only which part? I guess this is our chance to see, except . . ."

"Except what?"

"Except I keep thinking it should be *you* going out with Brian."

"Me?" Marilyn's eyes got huge.

They gave each other a long, silent look.

"Yes," whispered Lexa finally, "I want to see him with you. I think I have to." She slipped the black sweater from the hanger. "Maybe seeing you with him is what I need to . . . I don't know . . . unblock me. And maybe you being with him will give you some answers."

Marilyn's lashes lowered. "Is that what you really want?"

"What I really want is for whatever happens to be real. The truth."

At exactly ten minutes before 7:00 p.m., Lexa sat on the living room couch, a small purse clutched in her hands. She and Marilyn caught each other's eye; neither of them spoke. Even though they were expecting Brian, when the knock sounded on the apartment door, they both startled.

Touching the red scarf at her neck, she whispered to Marilyn, "Ready?"

With a now-familiar *whoosh*, she found herself on Marilyn's director's chair. She clasped her hands, watching her body rise from the living room couch, smooth the fuzzy black sweater over her belly, and walk, slow and swaying, to the door. Man, that Marilyn could walk.

When she opened the door, Brian gave her a quick up and down. "Hey," he said with a grin.

"Hey, yourself," said Marilyn through lips all at once impossibly full and glossy and spreading into a smile.

"You look amazing," he said, watching her as she slipped on a short, fitted leather jacket.

"You don't look half-bad yourself," she answered, stepping out, pulling the door closed. "You don't mind stopping into the shop to meet my daddy, do you?"

Inside her own head, Lexa almost fell off the chair. "What?"

Leading the way down the stairs, Marilyn winked at her.

"Sure, no problem," said Brian, "we've got some time."

Marilyn trailed fingertips down the railing. "Where are we going again?"

"Down by the lake. To the Waterfront Theater."

"Why, yes," Marilyn said, "I believe you said something about a film festival?"

"Yeah, I did." The quiet of his voice had Marilyn glancing over her shoulder. He lifted his eyes fast. That made her smile.

"He was checking out your butt," muttered Lexa inside. "I mean *my* butt."

"Of course, he was."

Before Lexa could say anything else, Brian was tugging open the door to Film Buzz.

She watched Marilyn introduce Brian to Dad, and how insane was that? Dad and Brian shaking hands, making a little small talk about college—Brian was heading to Southern Vermont University on a partial football scholarship. About the winter—yeah, he and his parents were already thinking about spring planting.

Then Brian was zipping the two of them out of the lot in his pickup truck, on their way to downtown. Marilyn looked out the window. "I can feel you," she said to Lexa, "champing at the bit for me to get talking to him. Relax! You wanted to see me in action. Now give me a chance." With a little impatient groan, Lexa sat back and did the lock and key twist in front of her mouth. At last Marilyn shifted her gaze to Brian. He concentrated on the road.

"What's our . . ." Lexa crossed her arms. "I mean, what's *your* plan?"

"I'm going to let him make the first move, sugar."

At a red light, Brian turned to Marilyn. "I'm really glad you decided to go out with me."

"That makes two of us," said Marilyn, her smile easy. "What movie are we seeing?"

"It's a surprise." He grinned as the light changed.

"A surprise?"

"Yeah," he said, pulling into a large parking lot. "Not for long, though." He angled his head toward the movie posters plastered on the sides of a funky, black-painted theater.

Marilyn laughed out loud, clapping her hands, speaking as much to Lexa as to Brian,

"*Some Like It Hot*? Why, that's the limit."

"When I saw that it was playing, I thought of you." His cheeks reddened. "Because of that birthday song you did. Hil—I mean—I heard you were copying Marilyn Monroe."

"Did you now?" purred Marilyn.

"Have you already seen it?" said Brian. "The movie, I mean."

"Why, you could say that."

Lexa dropped her face into her hands.

The next thing Lexa knew, Marilyn and Brian sat together in a dark crowded theater, munching from a large bucket of popcorn, bigger than life celluloid Marilyn Monroe right in front of them.

"This is what they call 'ironic.'" Lexa swallowed a sigh. "And really weird."

Marilyn inhaled a deep chest-filling breath and dug into the bucket of popcorn.

Lexa tucked her legs up on the chair, and soon she was caught up again in the cuckoo-nuts adventures of two guys hiding from the mob by dressing up like women and joining an all-female orchestra where—of course—one of them falls for the gorgeous band member Sugar Kane.

"This movie's pretty funny." Brian's voice: near Marilyn's ear.

"I always thought so—"

Even though Marilyn whispered, someone from behind shushed her, and she bent closer to Brian, turning her head. His face was right there, his mouth close. Inside, Lexa sat up fast. This felt like a chance. A chance to see. Almost without thinking, she pushed—*pushed*—with everything she had, and like a puppet Marilyn leaned forward, plastering her lips to Brian's. Like a blowtorch blast, heat and *zing* and shock blew through every part of Lexa, and then Brian's lips opened, Marilyn's too, her head falling back on the seat, one hand clutching the popcorn bucket, the other her purse. For a moment everything careened out of control, a Ferris wheel spinning too fast, blasting off its axis—

Thwap. A yelp ripped the air. Jerking away, Brian stared at Marilyn like she'd gone crazy and, popcorn flying, she lurched from the seat and hurried up the aisle.

The second they were locked in a restroom stall, Marilyn said, "Oh, honey, why did you make me kiss him?" She touched the purse to her forehead. "We both know I liked it. Liked it fine. Only it's not right." *Bam-whoosh* and Lexa was in charge of her own body again; inside, Marilyn curled in a ball on her leather couch.

"What the hell?" Lexa glanced down at the purse in her hand. "Did you actually *hit* him with this?"

"Naturally." Marilyn lifted her chin. "No better way to nip the octopus treatment in the bud, even if it was me, or really *you*, being the octopus." She wagged a finger at Lexa. "This is simply not fair to Brian. I could feel a tidal wave of his emotions in that kiss, and it wasn't like being onstage, acting. He's terribly confused, honey, about so many things. He kind of spilled over into me and well, I thought maybe that might be a two-way street. That's why I did what I did with the purse." She bit her lower lip. "I'd do it again, too. What we did was not fair to that boy. Not fair at all."

Lexa opened her mouth and closed it. Then she leaned to cool her cheek on the stall door. "You're right. I know you are." She blew out a long, loud breath. "What do we do now?"

Marilyn sat up, shoulders straight. "You go on out there and be yourself and talk to that boy. Talk to that boy, and treat him like a real, live person instead of a science experiment."

Out in the lobby, when Brian caught sight of Lexa, he gave her a confused, red-cheeked half-smile and held up their coats. "Uh, I figured you probably wanted to go home."

Nodding fast, she followed him out, ignoring Marilyn standing smack in the center of her brain with her hands on her hips.

In the few minutes it took them to reach the truck, Lexa kept stealing peeks at Brian. The hesitating way he walked, looking around the waterfront, at people, other cars. More than embarrassed or confused about the scene in the theater, he seemed kind of lost.

"Talk to him," Marilyn mouthed.

Calling on every bit of courage, Lexa touched his arm. "Hold up a sec." She cleared her throat. "I think we should probably talk about what happened, you know, in the theater."

He ran his palm over his head, but he was unable to meet her eyes. "I—I have no idea what happened. It was like my brain . . ." he shook his head, fast and jerky, like he was shaking off a chill. "Forget my brain. Why did you do . . . what you did? The kiss and the slapping bag thing?"

"I—I don't really know," she tried. "I guess I got carried away. Probably because of the play." She gulped. "Sorry."

They shared a quick smile and then he glanced around, saying, "I know it's kind of cold out, but any chance you want to, maybe walk a little?"

At Marilyn's fervent nod, Lexa said, "Sure, that'd be good."

Zipping and buttoning into their coats, they strolled to the boardwalk that ran along the lakeshore.

"There's something seriously weird about this semester," he began. "I know, I know. Graduation. Everyone heading off to college. The rest of our lives. It feels like more, though."

Lexa let out a laugh. "What could be more than all that?"

"Yeah," he said, echoing her amusement. "Except there it is. I feel like being in Mr. B's play has put me in this strange place. This place where I want . . . I don't even know what I want." His elbow nudged her arm. "You're in that place too, right?"

She made a quiet sound of agreement but couldn't speak.

"Ever since rehearsal the other day," he went on, "I've been thinking about our kissing scene."

Only it wasn't me. How Lexa wished she could say it.

"Only I know that wasn't you."

She stumbled, and Brian grabbed her arm.

"You okay?" he said, steadying her.

She nodded, mumbling, "How did you know?"

Cutting her a quizzical look, he said, "How did I know what?"

"That it wasn't me."

"Because." He lifted his brows. "You were being Cherie. Acting a part. That's what's so confusing. I'm not sure if it's because of our parts in the play, or because of what's going on with Hilary."

"What *is* going on with Hilary?"

His laugh was a short bark. "Hell if I know. It's like she wants to put me in a box, and the more she does that, the more I want out." He shook his head. "I still care about her. Everything seems really intense right now. With Italy this summer. Then going to different colleges."

"You're going to *Italy* this summer?"

"Yeah. Right after graduation. I'm interning on an organic farm in Tuscany."

Lexa could only blink.

"That's part of my big plan," he continued. "I know I want to stay in Vermont and take over our farm someday, so this summer is my time away."

"Wow," was all she could think to say.

They walked out on the pier, and when they were leaning over the railing at the end, he shifted to face her. "How about you? You're going to State, right?"

"Yeah. The whole college thing seems really far away, though," she said, "all I can think about right now is getting through the end of the year." She gripped the cold metal of the railing. "Getting through the play."

"I hear that," he muttered. They both stared down at the ice-covered shore, and then he bumped her shoulder with his. "This is cool. Talking to you is easy."

"Thanks," she said, and then she realized something that amazed her. "It's easy to talk to you, too."

Grinning at each other, Brian bumped her shoulder again.

"Hey," he said, "one of my buds is throwing a party, and I told him I'd stop by. Could be fun. Want to go?"

Lexa darted a look at Marilyn and wasn't surprised to see a hopeful expression. With a shrug, Lexa said, "Fun would be good. Why not?"

Why not hit her the moment she and Brian drove to ultra-rich South Cove and down a long driveway leading them to a huge house sitting all lonesome-like by the lake. As she got out of the truck, she looked up at three stories of glass and golden light, tons of bodies milling from floor to floor, thumping music and laughter drifting into the night.

Brian gestured for her to come on and, pasting on a smile, she followed him.

"Some bash," said Marilyn. She'd been lying on her couch, eyes half closed; now she sat up.

"Some bash," echoed Lexa under her breath.

Brian slapped palms with a couple of guys lounging on the front steps, and Lexa had the sudden sense that now he would do the obvious thing: leave her to fend for herself. He didn't, leading her inside where immediately a wave of heat and sound engulfed her: shrieky laughter and bubbling talk mixing with the vibrating electronic thrum of dance music.

Brian leaned whisper-close and still had to yell, "Want something to drink?"

"Um, sure," she yelled back.

They dumped their coats and he took her hand, threading them through the crowd. When they got near a wide archway, he stopped short and she knocked into him. Over his shoulder she saw the reason. Hilary, standing right there in the archway, looking at Brian with an expression so raw and full of longing that Lexa's heart pinched for the girl. Pinched until Hilary's eyes slid her way, and that sweet longing twisted and flash froze to a mask of fury. She burned Lexa with a look and strode over, whatever was in her cup sloshing a little over the rim.

"Well, well, well," she said, the shake in her voice the sole evidence of the instant she'd thought Brian was there for her. "Getting in a little *extra* rehearsal time?"

"Like you said a long time ago," Brian answered, "we need all the help we can get."

Hilary studied Lexa. "There isn't enough help on the planet to get your play ready in a month."

The way Hilary then smirked made a light go on in Lexa's head.

"You are right as rain, sugar," Marilyn said. "Good old Hilary had something to do with your auditorium-schedule mess."

Face going dark, Hilary went on, "Or ready to be at the Marquee. Unbelievable that you guys—who don't even care about acting—get to be on that stage." Scoffing, she took an angry swig from her cup. "What a waste. Nobody's even—" Hilary's eyes razored to Brian, an expression sliding over her features that Lexa couldn't read. "Wait a minute. Oh, Brian, I am so glad you told me I should help. I've got a brilliant idea." Slamming down her cup on a table, Hilary took a woozy walk over to a wall unit full of stereo equipment and flicked at the switches. The music shut off, the instant silence making every head crane her way. "Listen up," she called, her face going bright with all attention on her, "I have an announcement. You all know Mr. B's play is coming up and guess what? It's going to be at the Marquee. That's right, and let me tell you, from what I've seen it's going to be hella sexy. And . . ." She pointed a sharp finger at Brian and Lexa, "starring our own Brian McKinnon and surprise star Lexa Donovan as *lovers*. I know you all won't want to miss this red-hot show." Eyes fixed on Brian and

Lexa now, Hilary began to clap, her hands coming together hard. When others joined in, now hooting and yelling, Hilary slapped the music back on and sailed out of the room.

Brian held up a finger to Lexa. "Wait here," he said, his voice stiff with fury. He went after Hilary.

Music blaring in her ears, Lexa stood alone in the middle of the ogling, hollering crowd. She looked at Marilyn. "What should I do?"

Marilyn sat tall, her eyes huge and shocked. "Not that this isn't dramatic, but you might want to skedaddle."

Lexa backed up a step, bumped one body, two. She moved aside, craning her head. *Where had she left her jacket?* Then there was Brian, his mouth a grim line, a large plastic cup in each hand. He offered one to her and drank deep from the one he kept. Sipping from her own cup, she grimaced. Beer. Not her favorite. Still, the cool froth eased her dry-as-dirt throat. Before she could tell Brian she thought maybe they should leave, he leaned close.

"It's too loud," he said right in her face. "Let's go over here."

He led her across the sprawling pit-style living room full of couches and pillows and tangled bodies. She glanced around at faces, most she'd recognize but not tonight. Maybe it was the unknown house, full of ringing laughter, drifting smoke, some of it the acid stink of tobacco, some of it the sweet burn of weed. Maybe it was simply the night; most likely it was the Hilary show, and all the curious eyes drilling into Lexa now as she followed Brian through a set of sliding glass doors and onto a deck.

He leaned up against the wooden rail and looked up at the stars. "What the hell," he said. Then he laughed, quiet and unhappy.

Hugging herself against the chill, Lexa leaned over the rail too. "Did you—did you find Hilary?"

"Nah, she took off with her squad before I could talk to her." He flicked a hand at the night. "In her usual huff."

"Maybe we should go?"

Brian eyed her over his cup. "I think if we left now, it would make what she did in there too big a deal, you know?"

"Yeah. Okay." She trailed off as worry grew into a hot lump in the center of her chest. "Do you think . . . ?" She took a swallow from her cup, but the liquid did nothing to move the lump. "Do you think what she said will make a lot of those kids, um, come to the play?"

His face going sour, Brian said, "Who knows? I'm going to hope they're all too wasted to even know what she was talking about. Besides, the only reason Hilary said that was because way at the beginning I told her getting up on a stage dressed like a cowboy was going to make me feel like an ass, and I didn't want anyone, especially the guys to see—"

He cut off at the sound of the door sliding open behind them. Austin Blanco, QueenHi's star quarterback and their host, came toward them.

"Bro," Austin said, his arms wide and his grin beer-soaked. "You made it."

Brian slapped his palm. "Dude."

In that moment, a truth about Brian hit Lexa with a jolt.

"That's right," whispered Marilyn, "looks like he's just as scared of doing this play as you are."

Later in her room, Lexa sat on the edge of her bed. "What a nuts night," she said.

"Gee," said Marilyn, "it sure was."

"It's like I saw Brian for the first time. The true Brian, I mean."

"He's a real nice boy," said Marilyn.

"He is," said Lexa, "he really is. Somehow thinking about him being 'hot' seems strange now. I mean, don't get me wrong. He's still super hot, except it's different now. Or I'm different. Like everything I thought about him before was like—like having a crush on an actor or something. Not like knowing a real person."

"Well," said Marilyn, "you did say you wanted whatever happened to be real. The truth."

Letting out a tired laugh, Lexa said, "I did."

Marilyn pressed her lips together. "Do you think now that you know him a little better, you can do that kissing scene?"

"Man," said Lexa. She threw herself back on the bed. "I sure hope so. I—"

A rap on the door had them both jolting.

"Lexa?" Dad poked in his head, and the tight look of his mouth had her rising fast.

"Hey," she said, "I—I'm sorry I forgot to check in when I got back."

"I'll let it slide this time," he said. A worn smile creased his cheeks as he came all the way in. "How was your date? That Brian seemed like a good guy."

"Yeah," she said, unable to keep a small snort escaping. "That's exactly what he is."

"You okay?"

"Sure. Maybe a little tired." She yawned big, quickly slapping a hand over her mouth in case her breath was a beer cloud. "I'm glad you liked Brian."

"How was the movie?"

"Great." She shifted her feet, the weird sensation of trying to act normal now making it impossible to be normal. "How was—how was the shop tonight?"

He laughed. "Same old, same old. Hey, since we're both up, how about I make some of that tea you bought?"

Tea. Jeremy. In a flash Lexa's brain filled with an image of Marilyn sitting in a very familiar kitchen nook mirroring the time Jeremy poured tea from a very familiar green teapot. "Tomorrow," mouthed Marilyn with a wink.

Instantly Lexa's cheeks grew hot and, as Dad was now staring at said cheeks, she sputtered, "None for me thanks. I'm—uh—going to bed."

With a nod, Dad tucked his thumbs into the front pockets of his sweatpants. "I guess that's the best idea. You look a little flushed. I'm glad you had a good time, though. With Brian."

She couldn't look at him anymore. At that face that was nothing more than sleepy and content that his daughter had been out on a date. "I'll see you in the morning," she said, moving to her only available hiding place, behind the opened closet door.

What she wanted to hear was Dad leaving the room. What she heard was him standing there, breathing. Then he started whistling softly. Sweetly. The song was unfamiliar to her. No, no, at the very edge of being familiar. Heard-in-a-dream familiar. She peeked around the door. "Dad?"

He stopped whistling, his startled face whipping to hers.

"That song," she pressed him, "what is it?"

"Oh, an old Greek song. A lullaby." He sang then, his voice barely a whisper. "*Elá poi kontá, elá poi, eh. Elá poi kontá mou, elá . . .* I—I think the words mean 'come closer' or something like that."

He glanced at the Greece poster again, and she had to ask, "You used to whistle that song, or sing it to me, didn't you?"

"Your mom used to. When she was pregnant." Face clouding now, he backed toward the door. "'Night, Lexa."

Talking about Mom. With the play stuff, he'd been talking about her a little more lately and, even though that seemed good, Lexa could tell it hurt him, too. All at once she couldn't let him go. "Wait, Dad." What tumbled out of her seemed to come from nowhere. "Have you ever said you'd do something that you really didn't want to do?"

He stopped, half-laughed. "That's a funny question. What made you—?" His face dropped. "That Brian. He didn't—"

"No. *No.*" Horrified she shook her head. "I meant the play."

"The play? I don't understand."

She clasped her hands in front of her.

"Go on," urged Marilyn, "talk to him, sugar."

"It's coming up. Way faster than it was supposed to," Lexa murmured, "and I'm scared."

"That's totally natural." Dad was at her side now, touching her arm. "Acting is new for you. You've been working hard, though. It'll be great. No question." The pride in his voice lifted her chin.

"I wish I could know that," she said, "for sure." He patted her arm again, and she studied his face. "Have you ever wished for anything, Dad?"

"Boy, you're full of deep questions all of a sudden. What's going on?"

The truth wouldn't work, at least not now. "I don't know," she said, "maybe all the senior spring stuff. You know, what's next?" She looked him in the eye. "I want to know what else *you'd* like to do. Like in life."

Dad sucked in a breath, one hand scrubbing at his beard, as if he hadn't asked himself that question in ages and was only now wondering why. His gaze flicked again to the Greece poster, and all at once she understood what he'd been looking at when he'd been standing in her room all those nights ago.

"We always wanted to go to Greece. Me and your mom." He tilted his chin to the poster. "I know you know that she was half Greek. And going there was always one of her dreams. Then it became a dream for both of us. To check out the 'old country.' See if we could find any of her relatives." He grinned and sighed, already letting the dream go.

Zapped as if by lightning, she said, "Let's do it. This summer. After graduation."

"You want to go to Greece? This summer?" He stroked his beard. "I don't know."

"There's nothing *to* know." She reached for his hand. "We've never really done a big trip, and I could help pay. I've saved some money."

"That money's supposed to help with college."

"I'm not sure I'm ready for college." As soon as the words were out, she knew they were true. "Even if we had all the money in the world."

"You're accepted," Dad sputtered, "State—"

"I can—I can defer for a year."

"I—" His head shook slowly. "Why didn't you tell me this is how you felt?"

"I don't think I really knew I felt this way until right now," she said. "I guess maybe I didn't want to disappoint you."

"You could never do that, Lexa," he said. "So, a gap year maybe?"

"Maybe," she echoed, taking his other hand, clasping both of his tight between hers. "But going on a dream trip to Greece with my dad? Definitely."

He looked at their joined hands, his thumb stroking over the Greek key pattern of her silver ring. "You're really something, you know? Are you sure?"

She stole a glance at Marilyn, who mimed applause.

"Yes," she said, "this is one thing I am 100 percent sure of."

Chapter Twenty-Six

Em called late the next morning, waking Lexa from a dead sleep. Luckily Em talked so fast and so furiously that she didn't notice Lexa's massive yawn factor. She had finished costumes for Lexa to try and needed her to come over now.

After a quick breakfast with Dad, Marilyn and Lexa headed out.

"Your daddy is too cute," Marilyn said as they jogged down the outside stairs, "sitting at the kitchen table, looking at those pictures of Greece on that little computer of his."

Smiling, Lexa said, "Yeah, he's pretty jacked about our trip."

"You are too, honey."

"You're right," Lexa said, "I can't wait to check out some sites, and figure out where to go. I wish there was a Greek teacher at school, but guess I'll just get a Greek language app." She slowed. "Dad'll miss Mom. When we're there, I mean. I know that, only—only I think that's okay." She held up her hand, her ring catching the sun. "He told me this ring came from my mom's family, and that Mom always wore it. The pattern's called 'the Greek Key,' and it symbolizes love and devotion, and I think, like, the eternal flow of life." She rubbed her finger over the silver band. "Maybe when Dad and

I are there together, it'll feel like she's with us." She lowered her hand. "Anyway, that's all in the future. First things first. Getting through the play."

"Oh, you'll get through that fine," said Marilyn, squaring her shoulders and narrowing her eyes. "We'll make sure of that."

A razor thin shiver snaked up Lexa's spine. "Was that chill you or me?"

Marilyn didn't move.

"You don't know," Lexa said, "do you?"

Eyelids lowering, Marilyn shook her head.

Lexa gazed around at the Saturday morningness of the street, the quiet yards and houses, the people, families inside up to who could guess what. "The way my body feels sometimes," she murmured, "the way it responds. I can't tell anymore. It's been weeks and weeks since I was . . . only me."

"I know, sugar. I don't know if you can imagine this, but I'm in the same boat."

"I know you have to go back. I know it. Except I wonder what it'll be like after you're gone."

"You'll be fine." Marilyn crossed her arms over her chest. "We both will."

"I want you to be right. I can't help thinking about *you*, though." Lexa hugged herself, rubbing her arms as she walked. "What if what you said before is true? That the reason you're here is not about me."

"I wish I had an answer." Marilyn's lips curved, her smile not reaching her eyes. "One thing I do know is that worrying about it won't help. Besides, you have arrived."

Lexa stared at the front of Em's house: the diamond panes glittering in the morning light, and Ann, right there through a window, sitting at her kitchen counter and sipping a tall glass of bright pink smoothie. She caught sight of Lexa and gave her a cheery wave. Same old, same old. Hadn't Dad used those exact words last night? Only no. Nothing was ever same old, same old.

When Lexa came around the house, the back door was already open, Ann standing there glowing. “Good morning,” Ann called. Then Em was at her side. “Go on, dear,” Ann urged Em, “tell her before I burst!”

“Wha—?” The answer to Lexa’s unasked question was all over Em’s face. “Fashion and Design? You got in? Why didn’t you tell me on the phone?”

“Because I wanted to tell my best friend in person, dummy,” said Em, laughter bubbling as Lexa hugged and hugged her. Then Ann hugged them both.

Wowwowwow! Lexa held on tight.

Then Em was dragging at her, saying, “Come on. I’ll tell you everything while we work on your costumes.”

“Don’t forget about tonight,” Ann called after them. “Tell Alexandria.”

“What’s tonight?” Lexa asked as they clomped up the stairs.

“Ann wants to celebrate. Of course, she wants Kevin and you in on it. Probably your dad too.”

“That sounds awesome.” All thoughts evaporated as she caught sight of the clothes spread out on Em’s bed.

Costumes. *Her* costumes.

Rushing over, Lexa ran her fingers over a blouse. Lipstick red and lacy, with an ivory lining peeking through. Cherie’s blouse. “This is beautiful, and, man, look at this!” she snatched up a deep forest-green skirt, a version of the clingy but twirly-at-the-knees style she’d been wearing since their first trip to Golden Oldies.

“Why don’t we start with those,” said Em, “and this.” She held up a wide black leather belt. “I’ve got a red one too, but I’m hoping this one will work.”

Lexa unbuttoned her shirt. “Spill,” she said, “I want to

hear everything about F and D. When did you hear? *How* did you hear?"

"Well, I guess because it's rolling admissions, they have time to call people. So, I got a call," Em said, offering the lacy red blouse, "yesterday afternoon. Didn't you get my text about coming over?"

Lexa frowned, a dim memory of a text coming in, only she'd been so focused on her date with Brian. And then talking with her dad. "I—I guess I forgot to check."

"What were you doing?" Em said, her nose crinkled with curiosity.

"I was . . ." Lexa fixed her gaze on the blouse as she reached for it. "I was out last night with, uh, Brian."

"Hold up." Em pulled the blouse back. "You were out with Brian, as in, McKinnon?"

"Yeah. We were, um, rehearsing."

"Rehearsing?"

Reaching for the blouse again, Lexa said, "Yes."

"That's all?" Em let Lexa slip the blouse from her fingers.

"Mostly," said Lexa, giving Marilyn an inward eyebrow wiggle as she spread the blouse over her chest. "I love this. The color is awesome. Did you make it? The lace is really soft."

"Yeah, I did." Em batted her lashes. "And nice deflection. Wait." She handed Lexa a skin-colored tank top with a built-in bra. "I made this to go under both costumes, you know, for when you have to change on the stage."

Blouse, skirt, and belt in place, Lexa looked in the mirror and said, "Wow."

"Wow is an understatement," said Marilyn.

Em stood back, eyes sharp on her work. "Yeah. That black belt is the one. I knew it. Want to try the showgirl outfit next?" Without waiting for an answer, Em ducked to the bed, saying, "You know, in the portfolio I sent F and D? This is the costume they talked about on the acceptance call." She held up what looked like a sparkly pearl-colored bathing suit with a long gauzy tail of red, green, and black net. "Isn't it gorgeous?"

Lexa nodded, her throat squeezing at the costume's tininess factor.

"They said," Em went on, bringing it over, "they 'appreciated my use of color and texture to illustrate the duality of Cherie's inner and outer desires.'"

Light and super stretchy as the showgirl costume was, Lexa still had to shift around a bit to tuck herself all in. Swiveling, she caught herself in the mirror and stared, unable to take her eyes off the round humps of, well, of *her* spilling over the top.

"You look amazing," said Em, adjusting here and there. "Exactly how I pictured you."

"She's right," said Marilyn. Lexa rolled her inside-her-head eyes, and Marilyn fluttered her lashes and gave Lexa a slow smile. "You be as sarcastic as you want. Won't change the truth."

Touching the row of dangly sparkles draping down from both her chest and around the thigh openings, Lexa said, "I like how these are sexy but kind of soften the whole thing."

Em clapped her hands. "That's totally what I was going for. Sexy but fun sexy, glittery sexy. And it fits. That's the whole point of this. Fits the play. Fits the character." Her gaze came to Lexa's. "Fits the actor."

"Actor," Lexa murmured, "that remains to be seen."

Em opened her mouth but, in no mood for a life lesson, Lexa hurried on, "Will you help me undo this? I want to hear more about what the F and D people said, too. Like where will you live? When do you have to go?"

"They're sending me a packet," Em said, balling up the gauzy tail. "You should hear Ann. She's already talking about parents' weekend. And she is determined to celebrate tonight."

"Tonight?" As Lexa buttoned up her shirt, a flutter began in her belly.

"I wondered when you'd remember about that," said Marilyn.

"Wait," Lexa said to Em, "I—I kind of have plans."

Em narrowed her eyes. "Plans?"

"Yeah, I'm sort of invited to, uh, Jeremy's for dinner."

"As in Leith? Man, you are one busy girl."

"Ha ha," Lexa said, a jokey echo of Em's tone of utter amazement. "I'll tell him we have to do it another night, though. He'll understand." She hesitated, something nagging. She checked her phone. A blue dot next to the text from Em she'd ignored; no text from Jeremy, though.

"Good thing women are so independent now," Marilyn whispered. "Send him a message."

"I need to . . ." She waved her phone.

"Cool," Em said, "I'll run down and get us a couple of drinks."

"Hey," Lexa texted Jeremy. "Sorry, but tonight won't work."

The answering text came so fast that it was like he had been waiting for it. "No shit."

She frowned, typing, "What?"

Back like lightning. "No time for games."

Frowning, she called: her call went right to his voicemail. She didn't leave a message, instead sending him another text. "I don't understand."

His text came with only one word: "Waterfront."

A low, strangled moan brushed her mind. Marilyn stared at her, eyes wide, hand over her mouth. "The theater was jam-packed, honey," she said through her fingers. "I never saw him."

"Where are you going?" Em was back, a can of seltzer in each hand.

"There's something I've got to do," Lexa said, already out the door.

Chapter Twenty-Seven

Lexa stared out the bus window seeing nothing, her stomach bouncing with every bump, queasy from the sour smell of exhaust, from the bitter taste of . . . of everything she didn't know.

"You could tell him it was all a mistake." Marilyn bit her bottom lip, those tiny teeth like pearls against the glossy red. "A mistake that's all over."

"I don't want to lie."

"It's not a lie. It's simply not exactly the whole truth."

Marilyn's words settled heavily, stones sinking in water. *The whole truth.* Lexa swallowed hard. The bus cruised to a stop, the pressure swaying her forward in the seat. They'd arrived.

"Good luck, sugar. Whatever you decide."

Lexa walked to Jeremy's condo, images of what he could've seen her body doing with Brian flickering behind her eyes. At his front door, every bit of her except for one miniscule speck wanted to run. That one speck held her there, though, making her grab the brass door knocker and knock.

Silence, long, aching, infinite, then footsteps approaching, doorknob turning. She death-gripped the strap of her backpack as the door creaked open. A face appeared, owlish eyes blinking behind thick-lensed glasses.

"Why, hullo," said Mr. Leith, surprise lacing his clipped British voice. "Alexandria, isn't it?"

She gave a little wave. "Hi, Mr. Leith. Is, uh, Jeremy here?"

Mr. Leith opened the door wider. Before he could say anything, movement behind him had his head circling. "Jerz? Look who's here? Alexandria."

Jeremy and Lexa stared at each other, both of them shocked that there she was.

"Right, then," said Mr. Leith, looking from one to the other. He tapped the newspaper he held against his leg. "I'll leave you to it."

Jeremy came to the door, slowly enough that Lexa couldn't help but take in all of him: low-slung sweats, bare chest, sleep-messy hair, and those eyes. Long and blue and sharp as glass.

"Hey," she managed.

He crossed his arms. "Why are you here?"

"Because we have to talk." She pressed already numb fingers tighter on the strap. "Can we—can we talk?"

His eyes narrowed, and she was sure he'd say, "No," and slam the door.

"Please," shot out of her mouth. "We could—we could go for a walk."

Frozen silence, then Jeremy let out a loud, annoyed breath, muttering, "Let me get on some clothes."

All too soon, they were heading across the road and down the school drive to a completely Saturday-morning-deserted high school. Neither of them spoke, almost like they'd agreed on the need to be totally alone.

Except they weren't totally alone.

"Take a chance." Marilyn's whisper brushed warm. "Talk to him."

"I want to," Lexa's mind murmured, "could you . . . ?"

"Naturally," Marilyn said. She rose from her chair, tossing Lexa a fast, "I won't come back until you call me," before disappearing.

Then Lexa was alone. Or at least as alone as she could get.

"I thought you wanted to talk to me," said Jeremy, watching her now, his wrinkled-forehead confusion warring with tight-lipped anger.

"I do." She took a deep breath. "Tell me what you saw last night."

"Who cares what I saw? You want to be with Brian. And *clearly* he wants to be with you."

"No!" She stopped, grabbed his arm. "He doesn't want to be with me. He—"

Her hand fell away from him. Was there *any* way to explain this?

"I was there, Lexa! At the Waterfront Theater." He scrubbed his eyes with the heels of his hands. "Man, I'm such an idiot. I thought you were . . . forget what I thought." He turned those eyes on her again. Truth arrows. "I don't even feel like I know you at all."

"You do know me. You do." She pressed her palm to her chest. "I—I don't know exactly what you saw at the theater, but that wasn't me with Brian."

"Yeah, right."

"It wasn't!"

"That wasn't you laughing and eating popcorn with him? That wasn't you kissing him?"

"No," she said. She made herself keep looking him in the eye, even as his icy glare froze her. "No. Not completely. Okay, here goes." The truth came now, fast and unstoppable. "This is going to sound really crazy, but the spirit of Marilyn Monroe is, like—living inside me right now, you know, helping me with the play. Then Brian asked me out, but he really wanted to go out with her, so I let her take me over." She sucked in a breath, and Jeremy's face stopped her.

Astonishment. That was the definition of his expression: bopped between the eyes, open-mouthed astonishment.

"That is," he said, shaking his head, looking at the sky, "the stone-cold stupidest thing I've ever heard."

"I know it is. Do you think I don't know?"

He strode farther down the hill. She caught up fast, words spilling like a dam breaking. Starting from the beginning: from the second Mr. B pulled her name out of the jar.

They were way past the high school, and all the way down to the lake by the time she got to where Marilyn slapped out with the purse.

"I guess I left before that part of the 'show,'" he cut in.

Stung, she stopped her telling. Now both of them sat slumped on freezing stones, the winter lake churning dark and oily beyond an ice-rimed shore.

Jeremy never looked at her, just kept reaching down to pluck up small rocks and chuck them into the water.

"Do you believe *anything* I've told you?" she said at last.

He exhaled, sharp and scissory, and kept tossing stones, some of them skipping. The hollow roll in her belly told Lexa to get up and go—leave him—forget the whole thing. Only she couldn't seem to move.

"Believe you," he said, his voice too quiet. "Either you're the most amazing actress on the planet, or . . . no. I guess you're the most amazing actress on the planet."

"Don't you get it?" she said. "God. This is impossible." She stared at the lake. "That was the whole problem. I'm *not* the most amazing actress. I'm not even sure I'm *any* kind of an actress. And then I got that damn part! We're pretty sure that's why Marilyn came. To help me get through this idiot play."

His soft laugh had her shifting to meet his gaze.

"You won't stop," he said. "You act like you *have* to believe all this."

"I believe it because it's true."

His slight scoff of a smile hurt her more than any of his sharp, cutting looks.

"I am not lying," she said, everything in her wanting to jump to her feet, run away. No. She gripped the rock she sat on with both hands. Not this time. "Every word I told you is true."

In a rush, he stood. "I'm done with this." He stalked away from her.

Lexa looked after him, willing him to stop. To turn around.

He didn't.

Guess this was too unexpected even for Jeremy.

Chapter Twenty-Eight

Pressure. Building behind Lexa's eyes, in her chest. Hotter than the most sweltering mid-summer day. More and more difficult to think, to breathe. Like a covered pot of water, boiling on the stove. Boiling and boiling.

Marilyn. Marilyn waiting for Lexa to call her.

Only Lexa didn't call her, and not because she blamed Marilyn for what happened with Jeremy. She didn't. Truth was she simply didn't want to talk about it. Didn't want to have to *think* about it. And what else would they do? With Marilyn sitting in her chair, looking at her with those big eyes.

Marilyn wanted to come back, though. From wherever she'd tucked herself away to give Lexa and Jeremy their space. Maybe needed to come back. That had to be what all the heat, all the boiling in Lexa's body was about.

By the time Lexa was brushing her teeth that night, the pressure was unbearable. "Fine." She sighed and spat out a mouthful of toothpaste. "Come back already."

A *whoosh* had her holding tight to the sink to stay on her feet.

"Oh, my!" Marilyn said, striding fast, hugging her elbows. "I know all about needing privacy, but you have no idea what you've put me through. No idea!"

Pushing hair off her face, Lexa bent to rinse her mouth.

"I've been so worried about you," Marilyn went on, pacing now. "Worried to *death*."

Lexa scrubbed a towel over her lips.

"Please, honey, I know I could pick it out of your brain, only . . ." Marilyn paused, but the whip of her frustration was a fast follow. "Only I want you to tell me what happened, because *you* want to."

Slowly Lexa clasped her hands together in front of her. "I told Jeremy everything," she said, "everything about you." She lifted her laced fingers, let them drop. "He didn't believe me."

"Honestly," Marilyn said, eyes sparking, "we could probably take care of that in a jiffy."

"By having *you* do something?"

Marilyn opened her mouth again, and Lexa was about to say, "Of course," or "Why not?" but she shook her head, saying, "Maybe it was crazy to expect him simply to believe me, except he didn't give anything I said a chance."

"I'm so sorry."

"Yeah, me too." Lexa grabbed the toothpaste tube, jammed on the cap.

"If only . . ." Marilyn's lashes fluttered low. "If only I could've gone and left you alone, right from that first day."

"No," Lexa murmured. She wished she could actually touch Marilyn. Put a hand on her shoulder or pat her hand. Just once. "Maybe I wished that back then. I don't now. I'm glad you had to stay."

"You are sweet to say that. Still, the truth is the truth. If I'd left—"

"Everything would be different," Lexa cut in, "sure. Whatever. The truth is, me being in the play? You being here? None of that should have anything to do with Jeremy Leith believing in me, and—and I refuse to be that girl who falls apart because some guy is a—a—"

"Louse?" Marilyn offered.

"I think I'm more of a louse than he is," Lexa said on another sigh.

"All I ever wanted was to help you," Marilyn said, the back of her hand against her lips now. "I can't stand seeing you hurt."

"That makes two of us." Lexa let out a half-laugh. "It's not the end of the world. I mean, hey, I met a guy I liked enough to hurt over. That's got to be better than nothing, or—or what I was doing with Brian. Getting all noodly about somebody else's boyfriend. Worse, who when you come right down to it, I didn't even think of as an actual person."

Marilyn's lips curved, the smile blooming over her whole face. "You know something? You've got a lot more gumption than you think. I'm proud to know you."

"Thanks," Lexa said.

Marilyn gave her a sad little smile. "At least we didn't miss Em's celebration."

"Oh, yeah." Lexa mirrored the sad little smile. "So, you got that newsflash, did you?"

"I didn't mean to pry," Marilyn sputtered, "I—"

"It's okay," Lexa said, "Ann decided she wanted to plan a real party when the play's over. Good thing too, because I didn't feel much like celebrating today. Actually, I'm seriously glad this day is over."

"Lexa?"

Slow and sticky, Lexa's eyes opened to dark. Then a hand, shaking her shoulder.

"Lexa?"

"Dad?" She shoved up onto an elbow. "It's the middle of the night. What?"

"Ah, I'm hoping you'll tell me." He leaned over her, raising her window shade. "Pretty sure he's not here for me. Look."

Jeremy. Down on the ground. He whipped his arm, and a second later a sharp *plink* hit the window next to hers. Dad's window.

"Friend of yours?" said Dad, "or should I call the cops."

"Yes," she managed, "I mean, yes, he's a friend of mine." As she pushed up the window, she added, "Don't call the cops."

"I won't, but seriously, Lexa, two boys in one weekend?"

"Ha ha," she said, then she whisper-yelled down to Jeremy, "What are you doing?"

"Uh, trying to wake you up?" Jeremy looked from her to the window he'd been peppering with pebbles. "Crap. Wrong window."

She started to answer, but Dad's low chuckle had her head whirling. "Dad! Go back to bed. Please."

"And leave you alone with this desperate youth?" he laughed out loud.

"Dad!"

"I'm going already." Downright chirpy, he shuffled toward the door. "Feel free to invite the poor guy up."

"He's not a 'poor guy,'" she began, but Jeremy was now whisper-yelling at her.

"Can you come down?"

Before she could answer, Marilyn appeared, wrapping a white terry robe around her shoulders. "Now this looks promising."

Lexa clambered out of bed and grabbed her peacoat from the back of her desk chair. Heart beginning to pound, she slipped it on. Then she stopped cold. "Could you . . . you know?"

"Jeepers," said Marilyn walking away. "I'm going already. Honestly, I'm starting to feel like a yo-yo."

Lexa hurried from her room, what she was about to do making every part of her feel like the yo-yo here. A feathery, hot yo-yo.

The next thing Lexa knew, she was down in the yard, standing in front of Jeremy. This time it was her turn to ask, "Why are you here?" Her voice was soft, wary.

He ran a hand through his hair, his eyes even longer in the glow of the outside light she'd switched on. "You sound like me," he said, "at least like I did earlier."

"Don't make fun of me," she said, stuffing shaking hands—and not from the cold—deep into her pockets. "Please."

"I am not making fun of you." With a low laugh, he shook his head. "Man, this is the weirdest, most unexpected thing pretty much ever. Could we walk while we talk? I need to walk."

They hit the sidewalk, both staring at their walking feet. Finally, he blew out a long, slow exhale. "I tried not to, but I've been thinking of everything you told me. All day I've been thinking. I still think your Marilyn story is whack, except the thing is . . ." he paused, side-eyeing her, "I don't believe you were trying to yank me either."

"I would never do that," she whispered.

"I know." He stopped and reached for her hand. When their fingers touched, a spark flickered along Lexa's skin.

"Because I *do* know you," he went on, "even if I don't understand what happened last night. Forget that. What I really want to know right now is—what do *you* want, Lexa?"

"I . . ." Standing this near to him, holding his hand, made Lexa dizzy, as though she'd pulled up anchor and was adrift in a vast ocean, everything huge and rolling and bright. She swallowed hard and plunged. "What I want is this." She kissed him. Closed her eyes tight and let go.

✦

Kissing Jeremy.

On a dark, shadowed sidewalk, under that starry midnight sky. Lexa didn't want it to end. This moment. This deserted-street, out-of-time moment. Magic.

After a long while, he drew back, saying, "This is definitely not how I expected this day to end."

She had to laugh. "Me either."

They stood, foreheads resting together, their breathing ragged.

"I have to admit," he said, "that *was* a pretty cool story. The whole Marilyn thing? And you being possessed by her sure would explain some stuff. That dinner at Mr. B's? When you were talking to yourself in the bathroom? The acting exercises in class? Like when you sang to Brian that time?"

Her cheeks heated, and not in the unhappy hot way. Hot in the *wow-he-was-really-paying-attention* way.

"I think that's part of the reason I got mad before," he went on. "Even when I didn't believe you, I wanted to. I wanted what you said to be true."

"How come?"

He stroked her hair. "I was ten when my mum died. After, I used to do crazy stuff, like write her letters. I'd put one in an envelope, write her name on it, make up an address, and find a mailbox." He let out a short quiet laugh. "For those few minutes after I dropped the letter in the box, I could feel her, I don't know, out there, waiting, maybe even watching. Everything you said about Marilyn made me remember that. How it felt. How it hurt. How even though my mum's gone, sometimes I just wish so much that I could feel even for a moment like she's not gone."

Listening to Jeremy talk about his own wish for his mother made something open up in Lexa. A wanting that had her putting a hand on his chest to nudge him back.

"What's wrong?" he said.

"Nothing. I—I want to try something. Just—just give me a sec, okay?" She laced her fingers with his and closed her eyes, whispering in her mind, "Marilyn?"

The director's chair appeared from the shadows lit by a single golden light, followed by the click of heels. Then there was Marilyn in her black sweater and white capris, her makeup light, her blonde curls tumbled, fresh and morning. She sat in the chair, smiled. "You rang?"

"I want to ask you something," Lexa said.

"Anything, sugar."

"Is—is there any way you can 'visit' Jeremy? For a few seconds?"

Marilyn's brows lifted.

"No," Lexa said fast, "he didn't ask for this. I—I want to. Can you?"

"I don't know," Marilyn said, "maybe. Remember what happened with Brian in the movie theater? When you pushed me into that clinch?"

"Yeah," said Lexa, "you kind of spilled over into him, right? And you said maybe he could—I don't know—see you, too? Could we try it with Jeremy?"

"Anything for you." Marilyn stood, her eyes narrowing, considering. "You keep a hold of him. Don't let go and—and brace yourself."

Whoooooosh! As if jumping off the highest bridge, everything in Lexa dove, a whirling, tumbling free fall. Then she landed, thudding into the Marilyn-chair with enough force to make her feel like the chair would flip over. Before she could move or think, Jeremy's hands went rigid in hers, because this time Lexa was not only in her own head, but also somehow still in control of her body. Except for a pulling feeling, like she was caught in an invisible web that wrapped around her even as tendrils spiraled out from her.

Before she could complete a single thought about what was going on with Marilyn, Jeremy inhaled once, loud and sharp. Lexa held his hands tighter, ready to shout his name. He relaxed then, standing there, his expression far away, his hands going slack in hers. A second ticked, an eternity. The diving flight happened again, this time in reverse, like an arrow fired from a bow, hurtling and vibrating through space. Lexa landed firmly in her body with a bone-rattling thud.

"Well, how do you like that?" Marilyn was back in her chair, not a hair out of place. "You okay?"

"Yeah," Lexa said to her.

"Good, because that little trick took some effort," said Marilyn. She stood. "I'll leave you two lovebirds. Ta-ta."

The second Marilyn vanished, Lexa squeezed Jeremy's hands. "Are you—are you okay?"

"She was in my head," he mumbled, looking right at Lexa except not, his eyes unfocused. "Marilyn Monroe. In my head." Now he did focus on her. "How is that possible? How?"

"We haven't figured that out. Apparently, being a spirit is not an exact science."

"Why aren't you completely, I don't know, *unhinged* about it?"

"Are you?"

After a beat, he said, "No . . . I can't explain it, only I'm—I'm not."

"Yeah, that's one of the weirdest things. How *not* weird having her here is."

"She was really in my head. She—she *talked* to me."

"What did she say?"

He made a sound, light and soft and amazed, dropped his forehead to hers again. "She told me to treat you right."

Chapter Twenty-Nine

Floating into the apartment, Lexa explained to her waiting dad what she'd been doing with Jeremy—well, not *everything*—and went back to bed. She lay in the dark, covers up to her chin, only who was she fooling? Sleep would not be happening any time soon. As if Marilyn already knew that, she lounged in her chair, waiting.

"Other than you telling him to treat me right," Lexa whispered, "what else did you and Jeremy talk about?"

Marilyn's lips stretched in a slow smile. "I made sure he knew I was real," she said, "kind of like giving him a mental autograph. There's something I don't get. Seems like you two were doing fine without me. Why did you want me to visit him?"

"I—I think having you here's made me feel closer to my mom," Lexa whispered, "you know, knowing that some part of her is maybe still actually out there? I wanted him to feel that too, about his mom."

"That's sweet," said Marilyn.

"There's something else we decided," Lexa went on, "that we're going to wait to really hang out with each other until after, you know, the play's over and . . ."

"And I'm gone."

Lexa's tiny nod made Marilyn cock her head. "That's probably for the best. For all concerned." She sighed, and then said, "Are you in love, sugar?"

The way Marilyn asked, her face soft and open and curious made Lexa close her eyes, swim around in her warm Jeremy-blur.

"I don't know. It's too soon. Too big. It feels good, though. Real." She rolled to her side. "Do you think I'm in love?"

Marilyn smiled again, that easy bloom; her eyes were shadowed, though. "I can't answer that."

"But." Lexa hugged her pillow under her cheek. "But *you* were in love. A bunch of times."

"True," Marilyn said, "the beginnings were always nice and sweet, too." She leaned back on her chair, her pinky resting against her lip. "It hurts. Even now. To remember all that—all that *life*. Wouldn't you think I'd be over it?" Her voice was barely a whisper. "Wouldn't you think I'd be over all that life by now?"

Lexa swallowed hard, Marilyn's face, the texture of it, the expression, reminding her of the clip from *The Misfits*. How she'd looked sitting in front of that mirror, her brows dark, too defined, the black liner ringing her eyes heavy, her cheeks powdery and hollow. Sad. That's what her character had been in that clip, and she hated thinking of Marilyn sad. More, she hated thinking that spirits could be that sad.

Marilyn sat up then, her pinky dropping from her lip. "We should stop talking this way. It doesn't do any good, and I have spent too much of my time here fiddling around, and not enough time taking my job seriously."

"Your job?"

"Yes, my job!" Marilyn's eyes snapped, her voice rising. "The one that I want, no I *need* to believe brought me here. The one where I'm supposed to be helping you with the play. Not—not—"

Bright heat seared Lexa's insides, making her throw off her covers and writhe to loosen her T-shirt, even as the outside of her body chilled in the cool air of her dark room. Choking, she grabbed the water bottle on her nightstand, sucking water in as fast as she could swallow. She looked at Marilyn wildly. Marilyn who stood in her head unmoving, fingers covering her open mouth.

"Stop it," Lexa said, her voice a rasping croak. "Please!"

With a moan, Marilyn closed her eyes and slumped into her chair, her arms hugging her head.

Wiping her trembling mouth, Lexa whispered, "What was that?"

"I don't know," Marilyn mumbled, arms lowering. "Something in me fired up, like I was terribly mad at myself."

Lexa took another swig of water. "I don't think you getting mad at yourself is good for either of us."

"I can't help it," Marilyn said. "Don't you get it? I was sure I came here to help you with being Cherie, and instead I'm messing up, getting tangled up with teenaged boys. It's like being in this live body is bringing up old feelings I've forgotten, and throwing in some new ones I never had. I'm confused."

"You can't control everything."

"I—I'm afraid I can't control *anything*." Marilyn's voice was a little desperate. "And that feeling's getting stronger."

"Okay." Lexa took a couple of deep breaths. "Let's focus on what we can control. First, you *are* helping me with the play. Talking to me. Encouraging me. Just—just being here. You're why I've given *any* of this stuff a try."

Some of the sad pinch in Marilyn's expression dropped away. "Truly?"

"Yes, truly. Without you I so would've ditched out of the play." Lexa's pep talk dried up in her throat. "How is it possible I keep forgetting I still have to actually *do* the damn play?"

"Don't you worry," Marilyn said. She squared her shoulders and saluted Lexa. "From here on out, I am back to being your number one play helper."

"I'm counting on it. And—" Lexa couldn't stop a shiver. "No more getting mad at yourself."

"I'll try," Marilyn said, offering a quivery smile. "Honest."

Monday afternoon came, and with it their very first rehearsal at the Marquee. As the theater was in the heart of downtown, it was a fairly quick walk from QueenHi. Lexa chose the longest route possible.

"You're dragging your feet," said Marilyn.

"I know," Lexa muttered, "I wish all I had to think about was hanging with Jeremy, or—or graduation."

"I know, I know," Marilyn said, "or your trip to Greece, maybe. I read you loud and clear, but—"

"The show has to go on," said Lexa with a groan, "and way too soon."

When she pulled open the theater door, the hush of the grand lobby surrounded her, the only sound the click of her boot heels on the marble-tiled floor, echoing up to the ceiling where chandeliers glittered.

"Lordy," said Marilyn, "this is some elegant theater. A real classic."

"Yeah," said Lexa. She took a quavery breath, trying to smile. "Mr. B even got them to let us use a storage room for our sets and stuff."

A distant hum caught at Lexa's ears, and when she opened the doors to the actual theater, the buzz of set-building activity hit her in the face. Her old group of backstage buddies crawled around the stage, the clamor of drills and staple guns blasting, and the oily bite of freshly slapped-on paint filling the air. Graham was up there, filming with his phone, and so was Clara, on her knees painting what would become the diner counter. Em had a sewing machine set up on a nearby table, and she fluttered around a partially costumed Dani-Marie.

Lexa searched for Jeremy. She didn't see him onstage, but—*oops!* Hilary. In one of the front rows, sitting hunched over, one arm moving up and down, hand-sewing. A couple of rows behind her sat Brian, his head bent low.

Mr. B strode out onto the stage, black curls flying. Clipboard in hand, he chatted with one of the stage crew.

Dumping her pack on a seat, Lexa glanced around again and then up. Jeremy. In a balcony corner seat, practicing with a guitar. He lifted a hand, barely wiggling his fingers at her. Those eyes. On her. Her whole body vibrated, hard and fast. She could only manage the quickest and tiniest return wave. Wow! Why wasn't the whole theater going up in flames?

"Go visit with him, honey." Marilyn rose from her chair. "I'll—"

She broke off at the same instant Lexa heard a soft male voice.

"Lex?"

She came eye-to-eye with Brian and, even though they'd parted Friday night as friends, her brain fluttered over how she was supposed to treat him now, in the dazzle of Monday at the Marquee.

"Give him a smile," whispered Marilyn, "something."

Lexa managed a small curve of her lips and said, "Hey, Brian."

"Hiya," he said and, letting out a little laugh, he craned his head to take in the whole theater. "This place is intense." When he came back to her, his face went serious. "Hey, I just want to make sure that everything's cool with us."

"Don't worry," said Lexa, "all is cool."

Brian shook his head. "What a weird weekend." He ran a palm over his buzzcut. "I spent a lot of time thinking. About me. About me and Hilary. About, well, everything. And I guess . . . I guess I'm just trying to say that—confusion aside—I think I'm actually glad we got chucked into this play together. No matter how it ends up going." He nodded fast, as if putting a finish on things. "That's all."

"I'm glad too," she said, "we're going to be . . . great."

With a quick grin he returned to his seat and, the second he sat, Lexa noted Hilary's head circling to him, the dip of Hilary's chin, and the way she wrinkled her brow like billboards shouting her longing for Brian.

"Golly, that Hilary's as much of a backstabber as anyone I met in Hollywood," Marilyn mused, "but she sure seems to genuinely love that boy."

Before Lexa could comment, Hilary's head twisted her way. No. Lexa pivoted fast. She was beyond done with the Brian and Hilary show.

"That's right, honey." Marilyn's gaze went past her, over in the direction of Brian and Hilary, her lashes lowering as if she was remembering something. Something sweet and long ago. "They're on their own now."

Mr. B called out, "I see everyone's here. Join me on the stage, please."

Energy, fizzy and hot, raced through Lexa. Instead of heading to the stage, she turned to the balcony. Jeremy was gone. Then there he was coming down the balcony staircase.

"Hi," he said, tucking the guitar under his arm as he approached. "Everything okay?" His gaze flicked to Brian.

"Sure," she said, "except it's kind of sad he'll never know he was out on a date with Marilyn Monroe."

One side of Jeremy's mouth lifted. "She right there?"

"Yup."

"Cool. Hi, Marilyn." His voice went low, "Hey, any chance you could, uh, ask Elvis to help me with my singing?"

Marilyn giggled, and Lexa said, "She thinks you're a funny guy."

"Oh, yeah?" His whole face lit up.

"Miss Donovan, Mr. Leith," Mr. B, hollering, "please join us." He stood at the edge of the stage now holding a cowboy hat and, in that moment, him standing there looking so small on that huge dark stage with those deep red velvety curtains framing him, it was as though he was out there in front of a full audience: exposed, raw, performing. Clammy sweat chilled Lexa's skin, and she tried to swallow, only her throat squeezed, too tight to let even a drop of saliva go down.

"Come on," said Jeremy.

"You can do it." Marilyn and Lexa locked eyes. "Believe me. No. No. Believe in *you*."

Lexa wanted to; still she shuddered as she followed Jeremy.

The rehearsal did not go well. Lexa couldn't stop focusing on the seats. All those seats facing the stage. Again, she heard what Brian said at the party, about being embarrassed that "the guys" would come to the play and see him playing cowboy.

At the end of rehearsal Mr. B called her out. "Miss Donovan?"

With the sense of an axe falling, she turned. He sat on the edge of the stage, legs dangling.

"A moment of your time," he said, beckoning to her.

She headed down the aisle, fingers gripping her pack strap. Em popped her head out from the wing curtain and raised her eyebrows. Lexa tried a feeble smile, glad when she heard Hilary's voice calling Em back to whatever costume or prop emergency they were dealing with. Em gave Lexa a thumbs-up and disappeared.

Trudging up the stage steps, Lexa sank down next to Mr. B. Together they faced those rows and rows of empty seats, the cavernous theater hushed and quiet.

"It was my belief," Mr. B said, "that as a whole, the production was progressing nicely. Today, a new wrinkle with Cherie."

Lexa stared at the empty seats.

"You know what I'm referring to," he said, "yes?"

She nodded, the motion a dull ache.

"Anything to share?"

Twisting her silver ring around and around, she murmured, "I'm afraid."

"Ah," he said, "I sensed that. Please explain."

She took a breath and dove. "It was hard enough thinking that the rest of the class would see me, or that my dad would come, or other people from school would come, but—but being here at the Marquee? I don't think I really knew—really *understood*"—her hand swept out—"that maybe *other* people might come. Lots of other people. Strangers. Watching me." Shifting, she found Mr. B's eyes on her, dark brown bullets. She heaved out a breath. "Like you're watching me now."

"Yes," he said, "that's exactly what an audience wants. To watch the story through the actors. Through you."

"I know that," she said, "all those risks. Finding my Cherie." Her shoulders slumped. "Pretending at school was hard enough. I'm not sure I have it in me to do it here. On this stage. In front of a real audience."

"I know this is a bigger challenge than we expected. Nevertheless, here we are, and you have to know that almost every actor, no matter how famous, has these feelings."

"I do know all that. Except I'm not them." Her fist knocked her chest. "I'm only me."

"Yes. You are only you. All I can tell you is that I have every faith in you. That I believe you can do this." Mr. B sucked in a breath. "The truth is, however, that you have to believe it, Miss Donovan. You." He smiled at her. "And remember—perhaps the oldest truth in the theater—the show must go on."

She watched him rise, dust off his pants, and then followed his startled gaze to the wings behind. "Miss Poss?" he said, "I didn't see you there."

"I'm sorry to interrupt." Hilary ramped up her mega-watt smile. "You're needed backstage."

Lexa didn't move until the two of them disappeared, then she looked at Marilyn. "Do you think she heard what we were talking about?"

"Well, she is Hilary after all." Marilyn's eyes widened with worry. "What do you think?"

Three days later, Lexa stepped through the entrance of QueenHi and found Clara taping a good-sized poster to the announcement wall. Huge yellow letters screamed *Bus Stop*, and under them was a retro-looking, full-color drawing of a buxom showgirl standing on a table, surrounded by an audience of figures depicting waitresses, a sheriff, a man in an overcoat, a bus driver, and two cowboys. The younger-looking cowboy was on his feet, gazing up adoringly at the showgirl.

Lexa's surprised squeak had Clara looking over her shoulder.

"Lexa," she said, her face sunny bright. "What do you think? I kind of mashed up the original play poster and the movie poster. Gorgeous, right? It was Hilary's idea to make them."

"*Them?*"

"We've hung dozens. Around the school and all over town, too. Check this—we're going to sell tickets at the caf, you know, as a fundraiser. Half the money is going to Queen-Hi's drama program, and since I made the posters, the other half is going to the Wheeler School. Isn't that great?"

"Perfect," Lexa managed. "I've—I've got to get to class."

"See you at rehearsal," Clara sang after her. "Get psyched! The set's almost done and Em's bringing the costumes."

As Lexa hurried away, Marilyn kept looking in the direction of the poster. "I think she used my body."

"She sure didn't use mine!" Lexa hissed.

"She could've," Marilyn said with a chuckle. "Slow down, sugar, there's another one of those posters. I want a closer look. Or not," she said when Lexa raced by.

Everywhere Lexa went, posters and more posters. And kids. Teachers. Staring. Calling out, "Looking good, Lexa." "Did you pose for that shot?" "Can't wait for the play!" All she could do was smile and keep moving. Keep moving. Through the day, and on to the rehearsal where everyone else, Mr. B included, buzzed with excitement. Because posters for a play were a good thing. Selling tickets. Raising money for good causes. All good, good things.

Only not for her.

Chapter Thirty

Get through it. Lexa chanted those words to herself every morning as time ticked toward the day she'd be standing onstage in front of probably hundreds of people. Because, yeah, she'd found out how many seats were in the Marquee. One thousand four hundred. *One thousand four hundred!*

"My acting teacher Lee always told us to focus on the work," Marilyn would say, trying to help, or, "Concentrate on something on the stage, not the audience." She'd even quote from *The Idiot's Guide to Acting*, "Imagine everyone in the audience wearing their underwear."

Good advice. Professional advice. Didn't work, though. Screw it. Lexa was scared. Big, ugly chicken-scared. She couldn't hide anything from Marilyn but worked like a fiend to hide it from Mr. B and the others. Especially Hilary.

Impossible.

Over the next few days—before rehearsal, during rehearsal, after rehearsal—Lexa caught the others watching her, their eyes skittering away as soon as she looked at them. Except for Jeremy. He tried to talk to her about nerves; actually, tried to "encourage" her out of them, saying the same stuff as Marilyn. "Why are you so freaked?" he whispered to her. "It's only a play." He was swallowing his stage fright, why couldn't she? Lexa had no answer. Fear was a living animal inside her. And thank you, Hilary Poss, for setting that animal on a rampage.

Hilary. She went about her backstage business, a tireless champion, an ever-so-helpful little rabbit. Always positive, always chirpy and cheerful. Only Lexa recognized her smile from that day way back at that sixth-grade dance. That smug, triumphant smile as Hilary had stared at her in the girls' room all those years ago, raking her gaze over the tiny Em top and tinier Em skirt. *Bovinian*. Lexa heard that word in her head and saw that smile every time she saw Hilary now. At rehearsal when she spotted her passing out more *Bus Stop* posters to Dani-Marie and Graham, telling them which parts of town needed coverage. In the caf when she scurried by the table Hilary'd posted at the caf entrance, cringing when Hilary would sing out, "Tickets for *Bus Stop*. Come see QueenHi's newest stars in the hottest show ever. Support QueenHi Drama."

"Don't let her win." That's what Marilyn would whisper every time they saw Hilary selling and selling, and then later at the rehearsal when she would report in a loud swishy voice to Mr. B and everyone else about the hundreds of tickets she'd sold. How excited everyone was for the show. The show that had to go on.

Performance day looming, Lexa worked and pushed. To find her Cherie. Moving on the stage, learning the set, doing her costume changes, acting with the others. Acting. Even when she had to kiss Brian, she did exactly like Mr. B told her all those weeks earlier. She'd steal a glance at Jeremy, and then when Brian laid one on her, she'd imagine kissing Jeremy. In the dark. Under the stars.

Mr. B told her she was doing better, only something was missing. "The sweetness," he'd say, "the innocence. The flow. Try not to—to *try* so hard."

All she had was her "try." Except the more she worked to find the sweetness . . . the innocence . . . the flow, the more impossible they were to find.

"When I was struggling to find what I needed for a role, Lee would always say, 'take a minute.'" Marilyn's whisper fluttered against her mind at the end of the final dress rehearsal. "That little minute always helped me, you know, dig a little deeper. Take that time, honey, and I know that when you step out on that stage, you'll find what you need."

Lexa mouthed a silent scream. *How do you know?* Marilyn had no more answers. She'd already talked herself blue, and talking had nothing to do with actually being onstage. Nothing to do with Lexa actually being onstage. Acting. In front of hundreds of people, of strangers. Who would see her up there, pretending to be a sexy showgirl. Pretending to be the exact opposite of who she had always been. Who she was now. Who maybe she'd always be.

The clock ran out.

Lexa woke up that Friday—Performance Day—same as she'd gone to bed: lying on her back, staring at the ceiling. Marilyn appeared the second she opened her eyes. In her director's chair, wearing her simple black top and white capris, her feet bare except for her favorite pearly nail polish. Seeing her sitting there like that, her smile blooming, hit Lexa hard with a truth she'd buried way down under all her fear of being up on that stage.

"That's right," Marilyn said, "I've been thinking about that too. Me leaving after all this time."

"Maybe *that's* my problem," Lexa said, the effort of trying to be funny making her throat squeeze. "The real reason I don't want to do the play is because I don't want to say goodbye to you."

"That's a good one," Marilyn whispered, half-amused, half-sad. "I don't want to say goodbye to you either." The look they gave each other was warm and full, and then Marilyn said, "It'll be fine. Don't forget you have your dad and Em. And now Jeremy."

"I know," said Lexa, fiddling with her sheet. "Only talking to you is different. You know stuff about me that . . ." She trailed off and swallowed hard.

"I guess being inside your head would do that." Marilyn laughed. "You didn't always like that I knew stuff about you."

"Somehow I can talk to you in a way I can't talk to them." Lexa chewed her lip. "Maybe it's because I *didn't* know you. I don't know if this makes any sense, but having you around is kind of like how I'd imagine being stuck in an elevator for hours with a stranger would be. Like after a while, both of you would just start talking about the most personal stuff. And now?" Lexa shrugged, "I sort of like having someone to tell that stuff to."

"That makes perfect sense. Honest." Then Marilyn wagged a finger. "Right now, however, we don't have time to think about goodbyes. We have to get you ready for tonight."

Tonight. The word echoed in Lexa's head as a light knock hit her door.

"Lexa?" Dad. He poked in his head. Cute, morning-rumpled Dad.

"Hey," Lexa said.

"How's my star?"

"Hah!"

"If I forget to say it later." He clapped his hands once, his eyes bright. "Break a leg."

For a split second she wanted to tell him again how scared she was; his face, though—that proud grin spreading from ear to ear.

"Thanks," was all she managed.

The school day went by in a blur.

She got to the Marquee early, the silence of backstage eerie as she crept past the set and downstairs to the room where the costumes hung. Lifting her costume bag off the rack, she paused. Muted voices above, rising and falling. The others were arriving. She tossed the bag over an arm and ducked down the hall. Instead of going to the dressing room, she pushed into the backstage ladies' room and into the first stall. Dull, robotic, she hung the costume bag on the hook and leaned a cheek against the cool metal wall.

"I'm not going to give you any more advice, sugar," whispered Marilyn.

Lexa nodded, staring at the tile floor.

"I know you don't believe this but—you *know* what you need to do." Marilyn's eyes widened as she pressed both of her hands over her heart. "In here. You know what you need and," she paused, mouth curving up, "if there's nothing else, there's this: No matter what, it'll all be over in a few hours."

Something like a sigh slipped through Lexa's lips. "That's what I'm afraid of."

Unzipping the bag, she took out her first costume.

Backstage was crazy with activity.

"Lexa!" Em waved at her from the makeup table, her whole body a grappling hook reeling Lexa over faster. "Where have you been? Don't you ever check your phone? Oh, forget it." She took Lexa's arm, tugging her to a chair.

Luckily Em flipped her focus immediately, mumbling something about makeup. Nearby Hilary worked on Anton, and Clara on Dani-Marie. They'd only done full makeup once, at yesterday's dress rehearsal, so Em was like a psycho bee, buzzing around Lexa while at the same time fluttering around Hilary and Clara, making sure they followed her makeup sketches to the stroke.

Tipping up her chin, Lexa closed her eyes as a damp foundation sponge wiped across her forehead.

"I want to try something with the black eyeliner," Em said, her breath blowing warm on first one cheek and then the other. "Your eyes need to be a little more dramatic, but more innocent, you know?"

No, she didn't know. Since Em paused, Lexa figured she wanted an answer, so she gave her one. "You're the boss."

"Relax your face," Em said, dabbing and dabbing. "You're all squinched up. There's something else," her voice went breathy, almost as if she was running a race. Lexa guessed she was. Tiny scratchy sponges darted over her eyelids, then the slick of a wet brush near her eyelashes, the corner of her eye.

"Your friend is good," whispered Marilyn, her gaze focused as if she could actually see Em transforming her.

Lexa opened her eyes as lipstick, wet and sticky as clay, rubbed over her lips. Em pulled the tube back, and a tremor ran up Lexa's neck. Red. Bright and fire engine. Frowning, she said, "I thought we were going with a deep purple."

Em laughed, gleeful as a toddler. "We were," she said, "until yesterday, when Hilary gave me the most kick-ass idea." She grabbed a dark brown pencil, and then the sharp, sharp point made a spot above the left corner of Lexa's mouth.

"There, and I can't believe I'm saying this, but—" Em stepped back, cocking her head. "Perfect."

Lexa snatched up a mirror.

"Yes," Em went on, talking more to herself than to Lexa. "It totally makes sense. Marilyn Monroe would've been Cherie's idol! She would've so tried to look like her. But not completely. Not blonde. No. Cherie would've made her look her own."

Stunned, like her fear had finally stopped her heart, Lexa sat with the mirror gripped in her hand, staring. Then her eyes flicked to Hilary's station, fully expecting to find her watching, that full smug, triumphant smirk covering her face. The fact that she was nowhere in sight was small comfort.

Mr. B came over. "Ah, yes, there's Cherie," he said, his nod to Em satisfied. "You've outdone yourself."

He lifted an eyebrow as he and Lexa caught eyes, and she offered him a rubbery smile. With a wink, he tucked his tongue in his cheek and turned to Anton.

Em put her hand on Lexa's arm. "One more thing. Where's the scarf?"

"What?"

"The scarf," she said, "Ann's red scarf. Come on, you always have it."

Lexa's insides careened, like she rode in a car that took a fast turn. "I didn't—"

"In the pack, honey," Marilyn whispered.

Lexa rifled through the clothes she'd stuffed in her pack and, under them all, found the crinkly slip of chiffon. Em snatched it, and—*spritz*—Chanel No. 5 wafted.

"For Cherie," said Em, tying the scarf around Lexa's neck and kissing her cheek. "Break a leg."

Touching the scarf, she watched Em move on to her next victim: Brian. Right there in his leather and fringe cowboy-wear. He gave Lexa an up and down once-over and a thumbs-up, and then dropped into her vacated seat, saying to Em, "Goop me."

Dazed, Lexa drifted over to the wings. The main curtain was closed, the set behind looking thin and plywood in the too harsh glare of the backstage lights.

"It'll be over soon," said Marilyn, her voice small.

"I know." Lexa mumbled, circling her ring, around, around.

"I know you don't want to, but you should take your ring off."

"I know. Cherie wouldn't wear it."

"Cherie wouldn't wear what?"

Whirling, Lexa found Hilary. "Nothing," she said, stepping away.

Hilary put out a hand. "I need to say something to you." Her tone went soft, unfamiliar. "Brian came over last night and we—we talked. Talked like we haven't in so long . . . no." Biting her lip, Hilary shook her head. "No. That's not what I need to say right now. What I need to say is that you and I both know my being here, being part of this play, was to mess with you. With Brian. I guess with all of you. But mostly with you."

Marilyn and Lexa stared hard at each other, and then Marilyn said, "Smacking her right now wouldn't do a bit of good."

"Says you," she said to Marilyn, and then real quiet to Hilary, "Yes. We both know that."

"I was being a dick." Hilary swiped at her eyes. "I was mad about the play. About what was going on with Brian. I wanted to blame someone, and you were the perfect target. Then, I don't know, I saw how hard all of you were working, how hard Brian was working, and after he and I talked last night my mad kind of disappeared, and I really saw what I was doing. Please . . ." She waved her hand at the open stage. "Please tell me that I haven't wrecked this for you. For you and everyone, because—"

Lexa cut in, "Nothing you've done has wrecked anything." She pointed to her own face. "See? Em thinks your makeup ideas are brilliant, and she already told me you were doing a fantastic job with the props and stuff. And all the posters? The fundraiser? Who could complain about that?"

"But . . ." Hilary blinked at her. "But you know I only did all that to freak you and Brian out."

"Yeah, and I even know you messing up our schedule in the auditorium is the real reason we're doing this play at the Marquee," said Lexa. "Doesn't matter. Everyone loves that we get to perform here, and they all think you're a star."

"*You* don't. I—I wish there was something I could do to make it up to you."

"Go on, honey," said Marilyn, steepling her hands like a prayer, "show her what class really looks like."

"There is one thing," Lexa said. "Cherie wouldn't wear this." She pulled off her ring. "Would you take care of it for me?"

"Sure," Hilary said. She took the ring, surprise and something like relief coloring her face.

"One more thing," Lexa said, inspiration striking, "stop using 'bovinian' to cut people down. I mean, Vermont has, like, so many farms, and cows are super important, and—and you should remember that."

Hilary's eyes went wide. "You're right. I'm—I'm sorry." She backed away. "Break a leg, Lexa."

Lexa lifted her chin, managing a true smile and, with another one for Marilyn, turned back to the stage, now able to hear the dull roar of people entering the theater.

Break a leg. Those words, whispering around her, again and again, even from her own mouth. They were all wishing each other this kind of reverse luck, and she knew the others were nervous too, could practically see the anticipation rippling across skin, smell it in the charged air. None of that changed the fact that even now—*even* now—she wanted to be anywhere but here.

"A moment, please," stage-whispered Mr. B, waving his arms to gather them around. "The time has come," he began, eyes moving to touch each of them. "I want you all to know that this has been a voyage that I am beyond grateful to have been a part of. Your tremendous talent. Your passion. All the risks you have taken to bring these characters to life, especially in such a short time. I am humbled. Remember, theater is magic that happens only once, and each performance, each audience lives that single moment together." He clasped his hands to his heart. "Break a leg, each and every one of you. Take your places."

Crossing the stage, Lexa trailed a hand across rough wood painted to look like the diner counter, over the back of a chair, over the soft white cloth covering a table.

Her fellow "bus riders" joined her in the wings, Jeremy amazing with his hair grayed and his cheeks stubbly. Their eyes clung as he sidled by, and then lips close to her ear, he whispered, "It's supposed to be sunny tomorrow. How about we go down to the lake? I'll bring a thermos of tea."

She nodded, squeezing her eyes shut, breath shuddering in and out. *Tomorrow, tomorrow, tomorrow.*

Backstage went dark and quiet as a held breath, and then a thunder of applause. In the sliver of open curtain, she saw Mr. B stride to the middle of the stage, his voice booming an audience welcome. She caught sight of Dad, sitting front and center with Ann, both of their faces glowing, and had to look away, her heart beating too fast in her chest, a bird trying to escape a too-small cage.

Across the stage, Clara and Dani-Marie waited in the wings, their eyes gleaming in the near dark, their costumes and makeup making them unrecognizable. It was more, though. Clara, her hair darkened, a simple gray cardigan over her diner uniform, oozed innocence, only not her own dreamy innocence, instead an unsophisticated, untouched innocence. And Dani-Marie, her hand on her hip, lips bright orange and already smirking, gave off a hardened vibe brimming with years of knowledge and disappointment. Clara and Dani-Marie were gone. No, not gone—transformed into Elma and Grace.

Behind Lexa, Jeremy and the others rustled and shifted. Someone coughed.

Mr. B told the audience to "enjoy the show" and exited. The houselights swooped out, and Clara and Dani-Marie hurried to their places on the stage. A second later, the curtain gave a yank, the pulley-noise a muted *whir*.

Everything was moving too fast now, Lexa's heart rabbiting along. She pressed a hand to her chest. The stage lights dazzled on; Dani-Marie and Clara began.

Lexa'd kept from looking at Marilyn this whole time, only now she couldn't help herself. "I can't do this."

"Now, sugar—"

"No. No! I can't. I *can't*! I thought I could. I wanted to believe I could, that I had it in me. Only here we are and—and—I can't do it."

Marilyn didn't move, and she seemed smaller than usual, her face in shadow.

"Didn't you hear me?" Even in Lexa's head, her voice sounded too loud.

"I heard you."

"You have to help me!" The queasiness threatening Lexa's stomach moved up into her chest. Her cue was coming. Only a few lines away. "I need you." Panic choked her thoughts. There was only one way out, didn't Marilyn see? "I need you to be Cherie."

Jumping from her chair, Marilyn shook her head. "You don't want me to do that."

"Yes. Yes, I do! And you want to. Admit it." Desperate now, Lexa's chin jerked toward the stage. "Maybe this is why you're here. To save me from total humiliation, by doing what you were born for. Acting. Not me. *You.*"

"Born to act?" Hips swaying, Marilyn approached until they were eye to eye. "Maybe I was. Maybe I would love nothing more than to go out on that stage and dazzle one more time. Maybe that is why I'm here. I wish I knew. I wish I'd been able to figure it out for sure. Why I was allowed to come. But I didn't. All I know is who I am now." Her head tilted up slowly, eyes narrowing, searching. "Do you hear me? Whoever or whatever you are? This Marilyn says, 'Too damn bad, if the big plan is for me to ride in and save this girl's day. I won't do it.'" She looked into Lexa's eyes again, her expression softening, and Lexa's cheek warmed as if a hand cupped it. "It's up to you, honey. It always was." She stepped back then, fingers at her lips, ready to blow a kiss.

"No. *You cannot—!*" Lexa's brain revved, but Marilyn's eyes were cutting away from her, going wide, startled, as if she saw something, there, over Lexa's shoulder. Everything paused, a full, mind-bending stop, and then that slow Marilyn smile. "Well, how do you like that?" she whispered, and disappeared.

Lexa stumbled back, hitting Jeremy.

"Relax," he murmured, his hands steadying her. "We're almost on."

Her head nodded while inside she screamed, "Marilyn? No! You cannot do this to me! Come back! Please! *Please!*"

The silence in her head roared, so huge and loud and different. A slammed door. She was sure Marilyn was gone. Like *really* gone. She stared at the dark blank in her brain, wanting to be furious, wanting at least that, only a blazing snake of fear writhed around in her chest, choking everything except her terror. She ripped the scarf from her neck, balling it in her fist, squeezing her eyes shut, wishing, wishing she could disappear, too.

Slow as a sigh, the scarf fell from her fingers. She *could* disappear. She didn't have to wish. She could do it. Right now. She could bolt for the door. Be gone before anyone could stop her.

A taped sound effect like the *whoosh* of a bus coming to a stop made her head spin over her shoulder. The others stood there in a line behind her, waiting in the shadows, seconds until their cue. Seconds until all of them would be onstage. The whole group.

The whole group. They'd worked long, hard. Together. *Together, but*—images of her running out the backstage door strobed behind Lexa's eyes.

Onstage, Clara said the line that began Lexa's cue and right after, the thump of an imaginary diner door opening. A stagehand tossed a fall of fake snow onto the stage and moved out of the way, giving Lexa a double thumbs-up.

With a low wail, she ran—

Chapter Thirty-One

—onto the stage, to the very center, and froze, staring out from the hot glare of lights into the thick, heavy dark of the silent theater. She clutched her prop suitcase to her chest, her breath coming in deep, jagged gulps: staccato images from the front row—legs, skirts, pants, boots—stabbed her vision, sharp as knives. Her body began to shake and she opened her mouth, her lips sticky, trembling, everything in her boiling, boiling. The silence was deafening, as though the entire universe waited for Alexandria Donovan to do the one thing that would crown her humiliation for all time. A small moan escaped her lips. Then, from deep in the auditorium: a coughed, confused laugh answered by a soft, knowing giggle.

As if her brain, her heart, her body blasted open, knowledge blew in. This was what Cherie faced every night. Every night. And scared to death, Cherie went out on her stage every night, determined to sing her song. Whether the audience thought she was good or bad, that didn't matter. It was what Cherie believed. *Cherie*. There she was at last. At *last*. And—and there was Lexa, too. No magic. No special something inside. Just herself. Heat and electricity geysered through every part of her. Herself and this moment. She swung around, homing in on the shocked faces of first Grace and then Elma, and almost laughed out loud as she found her first line.

"'Is there someplace I kin hide?'"

From the second she spoke, the magic that is theater flared. Exactly like Mr. B promised.

During her costume change, Lexa whispered to Marilyn, hoping she'd come back. Marilyn didn't answer, though, and that silence drove Lexa back out on that stage again and again, all the way through the final scene.

At the end, the whole cast held hands, bowing through endless applause, endless hoots and hollers, looking at each other as they bowed again and again. When the curtain closed a final time, Jeremy kissed Lexa and hugged her tight. She hugged him right back, and over his shoulder catching eyes—surprised eyes—with pretty much everyone in the cast. She didn't care. She'd done it. *Done it!*

Out in the lobby, dozens of people patted her back, told her how great she was. How they had no idea she liked to act. All Lexa could do was smile. Especially at Dad and Ann after they took turns hugging her and handing her bouquets. And Em, who handed her a single perfect white rose, before crushing Lexa into a bear hug.

"I knew you could do it," Em whispered into her ear. She hugged Lexa tighter. "And really soon we are going to talk about how you figured that out."

"I know," said Lexa.

Em pulled back, "Promise?"

Lexa nodded. "Promise."

The final hug came from Mr. B. "I knew it," he whispered. "Brava."

"Thanks," was all she could say.

Mr. B told them then that they had to stay to strike the set, and that after they finished, they were invited to his house for a cast party. While he spoke, Lexa drew back and into herself. Marilyn should be at that party. *Marilyn*. Everything in Lexa, as if holding off until this moment, began to ache. Marilyn who in the blink of an eye had moved on. Moved on and was gone. Gone.

"Hey," Jeremy whispered in her ear, "you're so quiet."

"She's—she's gone." Lexa swallowed what felt like a lump of sawdust.

"Already?" He leaned close, lowering his voice. "Are you okay?"

"I don't know," Lexa managed.

Jeremy pulled her against his side, patting at her back.

Chilled and hollow, Lexa looked around at all the laughing, bright faces and then up into Jeremy's concerned eyes. "It's just . . . I can't believe she's gone."

"I'm so sorry, Lexa."

"Yeah," she said on a broken little laugh. "Me too."

The rest of the evening was a blur and too soon Lexa was home in her room, lying on her bed, quiet and alone. She draped the red scarf around her neck, Chanel No. 5, sweet and rose, tickling her senses. She touched her silver ring, back where it belonged on her finger. That's the way it would be. Tomorrow she'd wake up and everything that led to this moment would be back to the way it was. And yet. And yet. The memory of being on that stage, playing Cherie was alive in her. Alive and hers. Except Marilyn was gone. Just as deep down they'd both known she would be. Lexa stretched limbs that felt fragile out on top of her comforter. How strange it all was . . . that mix of sweet and bitter.

The rush of her bedroom door opening, and Dad poking in his head had her sitting up fast.

"Hey," he said, "I had to tell you again how great you were. The whole cast, but especially you."

"Thanks."

"I still can't get over it," he said. "Who knew you had all that acting talent in you?"

"Who knew?" she parroted.

"Makes me wonder," he went on, "and *really* look forward."

"Look forward to what?"

"Finding out what else you've got going on in there," he said, cracking a smile. "Hey, I've got a couple things to do down in the shop, and then I was going to put on the kettle. Want a cup of chamomile tea? Supposed to be good right before bed."

"That's okay," she said, "'night, Dad."

"'Night."

As the door closed, she sank back on her pillows and then jerked hard.

Marilyn. Right there on her director's chair.

"Hi, sugar," she said, her lips curving, slow and easy. "You sure were swell tonight."

"You—you saw?"

"Of *course*, I saw. What do you take me for?"

Thoughts and feelings swirled through Lexa, and she found herself wanting to truly answer Marilyn's offhand question. "Definitely a friend, but . . . more. I don't know." She swallowed hard. "Maybe, like a big sister?"

Marilyn tipped her head back, laughed her tinkling-bell laugh. "Oh, I like that. But when I said, 'no can do'?" Her shoulders shimmied. "Boy, were you sore."

"Yeah." Lexa let out a dusty laugh. "I was angry, all right. Only I was more scared. Even after everything we went through. Why was I still so scared?"

Invisible fingertips stroked her cheek. "Who knows? Fear

is a funny thing. How it gets ahold of a person. Why . . ." Their eyes met, held. "Why, any person at all."

"You're not just talking about me right now," said Lexa, the words coming slowly as a river of images from the past couple of months flowed through her brain.

"All that truly matters," Marilyn went on, "is that you didn't let that old fear stop you."

"I didn't, did I?" Lexa's fingers slid to her neck, touching the scarf. "Cherie and I, we simply took it along. Even though you . . ." she hesitated.

"Go ahead and ask."

"What happened? When you disappeared?" Lexa asked.

"Now that was some shocker," Marilyn said with a nod.

"You—you saw something, didn't you?" Lexa said, "about you leaving. Please don't go—" Her voice broke. "Please. Not yet. I—I'm not ready to say goodbye."

"Oh, sweetie." With a sad look, Marilyn stood and stretched, twirling slowly, the white dress she wore clinging, her fingers fluffing out her sunbeam hair. "I want to tell you about something I figured out on my—my little side trip." She turned to face Lexa and came closer. "I already told you this whole thing started with me seeing you and your silly red hat and wanting to know why I needed to watch you. Then when I got here, I was positive that the reason I *could* come was because there was a scared girl who needed my exclusive brand of help, and because the living wouldn't let go of me. I think I was right about those things, but you know what else I figured out?" She pressed her hands to her chest, her eyes going big and liquid. "In the end, it doesn't matter why I came. I did. That's all. Maybe that was the point, and maybe the living *do* need to let go of me, except here's the kicker: What I also know—and I don't need any 'higher power' to tell me this—is that I need to let go of the living right back."

Letting go. Everything in Lexa told her that truth. Her fingers tightened on the scarf, and she whispered, "I'll never forget you."

"I know, and that means the world to me. That tomorrow you'll spend a few moments thinking of me, of our time together. And then you'll keep moving, keep living. Now get comfortable, because I'm ready to play a scene I never got to play in my life."

Obeying, Lexa settled against her pillows, catching her breath as a numbing tingling sensation washed through her body, like when a foot or a hand fell asleep. Except her mind. There, everything was active and jumping, as if something was gathering, getting ready.

Marilyn was on her leather couch now. She leaned back, closed her eyes, the back of her hand to her forehead. "Goodbye, cold, cruel world."

A laugh snorted out of Lexa.

One eye opening, Marilyn laughed too. "Kidding." Then she stood up tall, squaring her shoulders and looking deep and warm into Lexa's eyes. "Goodbye, wonderful world." Her voice caught, her lips trembling. "Goodbye, wonderful life." Marilyn glowed now, points of light illuminating her, the glimmers stretching to golden stars that framed her: a screen legend coming in for a final close-up. "Goodbye, wonderful Alexandria Donovan." Smiling her famous-photo smile, Marilyn lifted her palm, ready to blow a kiss.

"Wait! Wait!" Lexa squeezed her eyes shut, hugging herself tight, holding Marilyn with everything she had. "You said being a spirit isn't an exact science, so, so maybe it's not goodbye. Maybe it's . . ." she opened hopeful eyes, "'see you later?'"

Marilyn's eyes went wide. "Of all the . . ." She burst out laughing. "You are the limit."

They laughed together and for one instant, there it was, warm and real—the deepest part of each of them holding the other.

"Well, then," Marilyn said, "here's hoping, honey. See you later." Fast as a snuffed flame, she disappeared.

Lexa took in a shuddering breath, and another. Marilyn was gone. Really, really gone this time.

An ache pressed behind Lexa's eyes, spreading deep in her throat and down, down to her chest. The weight of it grew heavy and insistent, her breath coming shallower and shallower. With a gasp, she rolled to her window and opened it wide. She stuck her head out into the cold night and took in breath after long breath of the freezing air. All at once soft, cold touches on her cheeks and forehead. She looked up. It was snowing. Snowing. She let out a laugh that came out more like a sob and lifted her head, opening her mouth and letting the snowflakes land on her tongue.

Lexa's lips spread into a smile. Slow and real. She pulled in her head and shut the window. Then she gathered up the red scarf, wound it around her neck, and stood up. Tomorrow would bring Jeremy and Em and everything that came after. But right now? She squared her shoulders, strode to her bedroom door, and opened it wide. Right now, she couldn't think of anything she'd like more than finding her dad and taking him up on that cup of chamomile tea.

Acknowledgments

This book that you hold in your hands was a labor of deep respect for and true super-fan love of the inimitable Hollywood screen legend—Marilyn Monroe. I grew up watching Marilyn movies, and several of them—*Bus Stop, Some Like It Hot, Gentlemen Prefer Blondes, Niagara*—are some of my most favorite movies ever. There is just something about her that keeps me glued to the screen, marveling at her beauty, grace, wit, and bottomless talent. When I began researching Marilyn's life, I learned a lot about her hardships, her dreams, and her hard, hard work. Some of the stories were incredibly heartbreaking to read. That said, reading about her life, from so many perspectives including her own, only increased my respect and admiration for her as a major acting talent gone too soon. Along with the millions of Marilyn fans out there, I will continue to hold a place for her in my heart.

Tremendous thanks to all the early readers—too many to name here—of all my dozens of drafts. My gratitude is infinite. Express thanks to Tim Wynne-Jones who provided invaluable feedback when the idea for this book was not much more than a glimmer in my mind, as well as tangible editorial feedback much, much later in the writing process.

Tim, your thoughts and advice gave me the courage to take the plunge at last and submit the book to my publisher.

Huge gratitude to She Writes Press and The Stable Book Group, without whom this book would not exist. Extra thanks to publisher Brooke Warner and to the entire She Writes Press team for collaborating with me on making a beautiful book.

And last—but never least—epic love and appreciation for my most important and needed supporters. My husband Charlie and our three children: Jack, Willy, and Marley.

About the Author

Photo credit: Karen Pike Photography

Half Greek half American, **Mima Tipper** and her writing reflect her heritage—a little bit old-country, a little bit rock and roll: one foot wandering through the dreamy realms of myths and faerie tales, the other running on the solid ground of fast-paced, contemporary story. She earned her MFA in Writing for Children and Young Adults from Vermont College of Fine Arts, and is the award-winning author of the YA novel *Kat's Greek Summer*. Beyond devoting most of her time to writing, Mima helps at Inklings Children's Books in Waitsfield, VT, volunteers at her local library, and is committed to promoting literacy and supporting the writing community. Currently, Mima lives in Vermont with her family.

KAT'S
A Novel
GREEK
SUMMER
MIMA TIPPER

Looking for your next great read?

We can help!

Visit www.shewritespress.com/next-read
or scan the QR code below for a list
of our recommended titles.

She Writes Press is an award-winning
independent publishing company founded to
serve women writers everywhere.

SWP